J.E. D'Angelo

Services Rendered

DOLCE BOOK PUBLISHING INC.

~ 2006 ~

Services Rendered

Copyright©2006 by J.E. D'Angelo

Published in 2006 by Dolce Book Publishing Inc.

First edition

National Library of Canada Cataloguing in Publication

J.E. D'Angelo

Services Rendered

ISBN: 0-9734656-3-8

PRINTED IN CANADA

Dolce Book Publishing Inc.

111 Zenway Boulevard, #30, Vaughan, ON L4H 3H9

905.264.6789 • 1.888.68.DOLCE • www.dolcebookpublishing.ca

Dedication:

To the Wads

In appreciation:

I'd like to convey my gratitude to my family and friends for their continued love and support. Your best wishes mean so much. Without you, attaining this goal would be meaningless.

A special thank-you to my 'sounding-boards': Anna A., Daniela D., Laura M., Linda B. and Tommi T. – thanks for the title! Ladies, your patience, your assistance, and above all your friendship, are invaluable to me.

PROLOGUE

Anger, resentment, and Ellis pride took the place of sheer admiration. She was no longer that little girl with a crush. The events of recent months had awakened her from her dream world. This was life, and it wasn't at all rosy.

"Is that what you call it!" she snapped, not intimidated by the fact that Mr. Madison towered over her by nearly a foot. Her fluffy blue slippers added very little to her height, or sophistication, for that matter.

"What would you call it, Miss Ellis?" Michael Madison asked her calmly. His tone was drenched in sarcasm and his eyes danced with laughter. And something told her that he was always like that.

"You, or your father, or *both* of you, took over my father's company. You're not going to lose on that acquisition. As for the sum of money that was required to pay all of my father's debts... unfortunately, my father never told us what was happening. I would never have accepted. I don't want your charity. You'll have your money back just as soon as we can sell this house."

"Sell the house?" Michael was incredulous. He looked at Frank, then at Joan and then back at her daughter. "Your father mortgaged this house a while ago," he said as he seated himself comfortably at the head of their dining room table. "That's why the banks would no longer help him. He had no collateral, nor credibility."

Jackie was furious when she turned to her mother, who was standing still, her fingers nervously clenching and unclenching. "What else haven't you told me, Mother?"

"I'll make some coffee, excuse me…" Joan spoke quietly. Turning, she walked hurriedly towards the kitchen. She couldn't stay there another moment.

"Actually, Miss Ellis, neither your mother or you, for that matter, would have a roof over your head right now if it weren't for my father's generosity. He took over the mortgage from the bank about eleven months ago. Your family has lived here rent-free since then," he informed her. "*And*, it's just as well that you don't accept charity, because I'm not about to offer it – not anymore. After all, your father made the bad judgements, not I. You can rest assured that I have no intention of paying for his mistakes. My father knew your father. In fact he had tried to come to his aid once before, but your father didn't accept his offer. He was too proud. In the end, however, it *was* my father who helped him, and substantially so. He has helped you as well. Any monies concerning your stay in this house have been cleared because he felt sorry for you. However, last month he decided to relinquish the helm to me. I am now president of Madison

Electronics. I am not my father, and after meeting you I absolutely refuse to chalk this all up to 'bad debts'."

"We don't want your father's pity or anyone else's!" Jackie declared, raising her chin. "When do you want us out?"

Michael took a moment to answer. He hadn't expected that. "You won't have to leave," he began, as he flipped through the papers of the large black book, a book, Jackie thought, that held all that transpired in their past and probably what was in store for them in the future. "At least not for now."

"Don't worry about your 'bad debt', Mr. Madison. We'll pay you the rent we owe you, plus this other loan! You'll have your money within the year!"

Michael's head jolted upwards, and he laughed out loud – something that infuriated Jackie to her limits.

"Within the year? And how do you propose to do that, Miss Ellis? I don't accept Monopoly money!"

"What are you talking about?" Jackie's eyes narrowed with suspicion.

"You obviously must not be aware just how much money was required to pay all of your father's 'debts', as you put it." Michael glanced at the figures in front of him. His eyes mocked her when they met hers once again. "As it stands, Miss Ellis, your accrued debts amount to nearly half a million dollars."

Jackie's mouth dropped, and Michael smiled with revolting smugness. If it weren't for the angry tension of her muscles, she would have dropped to the floor like a rag doll.

What had made her say that she'd pay him back without first asking for the figures? Stress must have shorted out the thinking mechanism in her brain, but it was too late to bite her tongue and she'd be damned if she'd admit defeat! She rebounded quickly.

"I'll have to find employment, won't I?" she answered with an extra-sweet smile.

Michael laughed again, sending her blood pressure soaring. "And what occupation will allow you to put aside that kind of money in less than a year? Unless, of course, you were planning on working evenings," he added suggestively, his laughing eyes scanning her slender body. "Worth thinking about."

"You disgusting, arrogant, self-absorbed, son-of-a-bitch!"

Without a second thought, she picked up the pitcher of water that her mother had earlier placed on the table and proceeded to pour the ice-cold contents onto his lap, shocking their guest to his feet, the heavy oak chair tumbling over in the process.

"Think about that, why don't you!" Jackie stormed out of the room, nearly knocking down her mother along with the tray of coffee she carried.

CHAPTER ONE

*T*he picturesque city of Nice was spectacular this time of year, but then, it always was.

The cloudless skies, the brilliant blue seas that shimmered in the sunlight from countless unspoiled coves and inlets, and the exotic plants and flowers that were everywhere; their fragrance enveloping the air, the outdoor cafés, fairs and festivals…

Every June, Michael Madison cruised his yacht along the French Riviera, stopping in every port, enjoying the foods, wines… and especially the beautiful women.

The Madisons were wealthy. Therefore, Michael squandered his money as though he had an endless supply, as if acquiring it was not a problem – and it wasn't. It never had been.

The recipients of his careless spending were women – women who were willing to share their time and their beds with him, eager to receive the lavish gifts he bestowed upon them in return.

A voluptuous brunette held a ruby-and-diamond bracelet to

the sunlight that shone through the portside window of the yacht. *"Oh cheri! C'est esquise!"*

Margot Deprix was exquisite too. Fine features, full pouting lips, thick lashes trimming expressive green eyes; features complemented nicely by the perfection of the rest of her body. Tall and overly blessed with feminine assets, she turned heads – both male and female.

Margot had been raised in a middle-class neighbourhood, by middle-class parents, and therefore she'd lacked the much finer things to which she'd recently become accustomed. However, her calculated self-induction into the life of the rich and famous had escalated her confidence. Her newfound sophistication matched that of any of the well-bred socialites that frequented the Riviera's most prestigious yacht clubs and hotels. She lived by the cliché, 'it's not what you know but who you know,' and Margot knew many, many men. They enjoyed her company; she enjoyed their gifts. She needed nothing more.

The non-committal clause in these relationships worked well for all those concerned. It most certainly worked for Michael, who had long ago decided that women were less inclined to commit than men were and therefore had given up the quest for that elusive, or perhaps non-existent, 'different' type.

Michael sat back against the plush pillows that adorned his king size bed and drew her to him.

Two days later he docked in Cannes. That evening he dined with yet another beautiful woman, this one a blonde. And he gave *her* sapphires.

From its sandy beaches to the quaint villages carved into the mountainous countryside, the Riviera is breathtakingly beautiful.

It's no wonder that it's known as one of the world's most glamorous holiday destinations, and its seductive appeal drew Michael to its shores, year after year. What better place to enjoy the luxuries that life and money have to offer? What better place to enjoy the company of beautiful women without annoying demands on his time, without the tiresome burden of his over-expectant father?

"Michael!" The deep baritone voice of Walter Madison sliced through his thoughts. "Are you listening to me?"

No, he wasn't really. In five months he'd be back in the South of France basking in the sunshine and the beauty that surrounded him. Perhaps get together with Margot or Claudette or...

Michael looked at his father sitting across the large ebony desk in one of the lavishly furnished executive offices of Madison Electronics. At sixty-five he was still a formidable force, an intimidating individual regardless of the grey hair and failing vision. Michael didn't answer him; he simply swayed back and forth in his black leather swivel chair, seemingly undaunted by his father's concerns. They were, after all, his father's concerns, not his, and besides, he preferred his daydream to the reality of the moment.

"For God's sake, don't you think it's time you found yourself a wife and had a few children? I want grandchildren, damn it! I want one before I die. Is that too much to ask?"

"If it's grandchildren you want, I can give you a dozen. Dad, if you think back, you'll remember that you don't have to be married to have children."

"You know," Walter continued, preferring to ignore his son, "I honestly thought that last summer you'd come back from Europe with a wife – or at least with news of an upcoming wedding. I've heard of your escapades, son. I know you've done your share of socializing. You can't tell me you can't find a woman to marry."

"Oh, I've socialized, Dad," Michael admitted with a smile, "but none of those ladies were the type to bring home to Papa."

"Damn it Michael, cut the crap! Aren't you at least concerned for your health? I know *I* am!"

"My health?" Michael was incredulous. He seemed to remember having this conversation years ago. It certainly wasn't warranted now. "I'm thirty-three, Dad; I think I know what I'm doing."

"That's not all. These women with whom you prefer to consort are robbing you blind! You mark my words: if you continue to live this lifestyle you're going to wind up penniless. I might be gone by then, but you mark my words," he repeated.

Michael was too old for the dreaded birds-and-the-bees lecture and too old to be told how to behave, so he shrugged indifferently at his father's obvious paranoia. "If you're gone by then what difference would it make to you?"

"What difference?" Walter's voice thundered. "I didn't work my butt off to bring this company to its present state only to have it flushed down the toilet. Maybe it doesn't mean anything to you, but it means a hell of a lot to me. I want to die knowing that you will pass it on to your children – not to these vultures you go out with!"

Tired of this conversation, Michael turned to look out the window and noticed it was snowing. Maybe he could take a drive up north to the chalet later, ski a little... He heard his father huffing and faced him once again. "Just what is it you want from me?"

Walter sighed. "I want a grandchild."

"Only if you're willing to accept an illegitimate one, because that's the only way you're going to become a granddad – Dad!"

"Why are you so stubborn?"

"I took after you I guess," Michael retorted.

"Find yourself a wife for God's sake! They can't all be the same!"

Michael glared at his father. "How can you sit there and make these demands when you've been divorced for the past – what is it – twenty-nine years? Why didn't you remarry? You could have had a whole herd of kids who would have been happy to procreate and provide you with grandchildren. You didn't. Now why do I have to pay for your regrets? You of all people know perfectly well that the adoring wife doesn't exist anymore. They went out of style. They're not barefoot and pregnant and in the kitchen anymore; they're either brainless adornments or executives in boardrooms! The two extremes. There's no happy medium – at least not that I've encountered."

"I'd like to leave you in a room full of feminists," Walter told his son, and Michael smiled mischievously.

"That might prove to be very interesting, actually."

Walter's cheeks became flushed suddenly. "You think you're funny, don't you? You think you've got it made. I just gave you the reins to the entire kit and caboodle; you're in charge now. So you figure your old man will kick the bucket soon and you'll just inherit everything – without really having done anything to earn it!"

Michael sprang to his feet. "Now just a minute! First of all,

I don't wish you dead and I resent the implication, and what do you mean by 'without having done anything'? You're saying I haven't worked – that I haven't pulled my weight?"

"No, that's not what I meant, but you've had it pretty easy. You have to admit that. I'm the one who created this company. I'm the one who struggled in the beginning. I'm the one who had to make, at times, difficult decisions in order to keep Madison Electronics on top. This was already a successful organization before you took over. You've set up shop over in Montreal. Granted. I'm happy to say that you've done an excellent job, but you didn't start it from nothing; there was already a base here in Toronto and I'm the one that put it there."

His father had a point. Michael was aware of that. Walter started the electronics company soon after graduating from university. It all began with the manufacture of computer boards. Walter had been lucky to form a friendship with the salesman of a large computer company. They gave him his first break; they'd ordered hundreds of boards within the first few months of business. From there came advancement in computer and video screens as well as TV screens, and naturally continuous improvement of the computer chip. His abilities along with his ample aggressiveness gained him the trust of the business world, securing contracts from companies across the country and abroad, thus allowing him to expand nearly every year.

Over a short period of time Walter Madison's name and his systems imaging company became synonymous with excellence. His product was in demand – and he delivered – consistently for the past forty-five years.

Walter had also had the foresight to invest in properties in the then outskirts of Toronto instead of the costly downtown sector. This section of suburbs became a city itself, the city of Vaughan, which had become known as the 'The City Above Toronto'. It was bustling with growth and development and it later supplied him with a substantial return on his initial investment as well as an optimum area to build the massive 400,000-square-foot facilities of which he was now so proud. His father had done very well. He had every right to be proud.

Michael sank into his chair again. Perhaps he should try to humour him. This conversation had to come to an end soon. "So is it my fault that I was born after you?"

"You joke, Michael, but you won't be laughing soon." Obviously it hadn't been the right time for wit. "You seem to forget, son, that I relinquished my directorial position here, I didn't relinquish ownership!"

Michael's eyes narrowed suspiciously as he watched his father slowly rise to his feet. Michael was taller than Walter, over six feet, but sitting there, his father leaning towards him over his desk, he suddenly felt as though he'd been propelled back through time – as if he were just a little boy.

Walter produced an envelope from the pocket of the navy blue suit jacket hanging on the antique coat rack by the large picture window behind his desk. He placed the envelope on the desk and slid it across towards his son.

Curious, Michael picked up the envelope and extracted the contents from within. They were legal documents. Not a will, but… Michael couldn't believe his eyes.

"Okay, this is a joke, right?" Michael laughed, but somewhere in the pit of his stomach was the feeling of impending doom.

"I'm giving you a year." Walter spoke slowly as he recounted what his son had just read. "You find yourself a wife – a real wife, Michael – I will know the difference – one way or another. If you don't, I will sell off this company in pieces. The proceeds will be diverted to whomever I choose, but be assured it will not be you. I want a grandchild – a legitimate one. No grandchild, no inheritance. Simple as that."

Michael was speechless. Perhaps he'd stayed away too long. His father had completely lost his mind. Michael flung the papers back onto the desk. "This is extortion!"

"Really? How is that, tell me? Look, the fact that you're my son doesn't necessarily guarantee that I'll just hand over all that I have."

"I seriously doubt I'll go hungry, Dad!"

"No, but you love your lifestyle, and for that you need me – you need this company to maintain it!"

"This is preposterous! You can't be serious!"

"Oh, but I am!" Reading his son's thoughts, Walter slammed his fist on the desk. "And no, I am not senile! I have had it with your cynicism and your annoying sarcasm. This is not a public company. It's *my* company and I will do with it what I damn well please. I've decided this is what I want and I *will* stand firm. My demands are clear; my decision is final. It's done. And no, Frank did not know of my intentions; I knew he would tell you."

He was right. Michael had been given 25 per cent of Madison upon his return to head office, but his father remained the major shareholder. Aside from trying to declare him mentally unstable – that thought actually occurred to him – he had no choice but to do what he was told or... He could be bluffing... No. Walter rarely bluffed. He meant what he said. He'd make good on his threat. Michael couldn't risk his inheritance on the odd – extremely improbable possibility of a bluff.

Michael raised his hands in the air as though admitting defeat. "All right fine, you'll have your grandchild, but I'm not marrying anyone."

"Yes you are. It's there in black and white. You must be married to the woman that will bear your child and it will be a real marriage, at least for as long as I'm alive."

"And you honestly think I can find such a woman within a year? You're right, you're not senile, you're just plain crazy."

"There are plenty of nice girls out there, Michael. You just have to stop looking in hotel bars."

"Is that where you found my mother?"

Walter's face became almost ashen in colour. "No, that's not where I found your mother, but I was painfully aware right from the beginning that the marriage would not last. She was not the wife I would have wanted, nor the mother I would have chosen for my son, but it happened."

"Yes, *it* happened all right. She walked out on both of us. I grew up without a mother. Although I'm certain that things wouldn't have been any different for me if she'd stayed." Michael shook his head in disappointment as he allowed himself to think back to his childhood for just a moment. "I can't remember her ever holding me, comforting me after a scraped knee or a bad dream. She was one hell of a mother – and wife for that matter. After what she did to us, you want me to put a child of mine in the same predicament. I won't."

Walter sighed heavily. He was willing to compromise somewhat. "Michael, if you meet a girl… as long as it's for real, I'll extend the time limit."

"How generous of you to allow me a possible stay of execution."

So much for compromising! "Don't push me, or I'll give you no flexibility whatsoever!"

Michael rose from his chair and turned to leave. "This is preposterous. You can't do this."

"No?" Walter called after his son. "Watch me!"

Michael slammed shut the door to his father's office, putting an end to their unbelievable conversation. He strode loudly across the dark hardwood floor, down the hall to Frank's office, ignoring the greetings of several of his staff.

Frank Atkins was the corporate lawyer for Madison Electronics. Nearly fifteen years his senior, Frank was someone Michael considered a friend, a startled friend who jumped when he suddenly burst into his office.

"Whoa! Who bit you?"

"My father! So help me, Frank, if you had something to do with this—"

Frank put down his pen and watched with concern as Michael walked determinedly towards him. "With what? What are you talking about?"

"He's had papers drawn up stating that if I don't provide him with a grandchild within the year he will sell the company and give it to charity! Oh, but that's not all. Get this: I have to get married!"

Frank burst into laughter, and made a mental note to visit

the gym on a more regular basis. Frank was not excessively overweight for his average height, but his belly jiggled just now, and it was not a pretty sight! "Come on, you're kidding!"

"Do I look like I'm kidding?" Michael snapped, and then suspicion drenched his tone as he watched his friend with narrowed eyes. "Did you know about this, Frank?"

Frank sobered immediately. "No! Of course not, Michael! All right, he can't be serious. He's probably trying to get you to settle down..."

This was incredible, even for Walter. Over the ten years that Frank had been employed by Madison, he'd come to learn that Walter was a very determined, ambitious man. Walter achieved every goal he'd set for himself in business and expected his employees to live by the same rule. Unfortunately, his advanced years now found him without much of a following as far as women companions were concerned. Understandably, loneliness in his personal life had blurred Walter's normally keen senses. Dulled by longing, his foresight in certain business matters had eventually caused him to sometimes act unscrupulously just to maintain excellence within the walls of Madison Electronics. Now his years at the helm of his empire were all but over, and it was too late to make changes to his personal life.

"But why, Michael? Why this sudden interest in marriage?"

"Sudden is right! Suddenly he doesn't approve of the way I choose to live my life! Suddenly he wants a grandchild... I offered to give him several – problem is he wouldn't go for it! He wants an heir... *and,*" Michael added, thrusting skyward his index finger for emphasis as he paced nervously across the room, "a daughter-in-law!" Michael began to laugh as well. It was just too ridiculous!

"Oh boy. You really got yourself in a mess this time, didn't you?"

Michael stopped pacing suddenly as he became serious again. "I beg your pardon? How did I get *myself* into this mess?"

"You do have quite the lifestyle, Michael. I can understand why you don't want to give up your freedom. Tell me, at what volume is your little black book now?"

"And what business is it of my father's or anyone else's for that matter? Besides, what has *he* been doing for the past twenty years? If you think my black book's thick, you should take a look at his!"

"I know Michael, but as I was about to say... perhaps it's, well... Walter's getting on in years, and perhaps he's realized the errors he's made and... he probably doesn't want to see you wind up old and alone..." Frank's voice trailed off. Knowing Walter as he did, Frank could actually see how this ultimatum might make sense to the old man – if that was indeed Walter's reason to force Michael into marriage.

Michael shook his head. "I can't do this."

"Michael, he's not asking you to cut off your... part of your anatomy."

"He might as well have!"

"Oh come on. I've been married nearly twenty-six years! It's not so horrible. In fact I've been quite happy and so has Irene."

"Well good for you. I'd rather have a root canal – without the Novocaine!" Leaning a hip against the desk, Michael sighed in exasperation, seeing no possible way to talk his father out of this ultimatum. "I wouldn't mind the kid, Frank. I just don't want to be married."

A few days later Frank walked into Michael's office.

"Hi Frank," he said absently, briefly diverting his attention from the paperwork on his desk. "What can I do for you?"

Frank sat himself in the round brown leather chair facing Michael.

Although Walter wanted to remain active in the operations of Madison, he had relinquished his office to his son. He had also insisted that Michael move into the larger, more elaborate office when he had retired. Walter felt that the office had to reflect the position of president, and it did.

Two large windows with dark, bold-coloured valances served as bookends to the rich mahogany bookshelves directly behind Michael's desk. The desk itself was an antique, massive in size and intricately carved. A Persian rug lay underneath, covering a mere portion of the hardwood floors. A couch in the same shade of leather as the chairs sat against one wall. Yes, the office was worthy of a president. As Michael had mentioned to Frank at the time of his move, however, perhaps the office was more suited for the president of a country!

"Actually, I might be able to do something for *you*."

Intrigued, Michael put down his pen. "Oh? Don't tell me you thought of a way to get my father off my back?"

"Possibly. Michael, I checked into his 'demands'... To tell you the truth, the first thing that came to mind was that your only solution would be to declare him mentally unfit."

"Yeah, I thought of that."

"Guess what he did. Before this brainstorm of his he went to see a psychiatrist – for a few months in fact. He's vouched for his sanity."

Michael watched him, impatience setting in. "How the hell is this revelation supposed to help me?"

"That wasn't my revelation, but this information may justify my suggestion."

"And that is…"

"What about a surrogate mother?"

Michael was less than thrilled with Frank's brainstorm. "I am not one half of a couple who is trying to have a child, Frank."

"I know that, but it could work."

"I don't think so. I'd go for it, but my father wouldn't. He wants me to be married, settled down with a real wife, so that he can die happy – and I can die young!" he added cynically.

"Is that what he said?" Frank chuckled.

"Yes!"

Frank leaned back in his chair, causing it to rock back and forth. "So, you marry the girl. What's the big deal?" Michael was about to protest, but Frank continued. "This is the age of prenuptial agreements. We draw up a contract," he explained excitedly. "You are married and she bears you a child. You pay her handsomely for services rendered and then divorce her. Naturally, I think in this case it would be better if we arranged that she doesn't see the child – just in case."

An incredulous smile spread over Michael's face. "Isn't that going a bit too far? I mean, who's going to agree to do something like this? I can't see anyone accepting these terms. And besides… my father wants this marriage to last as long as he does, so… so much for that."

"You'd be surprised what some people will do for money. All you have to do is act like a happily married couple for a few months. You make that stipulation in the contract. She either plays the part convincingly or she receives less money. We can discuss the particulars later. As for your father and the marriage being a farce, I'm certain that once Walter has his grandchild, nothing else will matter."

"And where am I going to find such a woman?" Michael didn't see the same light at the end of the tunnel.

"I'll handle that," Frank assured him confidently.

"You? Just how do you propose to do that?"

"I'm pretty sure I know what you like, Michael. I will take care of the preliminary interviews and give you a complete dossier on each applicant including, of course, medical records. You decide from there which ladies you'd like to meet or interview personally."

Michael laughed suddenly. "You're pulling my leg, aren't you?"

"No, I'm not. I'm quite serious. Can you think of a more feasible alternative?"

"No."

CHAPTER TWO

*J*ackie Ellis tried desperately to overcome the guilt that gnawed at her from within. She was fundamentally responsible for the mess in which they found themselves. Although, even in her state of self-condemnation, she was certain that she would have handled things differently given the chance. She struggled to understand her father's decisions, but it didn't look as though enlightenment had any intention of presenting itself anytime soon.

"Mummy, how could Daddy have done this?"

The petite woman sitting across the kitchen table shook her head wearily. "I don't know. I guess... I guess his back was against the wall. He had no choice."

"I don't understand. Didn't he at least confide in you that he was in trouble?"

"No!" she cried. "I told you! He... he had been a little preoccupied at that time. I thought something might not be right, especially since he'd been so excited about that new computer chip. I asked him about it, if there was anything wrong with it, if perhaps it didn't work properly, but he avoided my questions. He just told me not to worry and that everything would be all right. It was not all right, was it? He didn't tell you, he didn't tell me. He kept it all inside."

Was it her imagination, or had her mother aged five years in just a few months? At fifty-five, Joan Ellis was not considered old. A delicate, petite woman, her features were those of a porcelain doll. But her usually-coiffed brown hair now seemed dry and limp, combed simply back away from her face. Her hazel eyes, once full of laughter, were now dulled by pain, and her warm, welcoming smile had disappeared altogether.

"I'm sorry, Mummy. I don't mean to upset you. It's just that... it's just so overwhelming." Jackie put a hand to her forehead. "It's my fault, it's all my fault."

"Jackie dear, why would you say that? You know it's not true. You've been away for months..."

Still, the truth stuck in Jackie's throat. "How? How could all this have happened – and in such a short time?"

Joan looked confused suddenly, shaking her head, fidgeting with the placemat. "I don't know. The Madisons—"

"—I think, Mummy," her daughter interrupted hotly, rising to her feet, "that the Madisons just saw an opportunity and took it. Nobody does anything for nothing!" Jackie paced the white-tiled kitchen floor, all the while repeatedly pulling at the waistband of the faded jeans that had recently become oversized. "Couldn't the bank help Daddy? We were a good account. We never had any problems before. I can't believe that they wouldn't help him."

"Well they wouldn't!" Joan sounded bitter. Then in a quieter tone, "they couldn't. Our line of credit was cancelled. He owed too much. The Madisons were the ones who paid everyone. They are the secured creditors. We owe them now."

"Yes, and I'm sure they enjoy being in that position. Mummy, Madison Electronics is one of the biggest – probably now *the* biggest – systems imaging companies in the country. They didn't care about helping Daddy. Don't you see? For them it was purely business. The big fish eating the little fish, survival of the fittest – kill or be killed!"

"Jackie, stop it! If it weren't for them we'd be out on the street!"

"Mummy, I think they've played with your mind. Granted, they own our company, but they don't own us, nor do they own our home!"

Jackie sighed as her wide eyes took in her surroundings. She walked around the ample kitchen, raking nervous fingers through her shoulder-length brown hair.

This very kitchen held such fond happy memories. Jackie and her mother had cooked many a dinner in that kitchen. From daily meals to special events, the Ellis women were known for their culinary abilities. Birthdays and anniversaries were acknowledged with much fanfare, and holidays were especially happy occasions where friends and family members joined in celebration. No gathering was ever dull in the Ellis home. Now… it was quiet.

"I know how you feel about this house, but we'll have to sell it. You realize that, don't you? We'll have to sell," she shrugged.

"They will definitely want to be paid back—"

"—Jackie," Joan interrupted, her voice quivering nervously. "Please, I have such a headache. I don't know... I'm not sure about all the particulars. Mr. Atkins, the Madisons' lawyer, will be visiting this afternoon. He'll... he'll explain things."

"What things? Is there something else, Mummy?"

As if on cue the doorbell rang, saving poor Joan from any further explanations. "I'll get it," she called as she hurried out to the living room.

Jackie's stomach was in knots at the prospect of rehashing the sordid details of their present situation. In her head the knowledge of her culpability clashed noisily with the futile choices her father had made in order to resolve the problem, and this resulted in a massive headache.

Samuel Ellis was an intelligent man, a shrewd businessman. His company, which also manufactured computer components and video imaging, was a small company in comparison to Madison Electronics. Nevertheless, it had been moderately successful for so many years. This had been a terrible blow to Sam's pride – it certainly had been for Jackie.

Her father had graduated from Queen's University in Kingston, with an engineering degree. He had often spoken of the school during the summers when Jackie helped out at the office, and how he hoped his daughter would follow in his foot-steps. Queen's had an excellent engineering program, one of the best in the province. But moving away from Toronto and leaving her family would be difficult. Fortunately, the fact that her best friend had decided to study at the same university made her decision more appealing. The two decided to take a year to earn a little extra money to pay for their much-anticipated trip to Egypt. When they were ready to enroll they rented a small apartment near the university, sharing all bills as well as chores. Carol and Jackie were closer than most sisters and therefore the arrangement worked out wonderfully.

After two years of studies however, Jackie had decided to take yet another year off to work more closely with her father, and looking back now she wouldn't change that for anything. He had taught her so much. Sam had been so proud when he had shown his daughter the designs for a microchip that had the ability to quadruple the RAM memory on any computer at a fraction of the cost of standard RAM chips. Finally, Ellis Electronics would be acknowledged by the larger companies, and they would actually have a chance to earn a contract normally awarded to the Madisons.

"Daddy," she had pleaded excitedly. "You *can't* wait to market this chip!"

Sam's dark eyes had studied his daughter lovingly as he stroked his unruly grey-streaked brown hair. He smiled at her enthusiasm, her determination to put Ellis Electronics on the map, but he'd been skeptical. "I understand your eagerness, but I believe it would be best to test it for a few months, at least five or six—"

"—Dad, you are painfully aware of how volatile the computer business can be. This chip may very well be obsolete in six months' time. Either that, or someone else will beat us to the punch!"

Sam had not been completely convinced, but he'd been in awe of his daughter's determination, her complete confidence in his capabilities, and realizing that there was truth in Jackie's theory, he agreed to begin to market and sell his new invention – come what may.

Unfortunately, what came was not at all what he had hoped for. Preoccupied with returning to school, Jackie was unaware that something was drastically wrong and Sam made certain his daughter would leave knowing nothing of the chaos that lay ahead. He knew Jackie would hold herself responsible. He would not have that. She needed to continue her studies. In fact, Sam had listed the various benefits of accepting a job offer in Kingston during school break and the summer months. The experience of working for someone other than family would be an asset in the future, he told her. Jackie knew now why he had wanted to keep her away from the family business. During her weekend or holiday visits, her father never let on to his problems. Instead, he boasted about the vast number of new customers. He assured her that Ellis Electronics was not only on the map, but doing substantially well. She had no reason to suspect otherwise. Sam was determined to solve the problem without burdening his family.

However, his troubles had intensified rapidly. Within a few short weeks after installation, the microchip would corrupt the existing computer memory. Naturally, this caused companies to expect a refund as well as the cost for damages. He lost funds, then employees, and then contracts – one after the other. It all added up to one big mess! Sam owed the bank so much that they had finally closed their doors to him. He borrowed large sums of money from several unsuspecting investors, but it only made the hole he had dug himself deeper and deeper.

Apparently it was Walter Madison who finally bailed him out. He cleared all his payables, including the loans with the bank. Sam was debt-free, but there was a catch. Ellis Electronics had become a Madison-owned company. Sam Ellis had no say, no control. All this without ever mentioning a thing to his wife or daughter.

It had been too much to keep bottled up inside. During this time his body had run on pure adrenaline. The abrupt end to all his hard work had been his end too. One night, a mere week into the new year, Samuel Ellis died of a massive heart attack. He would have been fifty-nine the following week. He was gone before he could tell his family the truth – before he could tell them anything.

Jackie sighed heavily as she sat down again. Was it not enough that she'd lost her father? To learn that her haste for success, that the excess pride in her family business was the core of the problem, was perhaps even more intensely distressing. The fact that she had not insisted on returning home to work with her dad before her final year, only added to her guilt. But regardless, the initial error in judgement had been hers, and that realization was unbearable.

"Jackie!" Her mother brought her back to the present. "Jackie dear, Mr. Atkins is here."

Jackie reluctantly rose to her feet. She suddenly felt as though she was about to walk the plank. She took a deep breath and raised her chin in defiance. She refused to give Walter Madison and his company any indication that the remaining members of the Ellis family may be at their mercy! Jackie may no longer have had a penny to her name, but she still had her pride – maybe too much of it.

Jackie had expected to see only Mr. Atkins. She was surprised to see that he was not alone. At the sight of Mr. Atkins' guest, all her determination to be strong and unwavering was suddenly shoved somewhere to the back of her brain.

He was as she remembered... he was tall... with thick, brown hair combed away from his forehead, its length resting on the collar of the black overcoat that could not mask the broad shoulders tapering down to a flat stomach and narrow hips. It had been years since she'd seen him last – he hadn't attended the funeral; she'd heard he was away – but he hadn't lost the immense attraction that emanated from every pore of his being.

Her first encounter with the young Mr. Madison had been but fleeting. He'd slid behind the wheel of a sleek red convertible just as she and her dad had arrived on the Madisons' business doorstep. It hadn't been a meeting at all, and she would never dare ask her dad about him, but to an impressionable twelve-year-old he'd made an unwarranted and most likely unhealthy lasting impact. It was due to this encounter that she'd returned with her father on yet another occasion when she was the ripe age of seventeen. If it was at all possible he looked even better. That meeting was just as fleeting as the last, but... he'd smiled at her as he brushed by her, sending her reeling with emotions never experienced, never equaled, and regrettably, unsurpassed! She was in love... albeit in vain... but in love...

He was much older now – they both were, obviously – looks still intact, but he appeared... harder, colder, his features seemingly chiseled out of stone. And his eyes... his eyes mocked her obvious attraction!

Her mother's voice finally brought her back down to earth, before she embarrassed herself further. "Jackie dear, you met Mr. Atkins when you were here last."

Her mother could be so appeasing at times. It was frustrating! She meant the funeral; why didn't she just say so?

"This, dear, is Mr. Madison. He... he and his father, Walter... well, they are the ones who helped us..."

Immediately, anger, resentment, and Ellis pride took the place of sheer admiration. She was no longer that little girl with a crush. The events of recent months had awakened her from her dream world. This was life, and it wasn't at all rosy. "Is that what you call it!" she snapped, not intimidated by the fact that Mr. Madison towered over her by nearly a foot. Her fluffy blue slippers added very little to her height, or sophistication, for that matter.

"What would you call it, Miss Ellis?" Michael Madison asked her calmly. His tone was drenched in sarcasm and his eyes danced with laughter. And something told her that he was always like that.

"You, or your father, or *both* of you, took over my father's company. You're not going to lose on that acquisition. As for the sum of money that was required to pay all of my father's debts... unfortunately my father never told us what was happening. I would never have accepted. I don't want your charity. You'll have your money back just as soon as we can sell this house."

"Sell the house?" Michael was incredulous. He looked at Frank, then at Joan and then back at her daughter. "Your father mortgaged this house a while ago," he said as he seated himself comfortably at the head of their dining room table. "That's why the banks would no longer help him. He had no collateral, nor credibility."

Jackie was furious when she turned to her mother who was standing still, her fingers nervously clenching and unclenching. "What else haven't you told me, Mother?"

"I'll make some coffee, excuse me..." Joan spoke quietly. Turning, she walked hurriedly towards the kitchen. She couldn't stay there another moment.

"Actually Miss Ellis, neither your mother or you, for that matter, would have a roof over your head right now if it weren't for my father's generosity. He took over the mortgage from the bank about eleven months ago. Your family has lived here rent-free since then," he informed her. "*And*, it's just as well that you don't accept charity, because I'm not about to offer it – not anymore. After all, your father made the bad judgements, not I. You can rest assured that I have no intention of paying for his mistakes. My father knew your father. In fact he had tried to come to his aid once before, but your father didn't accept his offer. He was too proud. In the end, however, it *was* my father who helped him, and substantially so. He has helped you as well. Any moneys concerning your stay in this house have been cleared because he felt sorry for you. However, last month he decided to relinquish the helm to me. I am now president of Madison Electronics. I am not my father, and after meeting you I absolutely refuse to chalk this all up to 'bad debts'."

"Please..." Frank Atkins felt uncomfortable with Michael's stern words and tried to intervene. "There's no need..."

"We don't want your father's pity or anyone else's!" Jackie declared, raising her chin. "When do you want us out?"

Michael took a moment to answer. He hadn't expected that. "You won't have to leave," he began, as he flipped through the papers of the large black book, a book, Jackie thought, that held all that transpired in their past and probably what was in store for them in the future. "At least not for now."

"Don't worry about your 'bad debt', Mr. Madison. We'll pay you the rent we owe you, plus this other loan! You'll have your money within the year!"

Michael's head jolted upwards, laughing out loud – something that infuriated Jackie to her limits.

"Within the year? And how do you propose to do that, Miss Ellis? I don't accept Monopoly money!"

"What are you talking about?" Jackie's eyes narrowed with suspicion.

"You obviously must not be aware just how much money was required to pay all of your father's 'debts', as you put it." Michael glanced at the figures in front of him. His eyes mocked her when they met hers once again. "As it stands, Miss Ellis, your accrued debts amount to nearly half a million dollars."

Jackie's mouth dropped, and Michael smiled with revolting smugness. If it weren't for the angry tension of her muscles, she would have dropped to the floor like a rag doll.

What had made her say that she'd pay him back without first asking for the figures? Stress must have shorted out the thinking mechanism in her brain, but it was too late to bite her tongue and she'd be damned if she'd admit defeat! She rebounded quickly.

"I'll have to find employment, won't I?" she answered with an extra-sweet smile.

Michael laughed again, sending her blood pressure soaring.

"And what occupation will allow you to put aside that kind of money in less than a year? Unless, of course, you were planning on working evenings," he added suggestively, his laughing eyes scanning her slender body. "Worth thinking about."

"You disgusting, arrogant, self-absorbed, son-of-a-bitch!"

Without a second thought, she picked up the pitcher of water that her mother had earlier placed on the table and proceeded to pour the ice-cold contents onto his lap, shocking their guest to his feet, the heavy oak chair tumbling over in the process.

"Think about that, why don't you!" Jackie stormed out of the room, nearly knocking down her mother along with the tray of coffee she carried.

Hours later, Jackie ventured back downstairs to face her mother. Joan sat in her husband's favourite chair, absently caressing the armrest.

"Hi," Jackie said simply.

"Why did you do that?" Her mother's voice was quiet, her eyes focussed on nothing in particular. "We should be grateful to this man. Instead, here you are nearly drowning him, acting like a rude, hot-tempered child."

"Mother, if I'd wanted to drown him I would have at least aimed for his head."

"Jackie!"

Jackie rolled her eyes heavenward and sighed. "I'm sorry, all right?" Then, knowing that she had, more than likely, made matters worse for her mother, she asked, "Did he... did he change his mind – about letting us stay, I mean?"

"No, he didn't. Thank God."

"What *did* he say?"

"Say?" Joan looked up at her daughter.

She and Sam had waited nine long years to be blessed with children. Finally, after three miscarriages, at the age of thirty Joan gave birth to their one and only child. Jackie was their pride and joy. She was such a beautiful baby and she had become a beautiful woman. Her soft complexion, the long thick lashes that trimmed her big brown eyes, full lips that formed an enticing smile... but that mouth held a tongue that Joan wished her daughter would keep in check once in a while!

"Oh, nothing really," her mother continued calmly. "Just that he has accepted your offer to repay within the year, that's all. He hadn't mentioned a time limit until you did, Jackie. He hadn't mentioned that we had to pay him back at all!"

Jackie bit her lip. "Why did he come here anyway – to gloat?"

Joan was becoming increasingly agitated. "I don't think so Jackie, but you didn't give him a chance, did you? He had started to say that he had papers to sign regarding the house; the rent I think, but that's when I called you. We know what happened after that."

Jackie bowed her head. Why couldn't she control her mouth? "What else did he say? Afterwards, I mean."

"He said that you should watch your temper."

"Really?" Jackie fumed. How she could ever have found this man attractive...

"Yes, really!" Joan sprang from her chair. "Please! I know that this is a horrible situation. I know it was a shock to you. It was to me, too. And I know that damned Ellis pride runs through your veins as it did your father's, but maybe you should learn to control it! Your father left us in a bind, but you're not helping!" Jackie winced at her mother's words. "What were you thinking? How could we possibly pay them half a million dollars – and in just a few months!"

She hadn't been scolded like that since her teen years. "I'm sorry. I'll go talk to him. I'll apologize if you want."

"I don't want you to talk to him! I don't want you anywhere near that man! We'll end up owing double!"

Jackie sank into the soft floral couch, her head in her hands, and her mother sighed in exasperation. "Look, he obviously can't hold us to that time limit, nor can he possibly expect us to repay the full amount. It's absolutely impossible. But," Joan said, rubbing her temples. "I suppose it would be a good idea to find ourselves some type of employment. We'll pay him what we can. I'm sorry Jackie, but under the circumstances, you'll have to leave school, if only for a while."

"I know."

CHAPTER THREE

First order of agenda was to call the university and tell them she would not be returning. Next she called Carol, her roommate. It was difficult to recount the entire sordid ordeal, but Carol and Jackie had shared nearly everything since they were five years old. She couldn't keep this from her, she could tell her anything. And now Jackie had to tell her friend to find someone else to take her place in their apartment; she didn't know if she'd ever be able to go back.

Resumes were drafted and distributed to various companies. By the end of the following week she had been called for two interviews, but still she remained unemployed.

Her mother, on the other hand, had been more successful. She had found a part-time job at the corner bakery. Joan had shopped at Rose's Bakery for years. Mrs. Rose was happy to have an extra set of hands in the store while her husband baked. Joan was to work only weekday mornings. Mrs. Rose would let her know if she needed help evenings or weekends.

Jackie sold her car so that she might put aside that money in case her situation worsened, although she doubted if things could actually get worse than they already were. Joan would drive to work in the only remaining vehicle, leaving Jackie to face the cold March air on foot as she knocked on doors for possible work.

Try as she might to hold on to a small shred of optimism, things looked bleak and she was becoming increasingly worried. No one was hiring and she had to find something soon. Had he been right? Was she going to have to turn to the streets? "Over his dead body!" she said out loud.

"What was that, dear?" asked her mother, who had just come home.

"Nothing, I was just thinking out loud." Jackie tried to smile.

The telephone rang and Joan put her suspicions aside as she plopped her boots on the mat and went to answer it.

"It's for you, Jackie." Her mother's face suddenly paled. "It's Mr. Atkins."

What now? Jackie thought apprehensively, as she took the receiver from her mother's trembling hand.

"Miss Ellis, Frank Atkins here."

Jackie's tone bordered on crisp. "Is there a problem, Mr. Atkins?"

"No, no. There's no problem. Actually... I was wondering if you had found employment."

"No, but I'm expecting to hear from several firms. Why?" In reality, Jackie had little expectation that those firms would be calling, but she would never tell him that.

"I know of a position here at the Madison offices. It's a

secretarial position. I'm aware that you're much more qualified, but it's a start, I mean until a more suitable position is available…"

Jackie waved her mother away, assuring her that the phone call was nothing important. Sitting in the large easy chair, she twirled the telephone cord around her fingers, the vision of wrapping it around Madison's neck entering her mind. "Thank you, but I can't work for that man."

"I understand. Well, there are also a couple of openings in the plant. Actually, the pay is better than the other position. It's assembly work, you know, much like your—"

"—Yes," she interrupted, "I'm aware of the type of work, but like I said…"

"If you take the position in the plant you'd have less contact with him, if any. You'd probably never even see him."

"Does he know about this?" Jackie asked, her suspicion resurfacing.

"I did mention it." There was a slight pause. "It pays well and we both know that's what you need. What do you think?"

"But what did he say, Mr. Atkins?" Jackie was curious to know what Madison's reaction had been.

"Well… he said he didn't care, as long as the job was being done." Frank didn't relay Michael's opinion on the subject of Miss Ellis. "Besides, it was his father, Walter Madison, who suggested I call you. He's trying to help."

Could she actually contemplate accepting? "I don't know, Mr. Atkins."

"I'd take the job, Miss Ellis. Like I said, the pay is good. Plus, you'll have a full benefits package. I believe your mother suffers with asthma, does she not?"

"Yes."

"Plus a pension, even life insurance."

"Does he intend to bump me off?" Jackie asked sarcastically.

"Miss Ellis, really. By the way, I'll bring this up now and hopefully never again, but whether or not you take this particular job... when you do begin to work..." Frank was having difficulty finding the right words. "It will be up to you to determine how much you need to live for the month, but eventually Mr. Madison will expect some type of payment. When you're ready... payments in the amount you choose should be made payable to Madison Investments. I've sent paperwork in the mail; you should receive it shortly."

Jackie exhaled loudly. "Thank you Mr. Atkins, for reminding me of my situation."

"Miss Ellis, that wasn't my intention. I merely informed you—"

"—Yes, fine," she interrupted in a curt voice. "I'll take the job, Mr. Atkins. What do I have to do? Do I have to come in and actually apply?"

"No, don't worry about that. I'll handle personnel. Simply come in Monday morning at seven and report to Jerry Merrel, the plant manager. He'll have all the necessary papers ready for you."

"I suppose there is an employee entrance for the plant?" Jackie preferred to reduce the possibility of running into her new boss.

"Yes, of course. You'll see it as you come down the driveway to the far parking area. Jerry's office is at the end of the corridor, to your right. He'll be expecting you. Miss Ellis... I believe this is the right move."

"Right."

CHAPTER FOUR

*A*s she stood on the crowded bus early Monday morning, Jackie wondered if accepting the position at Madison Electronics was a wise thing to do. Her mother, on the other hand, thought that this was one more 'nice gesture' from the Madisons, especially after the way Jackie had treated Walter's son. How her mother could allow herself to be so easily taken in by those people was beyond her!

Jackie wanted to scream. Instead she sighed heavily, causing the woman next to her to look at her strangely. She supposed she *should* be grateful; she needed the job… and no one else had offered.

Jackie was hesitant as she opened the door marked 'Employee Entrance'. There was no one in sight. She looked down at her watch. It was ten minutes to seven. Due to missing the connecting buses, it had taken her over forty minutes to reach her destination from her home in Willowdale, which was yet another suburb of

Toronto. Tomorrow she'd have to leave earlier. She couldn't afford to be late.

Shoving her gloves in the pockets of her coat, Jackie walked down the corridor following Mr. Atkins' directions. She knocked on the open office door.

A young man looked up and smiled. "You must be Jackie."

"Yes," Jackie smiled back, self-consciously shrugging off her coat.

"I'm Jerry Merrel." He stood and extended his hand over the neatly kept grey desk. "Nice to meet you. I have a few forms here for you," he said, gesturing for her to sit down.

Jerry Merrel, she assumed, was in his thirties. He had very little hair, all of which he kept tied in a ponytail. He was tall and very thin and sported a long bushy blonde beard. He seemed like a nice man.

After supplying all the pertinent personal information, Jerry showed Jackie to the locker room to store her coat and purse, and then to her work area.

The plant was immense, much larger than her father's, but then this was a massive corporation with four plants across the country and interests worldwide.

The video imaging assembly department, Jerry explained, had seventy-four employees, counting Jackie. There were rows and rows of workstations; everyone with their own sets of intricate tools. The plant was also substantially noisier than that of her father. Aside from the obvious noises from the employees' stations, a distant humming of machinery could be heard throughout the department.

Jerry introduced her to the three other people at her station.

Marjorie's blue eyes held a mischievous sparkle, suggesting to Jackie that this young woman with the blonde bob might make the days at Madison Electronics slightly easier to bear. Jackie later learned that she was in her late twenties and had completed only one year of college. Lacking a commitment to any particular career, she had accepted this position until she made her decision.

Inga was Swedish, stereotypically blonde and blue-eyed. She had immigrated when she was eighteen. Learning the new language was difficult for her at first, but after six years she was able to read, write and speak English with only minor difficulties.

Hassan was of Albanian descent, but born and raised in Calgary. His family had moved to Toronto ten years prior. An electrical technician by trade, his father was soon hired by the Madisons. Hassan followed suit.

They welcomed her immediately, assuring her that they would be happy to answer any questions or help her with anything that she didn't understand. And Jackie accepted their kindness. She didn't want to explain that she was quite knowledgeable of the type of work that had to be done. She didn't want them to know her background or her reason for being there – forced into the service of the enemy.

Aside from the early wake-up calls and half-hour commutes to the Madison plant, her first few weeks progressed quickly and without incident, but Jackie couldn't help but feel uncomfortable. She was afraid that sooner or later *Mr. Arrogance* would walk into the plant and see her there. What would he do? What would he say? What would *she* do or say, for that matter! Nothing, if she knew what was good for her. Still, she hoped she'd never have to find out.

Naturally she did.

One afternoon, Jackie and the others were leaving the lunch-room, giggling at the antics of one of her co-workers, when her newly appointed enemy quickly appeared from around the corner and smacked right into Jackie. If he hadn't put his arms around her to catch her, she was certain she would have been sitting on her behind somewhere across the room.

His hands seemed to linger a little longer than necessary around her shoulders. Their eyes locked for a moment, as if he too was at a loss for words.

Finally it was he who found his voice. He excused himself and was on his way, leaving Jackie somewhat shaken. This strange reaction to his touch confused her immensely and that was something upon which she definitely didn't want to dwell. She was not that love-struck teenager anymore. She'd be wise to remember that!

Her co-worker enjoyed the little accident, however. "You lucky dog!" Marjorie told her, nudging her arm.

"What?" Jackie was determined to feign ignorance.

"Bumping into Michael like that!"

"Who?"

"Michael Madison! He's the owner's son. Actually, he's the boss now. Ooh! I'd give anything to bump into him!"

"Oh, give me a break," Jackie scoffed. She hated that she'd allowed herself to give him a second thought, but she *had* wondered what his name was. So what of it, she scolded herself.

"Come on! Don't tell me you don't think he's gorgeous!"

"I hadn't really noticed," Jackie shrugged.

"Yeah, right! Then you definitely need your eyes examined!" Marjorie concluded, and they returned to work.

The subject of Michael Madison's good looks was dropped, and Jackie managed to shove all thoughts of him to the back of her mind. With any luck they wouldn't resurface. Unfortunately, her luck hadn't exactly been positive lately...

Michael glared out of the large office window, oblivious to the snow flurries being whisked about by the wind. His mind was in another time, another place.

He sighed as he leaned against the frame, his white shirt-sleeves rolled up, his hands in his pant pockets.

It had been several weeks since the last applicant, and he doubted if there were going to be any more. These ladies were a far cry from his expectations. He couldn't force himself to be attracted to them, not even for his 'cause', and in any case, his father would never be fooled.

There was one woman, however. In fact, his father had mentioned her several times in the last few weeks...

Michael jumped suddenly, when Frank seemed to appear out of thin air.

"Sorry, I guess I should have knocked."

"That's all right. I was just daydreaming; I didn't hear you."

"Doesn't look good, does it?" Frank offered.

"No," Michael replied.

"What do you want to do?"

"Actually, there *is* someone," Michael started.

"Well then?"

"Well, she's not like the rest."

"What – she's not human?" Frank chuckled.

Michael gave Frank a wry smile. "I think she's human. What I mean is that she's not an applicant. However, I'm certain that given the amount of funds in question, she, like all the others, will at least be intrigued enough to ponder the possibility."

"Okay. You've met her?"

"Yes, so have you."

"I have?"

Michael pushed a file across the wide desk.

Frank read the name and looked up at him again, frowning, his brow creased.

"Oh, Michael..."

"Look into it, will you," he said, dismissing him.

CHAPTER FIVE

*J*ackie was worried. Why did Jerry call her into his office? Did she do something wrong? Perhaps the high-and-mighty *new boss*, Michael Madison, had simply decided to terminate her. Perhaps he was going to fire her and evict her at the same time!

Jackie mentally gave herself a shake. She'd know soon enough. Still, she couldn't stop her hand from shaking as she knocked on Jerry's door.

To add to her concern, it was not Jerry's voice that welcomed her to enter. Frank Atkins sat behind the grey desk. Jerry was not in the office at all.

"Miss Ellis," Frank said rising to his feet. "Please come in, sit," he motioned.

"Jerry said to come to his office. Am I early?" Jackie questioned, looking at her watch.

"No, no. *I* wanted to speak to you, and I thought it would be a little more private, more comfortable for you here in

Jerry's office."

Jackie walked slowly toward the desk. "What's happened, Mr. Atkins?"

"Nothing's happened! Nothing to be alarmed about, anyway," Frank smiled, as he sat again in Jerry's chair and urged her to sit as well. "Actually... I have a proposition for you."

Jackie's eyes rounded in surprise, and Frank hastened to explain.

"What I have in mind, if you agree that is, will end your financial problems."

"Oh?" Now she was suspicious. "What *do* you have in mind, Mr. Atkins?"

Frank was suddenly feeling a little uncomfortable. He should just get it over with, quickly. "Do you know what a surrogate mother is, Miss Ellis?"

Jackie started to feel her temperature rising. "Yes, of course. What does that have to do with me and my financial status?"

"It's not an uncommon practice nowadays," he informed her, giving himself a little time to find the right words. He had thought it would be easier.

"Mr. Atkins, I don't think I'm interested in what I think you're implying—"

"—Miss Ellis, if you would just hear me out."

Jackie shook her head slowly, but didn't leave. She decided to listen to what he had to say.

"There is a gentleman who wants a child," Frank began.

"His wife can't have children?" she asked offhandedly.

"No... he's not married," he said quietly.

Jackie's eyes narrowed. "I don't understand. I didn't realize that this company dealt with family planning."

"It's a very awkward situation, Miss Ellis… You see, this gentleman never intended to marry. However, h-he would like… an heir. So would his father, as a matter of fact. He's told his son that he wants a grandchild before he dies," he told her, striving to sound dramatic.

"Is he dying?"

"Well, no, I don't think so, but—"

"—Where do I fit in, Mr. Atkins?" Jackie's blood pressure was nearing boiling levels… but she had to admit she wanted to hear the rest of it.

"We've interviewed several women, but they just didn't work out. Actually, Miss Ellis," he said, finally getting to the point. "I thought that, under the circumstances, you might consider this proposition."

"You're not serious." Jackie sat upright, a smile on her lips.

"Yes, Miss Ellis, I'm quite serious," Frank replied, and her smile quickly disappeared. "The only stipulation is that you are married during the time of conception."

"Married? *Conception?* Mr. Atkins, what are you saying?"

"Well, artificial insemination is out of the question," he rambled on. "And his father is not to know about this entire transaction; hence the marriage. You can be divorced immediately afterwards, and continue with your life."

"And leave him the baby, of course! You're not asking me to help a couple who is unable to have children; you want me to sell my baby!"

"I assure you what I am proposing is quite legal, Miss Ellis."

"I don't care if it is! I just couldn't do that! I can't do it, Mr. Atkins," she said firmly as she rose from her chair. "You'll just have to keep looking."

Frank stood as well.

"Miss Ellis, perhaps you should think it over. Remember what is at stake here. As well as helping this gentleman with his problem, you'd be helping yourself and your mother. Let's be realistic, do you really think you can clear your debt in just a few months? Maybe you should at least consider this option."

"Look, I know I said I'd rather not see Madison, but I'd be willing to speak to him. I mean this is ridiculous. He must know that I can't possibly pay him back in such little time, if at all, but this idea of yours is outrageous to say the least!"

"Unfortunately Michael is determined to hold you to the time limit you suggested. He knows it's impossible, but since your… conversation, he's quite adamant. Believe me, I've tried to change his mind, but to no avail. He won't budge. And so, time is running out. Where are you and your mother going to go when you're asked to leave your home? Think about what it would do to her."

Jackie listened. He was right; it would solve everything. But would she be able to do such a thing? And what would she tell her mother?

"What would it do to my mother when she found out what I'd done, Mr. Atkins?" Jackie voiced her thoughts. "That would surely kill her."

"She need not know, Miss Ellis. Remember, you would be married. His work takes this gentleman out of town, sometimes out of the country. I'm sure that you can orchestrate a plan to stay out of sight for a few months. Your mother wouldn't have to know at all." Frank repeated.

Jackie put her hand to her forehead. "I can't believe I'm actually listening to this nonsense. Who is this man, anyway?"

"Please," Frank gestured for her to sit down. "Would you like a glass of water or a cup of tea?"

"No. No, I don't. I want to wake up from this horrible dream." Jackie sank into her chair once again.

"I don't think I should disclose that information until I know that you're interested in this proposition. I assure you, though," he added with a smile, "he's quite handsome."

"If he's so handsome, why is he having such difficulty finding someone to have his child?"

"Procuring a woman to have his child is not the problem. Attaining a woman who will agree to the marriage, the farce... that's the difficulty. Besides, he's also very picky."

"You sound as though you think you've found the right candidate in me. What makes you so sure he'll feel the same?"

"I know what he likes, Miss Ellis," Frank said knowingly. "Naturally, you would have to supply medical records, but I'm certain that wouldn't be a problem."

"No..." Jackie sighed.

"Does this mean you're considering..." Frank jolted forward in his chair.

"What? No! I... I don't know!" Jackie put her hands to her cheeks and closed her eyes. "I can't... it's crazy. I couldn't do something like this. I can't marry someone I don't know – someone I don't love. And to actually conceive a child... and to leave him behind! This is preposterous! I realize you're trying to help – I suppose – but I'm sorry, I can't, I just can't..."

"Tell you what... why don't you think about it for a couple

of days. Give me a call; let me know either way."

Jackie stared at him for a moment. She stood slowly, and without another word, left the office.

Handsome? Procuring an heir in such an unorthodox manner? A father kept in the dark? Frank Atkins playing go-between? Why did she get the sickening feeling that she'd already met the man capable of such underhandedness? No. No, it couldn't be…

Jackie did just what Mr. Atkins had suggested. She thought about his proposition. How could she not, especially when she'd find her mother walking through the house, gazing lovingly at her belongings, touching them as if for the last time…

One night, after dinner, Jackie joined her mother in the living room. Joan was sitting in her husband's chair, and as usual, she was crying softly.

Jackie sighed. It broke her heart to see her like this.

"What's the matter, Mummy?"

"You have to ask?" she sniffed. "Oh… I'm sorry, dear. I'm just, I'm just so angry! How could he do this to us!"

"Who? Madison?"

"Your father! That's who!"

This had been the first time that Joan actually voiced any negative thoughts about the state in which her husband had left his family.

"Mummy, I'm sure he didn't mean for this to happen. He tried to turn it around, but… well, for sure he didn't plan on dying! Besides, I told you before. I'm to blame." Jackie bowed her head. "You see… Daddy wanted to wait and test the chip for a few months. I talked him out of it. If he'd waited, he may have learned of its faults and corrected them. Once they'd been installed... it was too late, and well, we know what happened after that..."

Joan listened quietly. She understood now why her husband had remained quiet. "Jackie, dear. If it was defective, then it was defective. You don't know that the problem would have arisen during that testing period."

"I'd wager that it would have."

"But you don't know," Joan insisted. Jackie shrugged, and her mother continued, her voice quiet once again, her head bowed. "I'm sorry. I shouldn't be angry with your father. I ... just wish he'd told me. Now look at us. We owe our lives, and before long we won't even have a home, a home we've had since we were married. Sam carried me over that threshold," she cried, shaking her head sadly. "All the memories..."

Joan's attempt at relieving her daughter of the blame had not worked. Jackie's lips contorted into a wry smile. Her mother was right. They'd be kicked out soon. Her big mouth had made certain of that! It was up to her now to see that would not happen.

CHAPTER SIX

*G*rudgingly, Jackie called Frank Atkins. He told her to meet him in Jerry's office after her shift the next day.

"Am I correct to assume that you are considering the proposition?" Frank asked tentatively as once again he motioned for her to sit down.

"I don't have any alternatives at the moment. I'll have to explore all my options, won't I?" Jackie returned.

"I think it's in your best interest to do so."

"Yes, well... before I agree to anything, I want to meet this guy. Can you set it up? Would that be a problem?" Jackie's previous thoughts on the identity of the individual with the crisis returned.

"No. Not at all." Frank Atkins picked up the telephone receiver and pushed one of the buttons.

Jackie's stomach turned. Had her suspicions been correct? And why did she suddenly feel as though all of her blood had rushed to her head? Her face felt as hot as the embers of a raging fire, the veins at her temples pulsated rapidly, each beat pounding in her brain. Yet her hands, her legs… were cold and numb as though the lower portion of her body had been immersed in the centre of a glacier. Was it him? How could she confront him? Better yet, why was she still there? Before she could stop Mr. Atkins, he was speaking to the person on the other end.

"Do you have a moment?" Frank was saying. "Yes. Well, no. All right. I'm in Jerry's office." He ended the short conversation and replaced the receiver. "He'll be right in, Miss Ellis."

Her panic intensified. "But I – not now! I didn't mean now!"

"It's best to get the introductions over with as soon as possible. There's no use prolonging this further."

"Wh-who is it?"

Frank Atkins was evasive. "The gentleman in question."

"No. Who is he, Mr. Atkins?" Jackie's anxiety had peaked. Cardiac arrest – or at least a seizure – was imminent! She had time for neither.

"Well, Miss Ellis, I—"

Frank Atkins didn't have the opportunity to finish his sentence, nor was Jackie able to voice any more of the questions that crowded her mind. There was a rap at the door and the sound of footsteps coming towards the desk. She couldn't turn her head. She couldn't move. She was paralyzed!

Frank stood.

"Miss Ellis…"

Jackie turned her face toward the man who was already within steps of her. She wanted to die!

Michael's expression was blank; he was the first to speak, but his words were spat out toward his friend. After all, he had to sound convincing! "How dare you, Frank?"

Frank played along as he'd been instructed and put out a hand to compel his boss to calm down. "Michael..."

But Michael turned to leave. "Forget it!"

Jackie stood on wobbly legs. And when it finally surfaced, her voice trembled with emotion. "This was all planned, wasn't it?" she said, stopping Michael at the door. "Just how far will you go to get your money back? You have our business, our home – now you want my firstborn! I'd sooner walk the streets, as you suggested, than do this – with you!"

"This was not my idea," he sneered, but he suddenly had doubts as to whether or not he'd be able to fool this woman. "But as far as your current financial situation is concerned, you had better start walking, because at the rate you're going you'll be out on that little butt of yours by winter – and they say it's going to be a cold one!"

Frank had stood, quietly watching the exchange between them. It was time for him to intervene. "Look, let's just calm down, shall we?" He motioned with his hands. "I didn't tell either of you about the other because I knew that you never would have agreed to a meeting."

"I can't believe this." Jackie shook her head, her brain filled with questions, questions for him and for herself.

"Let's face the facts; you're both in a bind. You, Michael, haven't found anyone who even comes close to your expectations—"

"—And *she* does?" he asked, his sarcasm credible.

"She's perfect!" Frank told him. Michael just shook his head and went to stand by the desk, leaning against the wall.

Jackie's legs wouldn't hold her weight any longer. She sank

down onto the chair again, trying desperately to keep her composure. This was just too much! And now they were talking about her as if she wasn't even there. That was just as well though; she certainly would have preferred to be elsewhere! She only wished she had the strength to leave!

"You, on the other hand, Miss Ellis," Frank continued, bringing Jackie out of her thoughts. "You and your family owe Mr. Madison here a great deal of money. We both know you won't be able to pay him back, not unless he's willing to... let it go?" Frank said hesitantly, looking toward Michael.

"Not a chance," Michael snapped rudely.

"Right. That's what I thought. So under the circumstances, this proposition works for the both of you. I'm sure that in this instance, the child will cancel your debt." Frank looked at Michael again, but Michael didn't comment, so Frank continued. "It'll clear the slate, so to speak."

Jackie was furious. "Clear the slate? What about the baby? You expect me to walk away from my baby?" Frank wasn't quick to answer this time. He looked over to Michael again and sat down. "What if you remained married to Michael?"

Her eyebrows shot up, but Michael was a little more expressive.

"What?" Michael didn't appreciate the fact that Frank might be getting ahead of himself. "I'm not that desperate, Frank! I told you I don't want a wife! And if I did, I could think of at least two dozen other women I'd rather marry. Don't go changing things for her, or anyone else for that matter!"

"Michael, I spoke to your father. He means business. He's determined to make good on his threat."

"That doesn't give you the right to change the rules," he

reprimanded. "And must you discuss my personal life in front of her?"

"She might very well be part of your life. She's going to know anyway – if she agrees."

"Well, if and when," Michael said pointedly.

"Look, I'm only trying to help you – both of you. This is none of my business. I'm not a matchmaker, nor am I in the baby-selling business, Miss Ellis, and if my wife found out about this I'd be living in the doghouse for the rest of my life, but Michael, you agreed to my suggestion and you asked me to find you someone suitable. I did. Now, you must not let your respective prides obstruct what's clearly in front of you. I truly believe this would be the best thing for everyone!"

"But he gets to keep my baby!" Jackie adamantly pointed out again.

"*Your* baby? Are you going to do this by yourself?" Michael exclaimed.

"If that were a possibility – I'd actually consider it!" she retorted, and Michael smiled cynically.

"You know, Michael," Frank said in a persuasive tone. "Perhaps you can come up with some sort of arrangement regarding the child. For instance, you might agree to, perhaps… visitation rights?" Frank raised questioning eyes to Michael who chose to remain quiet for the moment. This possibility had not been discussed.

Jackie wasn't listening at all. "I don't understand why you have to do this. How can you deceive your father like this?"

"It's not your concern."

"Hey, I didn't ask to be dragged into your personal problems;

I have enough of my own, and you're the biggest! And Mr. Atkins, you know perfectly well about the animosity between us. How you came to ask this of me, of all people, is beyond me. As for him," Jackie's head gave a slight tilt in Michael's direction, "I had the sickening feeling that he was *the man in question*—"

"If you were so sickened, why are you here?" Michael couldn't help himself. He nodded knowingly as though he'd just read her as easily as a two-item menu, as though he'd seen right through her brain to thoughts she had not yet realized she had.

More blood rushed to her face. There was a definite concern that she would tip over soon. Either that or her head would explode! "I suppose I had to give you the benefit of the doubt. This just confirms what I've thought of you since I met you."

"And that is?"

"You're selfish, arrogant, and will do absolutely anything to get what you want."

A muscle twitched at his jaw. "Then I'll repeat: why are you here?"

"Not for long. I think you'd better find yourselves some other desperate soul!" Jackie rose again and turned to leave, but Frank stopped her once more.

"Miss Ellis, I understand how devastated you must have been upon learning about your father's situation, and although you mentioned you want no pity, my heart does go out to you. Nevertheless, I must remind you that you decided not to listen to what Mr. Madison had to say. You, however unwillingly, made matters worse." Jackie swallowed this piece of truth. "Now... I think it would be in your best interests to try and call a truce – both of you. Give this a try. Go out a few times, spend some time together. It would be best, naturally, if you refrained from killing each other." Frank tried to sound flip, but sighed heavily. "Give yourselves a couple of weeks. Who knows, you might even learn to like each other – under all the hostility."

"I doubt it!" they said simultaneously.

"And if not… perhaps you might come up with other solutions to your problems. Having dinner, or only a cup of coffee in a public place, will at least force you to be somewhat civil to each other. If you still feel the same, Miss Ellis, then by all means walk away. You will not be penalized in any way, I promise you. All we ask is that this information goes no further than this office. As for you, Michael, you have absolutely nothing to lose, except time. What do you say?" Frank urged.

The small office fell silent. Could she possibly consider this? She should have simply bolted, but her feet seemed planted into the stone floor beneath her. And as much as she'd stressed her hatred for this man, she had to admit he'd been right – at least in one observation. Why *was* she there? To confirm her suspicions? If so, why had she not left when Madison had entered the office? Mr. Atkins' reference to her father's ruin had reminded her of the truth with stark clarity. It was Jackie's responsibility to save what little was left of her mother's dignity. She knew that she had to agree – she had no choice.

Michael, surprisingly, was the first to answer. "All right. I'm game, if she is."

Jackie's incredulous eyes turned toward him as she was leaving. Her shoulders gave an almost undetectable shrug. She did not voice her opinion on Frank's suggestion; she only needed to leave the office before she lost her mind completely. "I have to go," she said simply and walked out the door.

Behind closed doors, Michael and Frank exchanged a handshake.

The bus was excessively crowded, as it was every Friday evening, but Jackie was unaffected by all the pushing and shoving. She had too much to handle in her head.

This would certainly solve her problem. Her mother would be able to keep her home and all her belongings and she would never have to worry about whether or not she could afford the mere necessities. All debts would be paid and everything would be fine again – wouldn't it?

The elderly gentleman with the Elmer Fudd hat standing next to her looked at her when Jackie shook her head, and she smiled at him.

She couldn't believe she was actually thinking of accepting that ludicrous proposition. But it was Jackie's responsibility to try and right the wrong she had created. She had to accept. She had to... for her mother's sake.

Jackie shrugged, and the old gentleman looked at her again.

Maybe all this was in vain. Michael Madison didn't exactly jump for joy when he saw Frank Atkins' new candidate, but surprisingly he had agreed to 'give it a try', as Frank had put it. Naturally, since she was nothing like the women he normally dated, he'd most likely decide he wanted nothing to do with her, which would leave her in exactly the same predicament, except perhaps he'd have even more reason to be vindictive toward her.

However, if they went through with it, she would have to give her mother some indication that she was seeing someone. She wouldn't want to shock her. Although, 'shock' might not fully describe her mother's reaction if Michael Madison ever showed up at her door asking for her daughter!

"You're seeing someone?" Joan Ellis was saying several days later. "Why haven't you told me?"

Jackie's guilt was threatening to choke her. "Sorry, Mummy. I... it's nothing serious or anything. We... we've just been talking... with all that's happened—"

"Where did you meet him?" Joan interrupted, excited to hear this news. "What's his name? I'd like to meet him."

Now what? Did she dare tell her? What if it never came about?

"Well, actually you've already met him," she started.

"I have?" Joan looked puzzled. "But... you never go out, and there hasn't been a young man in this house for months. And even then, Mr. Madison was the only one and you called him an arrogant jerk!" Joan reminded her, as she took a sip of her tea.

"That's the jerk – I mean, he's the one I'm seeing," Jackie blurted, and Joan choked on her tea.

Jackie jumped up and patted her mother's back. "Mummy! Are you all right?"

"Yes, yes. I'm fine!" she coughed. "I thought you said—"

"—I did, Mummy."

Joan looked at her in astonishment. "Your boyfriend is Michael Madison?"

"Mummy, please don't get ahead of yourself. I wouldn't call him *that*. Like I said, we've just... talked, sort of called a truce – for now."

"I see." Then she looked at her daughter suspiciously. "Are

you trying to get him to reconsider that time limit?"

"Actually, I had contemplated going to beg him for that... but I didn't have the chance. He... he came to me."

"And?"

"And what? I don't know. Mom, we haven't really discussed our problem, and… it might stop at any time, so don't go reading more into it. Right now, we're just talking," Jackie repeated, shrugging, trying to sound indifferent.

"Well, I suppose that's better than being at each other's throats."

"I suppose." Jackie hated lying to her mother, yet there'd be plenty more lies to come.

CHAPTER SEVEN

A week had passed and Jackie had neither seen nor heard from her new 'friend'. Perhaps he'd changed his mind, she thought as she squeezed her hands into the yellow rubber gloves. The problem was that she couldn't figure out why she hadn't breathed a sigh of relief.

It was Saturday, and since both ladies worked now, a major cleaning day. Jackie had her head in the oven, wiping off the overnight cleaner, when the doorbell rang.

"I'll get it!" Joan called from the living room.

When she heard footsteps in the kitchen Jackie assumed it was her mother and didn't bother looking up.

"There's someone here to see you, dear."

Jackie hadn't had visitors in months, and in her haste to learn the identity of her surprise guest, the guest who'd suddenly made her mother sound nervous, she bumped her head on the roof of the oven.

"Morning," Michael Madison greeted her casually.

She knew she had a bump on her head – in fact she was rubbing it – but she was oblivious to the pain. She was too busy feeling embarrassed. How could he show up at her home – without warning? He had indicated that he wanted to pursue what they had discussed, but he'd never called to confirm it. Now he was assuming it was all right to just show up... looking the way he did... while she looked like a complete wreck in ripped sweats and an old T-shirt. He had her at a disadvantage, and it wasn't fair.

"What are you doing here? I mean, what brings you to this part of town?" Jackie corrected herself, realizing that her mother was still there, next to him.

"You," he said simply, leaving Jackie momentarily speechless.

"I'll get back to my dusting," Joan announced. "It's nice to see you again, Mr. Madison."

"Michael," he corrected.

Oh brother, thought Jackie.

"Michael. Well, I'm certainly happy I don't have to call in the guards. I'm glad you've made peace."

Michael just smiled and watched her return to the living room. Then he turned his attention back to Jackie.

There should be a law against looking so good. He was dressed in black jeans, and a white sweater was visible under a black leather jacket. She had not seen him in casual clothes since their very first encounter thirteen years prior, and she had not imagined it would make a difference, but it did. He still looked menacing, towering over her as he did, but with the business attire gone, he seemed more... human. Well, almost. And if anyone had told her that the young man she'd become so infatuated with so long ago would one day stand in her kitchen with the possibility of a relationship – however outrageous…

Jackie rose to her feet and stood at the sink as she removed the rubber gloves and washed her hands. "What *are* you doing here?" she asked quietly, knowing that he was standing behind her, taking her in.

"I told you that I was willing to give this a try – your reply was a little cloudy, to say the least. I came to ask you if you have given it any thought."

"Don't you own a telephone?"

"I thought it might be more effective – a personal call, I mean. Judging by your mother's reaction," Michael tilted his head, "am I correct to assume that the answer is yes?"

Jackie turned to face him, but she had difficulty making eye contact. "I have pondered the possibility," she breathed, the words sticking in her throat. Jackie allowed herself to look him in the eye now. He was a jerk, an arrogant jerk; but as Marjorie had put it, he was a gorgeous one. She definitely had to try to push that fact out of her mind!

"And?"

"I don't have much of a choice, now do I?"

"No one's stopping you from saying no," he said quietly.

Jackie searched his eyes. She wasn't quite certain what she hoped to find, but there was nothing. All she learned was the colour. They were green, olive green. She hadn't noticed before.

Jackie snapped herself out of the trance. "No one's given me an alternative either," she returned finally, and a muscle twitched at his jaw.

"Is that a 'yes'?"

" …Yes."

"Fine. I thought we might go to dinner."

"When?"

"Tonight. Unless you have other plans."

"No, I have no plans." She wished she could tell him that she was booked solid for the next three years!

"Fine." Without waiting for a response, he turned and preceded her out of the kitchen.

The cold March air swooshed inside as he opened the front door and Jackie caught a glimpse of Mr. Henrich across the street, shovelling the freshly fallen snow. Michael turned to look past her, to Joan.

"It was nice to see you again, Mrs. Ellis," then to Jackie, "I'll pick you up at seven."

Then to her utter surprise and discomfort, he bent and kissed her firmly on the lips. He was already gone by the time she realized she was still standing by the open door.

"Earth to Jackie!"

Blinking several times, she closed the door quickly, and turned to lean on it.

"I suppose I don't have to wonder anymore if you really do like him."

"What? What do you mean?" Jackie snapped, unnerved and annoyed with herself.

Her mother smiled. "You're glowing, Jackie!"

Jackie put her hands to her cheeks. They were so hot! Her lips still tingled from his kiss. She knew now which of the two would be the better actor.

"I'd better finish cleaning that oven," she said absently, as she disappeared into the kitchen.

CHAPTER EIGHT

J ackie's bedroom was bright and cheery. The butter yellow of the walls was the exact colour of the daisies among the other flowers on her quilt. The sheers that hung on her bay window were a pale blue, picking up the colour of another flower. Her beaded lampshades and various picture frames were also multicoloured. Her furniture was still the same light maple set her parents had purchased when she was a little girl. As a teen she'd painted flowers on the centre of every drawer and now they too matched perfectly with her flowery theme. It was a little juvenile – perhaps extremely juvenile – she admitted, yet when her dad had offered to buy her a new set when she graduated high school, Jackie wouldn't hear of it. She loved that furniture and all the happy memories associated with it and her childhood. Come to think of it... many a night she'd lain awake on that very bed thinking about young Mr. Madison, imagining what it'd be like to be kissed by him... Jackie shook her head. She knew now – firsthand,

and she grudgingly admitted that the real thing was much more enjoyable than anything her imagination could muster. Her lips still tingled… but those were not the memories she was referring to!

She had stood in front of her closet for fifteen minutes before finally deciding on the black silk-knit dress that her parents had given her on her last birthday. It had a high neckline and long sleeves. It had only one flaw – no, two flaws; it clung to her every curve and it was quite short. She wrinkled her nose at the hemline and tried to stretch it downwards. "Oh, don't be an idiot! It looks good," she scolded herself. She needed something to boost her spirits; it may as well be the dress!

Her heart was in her throat when the doorbell rang again. Jackie hurried down the stairs, but Joan had already answered the door.

Michael's eyes scanned her body, but he made no comment. "Ready?" he asked, declining Joan's invitation to enter.

Jackie slipped on her coat and reached for her purse. "Yes. Mom, don't wait up. Go to bed, okay?"

"Don't worry about me," Joan waved a hand. "Have a good time."

Michael led her to his car and held the passenger door open for her. Jackie hadn't been exposed to many exotic cars in her lifetime; she couldn't tell what make it was, just that it was black and sleek and obviously expensive. Once inside, she saw a Fiat emblem, although she'd never seen a Fiat that looked quite like that one. Nevertheless, she was not going to ask. This was not a common date. She was too nervous for small talk!

Neither spoke during their ride to the restaurant. Michael had chosen the route towards the Don Valley Parkway, which led

Jackie to believe they were heading downtown – and they were.

Jackie was born and raised in Toronto, so a shopping trip downtown to the beautiful shops in Yorkville or a stroll along Harbourfront in the exclusive Queen's Quay area was not an uncommon occurrence on a summer weekend. The marina would be bustling with weekend sailors docking beside vendors and musicians displaying their crafts to the tourists. Restaurants would be filled to capacity, often entertaining celebrities in town to film their movies in the city that had recently become the Hollywood of the north. Residents and tourists alike enjoyed the numerous theatres, not to mention a vast array of concerts. During the summer, on baseball nights, tens of thousands of fans would flow from the Rogers Centre and onto the streets, often mingling with yet more thousands exiting The Air Canada Centre after a concert. Hockey and basketball would be the cause of commotion during the colder months.

Jackie couldn't deny Toronto was a beautiful and exciting city, but the intense auto and pedestrian traffic and the tall, almost ominous office buildings compelled her to prefer the quieter suburbs for everyday life. She always felt microscopic amidst the busy city, even a little uncomfortable, just as she did now.

The disturbing fact, however, was that her geographical surroundings were not the only cause in this case. Her companion was the root of her sense of panic this time. Jackie had wanted to tell him several times to stop the car and let her out, but had held her tongue. In fact, it felt bruised from biting it for so long.

Finally they arrived at the restaurant she'd heard so much about. She'd never dined at The Bistro, but her friends had offered excellent reviews.

There was a bar to the left of the front entrance. The main dining area was further along. The tables were covered with soft damask cloths and their place settings sparkled in the dim light, and they were immediately escorted to a quaint and romantic table for two.

"May I offer you something from the bar, Mr. Madison?" the waiter asked, and Michael looked her way.

"I don't drink." Jackie was almost apologetic. "I'll just have water, thank you."

"Campari and soda. And a Cosmopolitan for the lady." And the waiter disappeared.

"I told you I don't drink."

"It'll help you calm down," he told her offhandedly.

Jackie was unnerved at his perception. "Did I say I needed calming?"

"You didn't have to," he replied, and Jackie looked away from the mocking green eyes.

Naturally, he was right. She did need to relax, but sipping that drink had not helped. Although she had to admit she'd liked the taste. Later she forced herself to sip a bit of the wine that Michael ordered with dinner, and now the two were beginning to take effect. She felt a little more relaxed and he noticed, although he hadn't commented. In fact neither had tried to make conversation as yet, and she was beginning to fidget.

Jackie was hoping they would have been seated at a larger table where she could have chosen to sit at a 45-degree angle rather than directly in front of him; she cringed at the prospect of looking into those eyes all evening.

Michael leaned back against the cushioned chair, the discarded cork rolling between his fingers. "Your mother mentioned you were in school. What were you studying?"

Jackie didn't want to engage in idle conversation, but she had agreed to this; she'd have to try. "Engineering. I wish now I hadn't gone back to school," she said absently.

"Gone back? What do you mean?"

"I took a break to work with my father after my second year."

"When was this?"

Jackie shrugged. "Year before last. This would have been my final year."

"Do you think your father wouldn't have made the decisions he made if you had been there?" His tone was surprisingly not sarcastic. In fact it sounded more like he was trying to relay to her that she was not at fault.

"I don't know. I can't help wondering if I may have been able to help in some way…" She had no intention of divulging too much personal information.

The waiter took away their dishes, along with the cork, leaving Michael's fingers idle. "So do you intend on returning to school?"

Jackie shrugged, refusing a refill of wine that the waiter offered. "This year is over. I'd need at least a semester to graduate."

"You can go back, you know. Naturally you'd have to attend school here, but you don't have to continue working. Money won't be an issue."

Jackie looked at him. How could she concentrate on school if she consented to be his wife? She could barely keep her mind on anything else at this point of their liaison. "I don't know. My future looks pretty bleak right now," she concluded, pushing forward her wineglass. She'd had enough.

This also concluded their conversation for the evening. She didn't know what to talk about, what to ask, and obviously neither did he. Coffee was served and drunk in silence. When Michael suggested that they call it a night, Jackie agreed. This meeting had been more than enough for a 'first date'.

Michael drove her home, and walked her to the door.

Jackie fumbled with her keys and dropped them. Should she ask him in? She'd really rather not. Naturally her decision would be made for her if he simply decided to follow her inside. She was relieved that her fears were unwarranted.

Michael picked up the keys and inserted the correct one into the door, but stepped back and returned the keys to her. "Are you busy Friday night?"

"I wish I were," she said honestly, and laughter returned to his eyes.

"I'll pick you up at the same time. If you get a better offer by then, be sure to let me know. You know where to find me."

"Unfortunately."

Jackie closed the door behind her. Grateful to find that her mother had heeded her wishes and gone to bed, she did the same.

Well, she thought, as she tossed and turned. She hadn't expected it to go so smoothly. Jackie had imagined they'd be at each other's throats by the time they reached the restaurant. The evening hadn't been too painful – this time.

CHAPTER NINE

*T*he following Friday arrived before she knew it. This time she promised herself that she wouldn't appear nervous at the prospect of seeing him again. She'd stay in her room until he arrived, she vowed.

Jackie lay down on her bed and held her favourite pink rabbit, a stuffed animal she'd had for as long as she could remember. Hugging the toy to her chest, her eyes took in the cheery colours of her room. She wished that some of that cheer would creep into her brain, her heart. She felt tortured, torn between wanting to help her mother and desiring happiness for herself. By marrying Michael she'd be righting a wrong that she had caused, but the price would be extremely high; a price she wasn't sure she'd be able to pay.

"Jackie! Michael is here!"

Jackie jumped!

She had been ready for at least half an hour, but having been summoned downstairs, the butterflies returned. She picked up her brush and brushed her hair one last time, contemplated changing out of the grey plaid skirt and plum-coloured sweater, and finally deciding against it, made her way to meet her date.

Michael's greeting was nearly inaudible, but it was enough for her mother. "Have fun, you two!" Joan was far too happy about this association. She wasn't going to like the way it was meant to end.

Michael drove her to another restaurant, this one situated in midtown, still busy, but certainly less so than the downtown core.

This restaurant was also darkly lit, but it had a lounge suitable for dancing adjoining the dining area.

Again he ordered drinks, again he ordered wine, and again she forced herself to drink the awful liquid with the hope that her nerves would be a tad less frayed.

Michael was still the first to break the uncomfortable silence. "So I gather you had no better offer."

"Obviously neither did you."

Michael smiled. "I suppose not."

Dinner was being served before she decided to speak again. "Look... I don't know if I can do this..."

Michael shrugged. "Do what? Have dinner with me?"

"You know what."

"You don't have to. But I thought we were just supposed to meet a few times to see if we could stand to be in the same room without having to suppress any urge to commit murder."

"You think that's possible?"

"Unless you just poisoned my wine," he said, his eyes sparkling, "we've survived two dates already. Actually, that's more than I can say for most couples..."

Jackie tore her eyes away from his. What was it she was saying, anyway? "Did... did you mention anything to your father?"

He looked at her lazily across the small table. "No, I didn't. But I understand he has a business meeting here tonight. As they say, a picture is worth a thousand words. He'll ask me about our... association... before I have a chance to tell him. This way, if this continues, he'll have already seen us together and he'll assume that we've been that way for a while."

"You seem to have everything planned," Jackie observed, somewhat annoyed at his businesslike attitude.

Michael didn't answer her. He just glared at her, until the corner of his mouth curved into a smile.

Jackie's eyes scanned the room. There was a table with five men having a heated discussion about some business deal going awry. There were several tables with two or three couples enjoying a relaxing evening and there was one couple in particular that had chosen that night to 'pop the question'.

Feeling his eyes upon her, she looked towards him again. "Well? Has he seen us?"

"No, but he's about to." Startling her, he reached over and took her hand. "You know, you're going to have to get used to me touching you, if this is going to work. Try to act as though you enjoy my company, will you?"

Jackie tried to pull away, but he wouldn't let go.

"Are your hands always so cold?" he asked as he snuggled her hand in both of his.

"Yes, sorry," she returned as sweetly as she could.

Michael smiled at her discomfort. He was enjoying this. "Do they always tremble, too?"

Jackie attempted to pull away again, but his grip tightened. Then he raised her hand to his lips and lightly kissed it. She couldn't take much more of this!

"Do I make you nervous, or have you never been out with a man?"

Now he was being mean and her voice was curt when she answered him. "You make me nervous." Jackie decided that the truth was better than letting him think his other assumption was correct!

"When was the last time you were out? I mean, on a date."

He probably knew everything there was to know about her. It was no use lying. "It's been a while, but I haven't exactly been in the mood to spend an evening socializing with anybody. It's not that no one's asked."

"I didn't mean to imply that," Michael told her, surprisingly, and changed the subject. "I've been speaking to Frank. Just so you know… if this, if you decide to go through with this, I did agree to clear the account. Naturally insurance will pay for the medical expenses, but I will take care of any other costs that may arise during or after."

"How extremely generous of you," she said, finally retrieving her hand, and his smile mocked her again. "Just what is your father threatening you with, anyway?"

Michael's expression sobered. "That doesn't concern you." *Oddly*, he felt a little embarrassed with the situation. Odd…

"I beg to differ."

Michael watched her intently, the candlelight giving her complexion a golden glow. "He's threatened to disown me if I don't give him a grandchild – and the sooner, the better."

Jackie's eyebrows shot upwards. "This is not meant as a compliment, but you don't strike me as someone who has trouble finding a mate."

"I have known my share of women… but the women I know would never consider becoming mothers, if only for nine months."

"How selfless of them. Funny how this piece of information doesn't surprise me though." Jackie exaggerated her pensive tone.

"We've always had similar views on commitment. Not everyone was meant to be parents – or married for that matter."

"And what about parenthood? What are your views on that? Obviously you intend to raise this child without its mother. Who will raise him?"

"I will."

"You."

"Yes. Naturally I'll have to hire a nanny."

"Naturally. And then send him to boarding school the moment he learns to walk."

Michael sighed. He didn't like being grilled. "No."

"And what will you tell him when he asks for his mother? Will you tell him she deserted him?"

Oddly, he found himself thinking that a relationship with her would never be boring… she certainly had spunk! "That'll depend on his mother." This statement drew her eyes to his, but he changed the subject quickly. "What are we going to do for the rest of the evening?" he asked now, glancing at his Rolex watch. "It's only nine-thirty."

If he expected a suggestion from her, he'd have a long wait.

He signaled to the waiter for their check, and after paying the sum, rose from his chair offering his hand to Jackie.

"Where are we going?" Jackie asked as he guided her across the restaurant.

"We'll go sit in the lounge for a while, unless you have a better idea," he asked suggestively.

"No, I don't," she said firmly. She could guess what better idea he had in mind.

The lounge adjoining the dining area was small but quaint: a bar with stools on one end and a dance floor in the centre. Surrounding the dance floor in a semicircle were twelve intimate booths and small tables. Michael chose a booth. He sat close to her, but he was not touching her – yet. Her hands were trembling worse than before, so she held them on her lap, hidden from his scrutinizing eyes.

Thankfully he had ordered more coffee instead of drinks. She didn't think she could handle another alcoholic beverage. Her head had started to spin and everything seemed a little blurry.

The coffee hadn't arrived yet when he suddenly reached under the table, and taking hold of her hand, he asked quietly, "Would you like to dance?"

"Is this a request or an order?" Jackie was being stubborn, but she couldn't help herself.

"Let's call it an act of charity." There was a smile on his lips, but his eyes told her not to push him too far. "Shall we?"

On the dance floor, one arm was around her back, holding her firmly against him, while the other hand held Jackie's against his chest.

There were several other couples dancing as well, but they looked a little happier and considerably more comfortable than she felt. Her eyes searched the lounge to find something to focus on; finally resting on the tiny stitching on the shoulder of his charcoal coloured jacket.

It had been so long since she danced, and considering with whom she was dancing, she was surprised that her steps had not yet faltered. But then she was too busy inhaling the seductive aroma of his cologne. His arms around her, his closeness, did not revolt her. In fact...

Michael left her hand for the soft curve of her chin. He tilted it upward, forcing her to look at him. His thumb gently caressed her lips. Yes, he was definitely enjoying this.

"My father just walked in."

His eyes had an almost hypnotic effect on her. When his mouth covered hers in a soft, sensuous kiss, she found herself responding. It had been a long time since her last kiss too...

"That's better," he whispered against her lips.

Her eyes shot open. Only then did she realize that she had returned his kiss.

"What?" she breathed.

"You said you haven't been out; where did you learn to kiss like that?"

Michael's breath was warm against her cheek, and she shuddered involuntarily.

Jackie was angry with herself. She had wanted to tell him that he shouldn't have kissed her when he'd come by her home and he should refrain from doing so in the future. *Future?* But she hadn't said a word. Instead, she not only allowed him to kiss her again, but also responded to that kiss. She'd... enjoyed it. This was not good.

"I took a correspondence course."

"I'll bet!" he chuckled.

The song had ended, and Jackie was grateful. She definitely had to distance herself from him. She also had to set him straight. She did so the moment they arrived at their table, before she lost her nerve.

"I agreed to go out with you – to call a truce – as Mr. Atkins suggested, but I don't remember agreeing to accept your advances."

To her annoyance, Michael laughed. "You didn't seem to mind when I kissed you just now. In fact, I believe you enjoyed it."

"Wishful thinking on your part, perhaps."

"No. I don't think so," he said knowingly, his eyes sparkling. "So what's your excuse?"

"My excuse?"

"Granted you were probably imagining someone else, but the kiss was reciprocated."

Jackie shrugged, trying to act indifferent. "Like I said, it's been a while… in any case, this is just a trial relationship; you don't need to touch me, and I prefer that you don't."

Michael watched her for a moment. "All right. I won't touch you." This was different. No woman had ever made such a request. On the contrary, the women he was used to dating wanted nothing more!

It was soon afterwards that he suggested they leave and Jackie was glad to put an end to the evening.

When they arrived at her home he took the keys from her trembling hands. "Have you considered taking tranquilizers?" he said sarcastically.

Jackie just made a face, desperately fighting the urge to stick her tongue out at him. "You're not coming in, are you?"

Michael smiled, knowing full well that she wanted him to

leave. "Just to say good night if your mother is up." He opened the door and stood aside to let Jackie enter.

Jackie recoiled with unwarranted anger when she saw her mother sitting on the couch watching TV. Why couldn't she just have gone to bed?

She shrugged off her coat and draped it over a chair, and Michael followed her into the living room.

"What are you doing up so late, Mummy?" Unknowingly, Jackie was speaking through clenched teeth, but Joan decided to ignore her daughter's tone.

"Oh, hello. Did you have a nice time?"

Michael answered before Jackie could think of something to say. "Yes, we had a very nice time." Then startling her, he stepped up directly behind her. He did not touch her, but he was close enough for her to feel his breath on her neck, to smell that cologne…

"Well, I'll leave you two alone. Good night."

When her mother disappeared up the stairs, she took a few steps forward to set her purse down on the coffee table, putting a little more distance between them, before she turned to face him.

Jackie hoped she didn't look as nervous as she felt, but the mocking look on his face told her he saw right through her flimsy facade and wasn't about to pretend otherwise. She was praying he would leave – now!

Instead, he just stood there watching her. His gaze slid down to her mouth when the tip of her tongue came out to moisten her dry lips. This was not the way his dates ended. His lady friends would be in his bed by the end of the first evening together – sometimes sooner. This was definitely different!

Jackie's heart was pounding so loudly in her ears she was certain he could hear it as well from where he stood.

"I'd better be going," he stated simply, though he was certain that if he took her into his arms she would melt like butter. But her mother's close proximity, along with the whole situation, warranted that his advances best be kept in check – at least for now.

She wanted to move, but his eyes kept her there. Should she say something? "I... umm... thanks for dinner."

Michael took a moment before answering, trying to disperse the clear vision of the two of them... "You're welcome." He turned to walk to the door and Jackie followed him.

He stood in silence, his hand on the doorknob. "So, do we go on with this? I mean," he asked in a low voice, "do you want to go out again?"

Jackie searched his face again, but his eyes were averted; she couldn't read his expression. It perplexed her. Regrettably, she actually found herself wanting to go out with him, but she knew why he was asking; and to this she couldn't appear enthusiastic. "Like I said, I don't have much of a choice."

He exhaled. "Fine. I'll be in touch."

Jackie stood with her arms crossed in front of her protectively. For a moment she thought he was going to kiss her again, but he made no attempt. Instead, he reverted back to business.

"Don't forget to give a medical report to Frank."

Jackie fumed. "I'm perfectly healthy."

"Then it won't be a problem, will it?" He turned and left.

Jackie leaned against the door. He definitely should not be affecting her this way. She didn't like him. She couldn't like him.

He was an arrogant jerk!

She shook her head vigorously and ran up to bed. Maybe it was the wine playing tricks with her mind and her emotions. She'd see things more clearly in the morning.

Walter arrived home just as Michael returned from dropping off Jackie. He waited at the door. Michael greeted him and would have continued toward the stairs, but his father stopped him.

"I'd like a word with you."

Michael was expecting this. "'Bout what?"

"The girl you were dining with this evening."

"What about her?"

Walter walked through into the living room, forcing his son to follow. He sat down in his oversized chair, inviting Michael to do the same, but he chose to stand.

"That's Sam Ellis' daughter."

Michael tried to remain indifferent. "Yes, I know who she is."

"So what are you doing?"

"What do you mean, what am I doing? Wasn't it obvious? I took her out to dinner."

"Michael, last I heard you had a little bit of a run-in with her. What are you trying to pull? She's a good girl. My God, I remember her when she was just a little girl in pigtails, climbing trees... I want to help her, that's why I was happy to learn you'd hired her, but I don't want her hurt."

Michael's fingers made a circular motion around his temple. "Dad, I see the wheels turning. Granted our first meeting made some wartime battles seem mild... she's undoubtedly feisty, but—"

"—That she is. I like her."

"Yeah, well… so do I. I… don't know if this can go beyond a few dates, but I'm trying to do what you suggested. I'm trying to look for a different type of woman. Maybe I've found her and maybe not. I don't want any pressure from you. Got it?"

"Listen Michael, what I said to you… my requests—"

"—Your demands."

"Yes, well… I'm only trying to look out for you."

"I suppose, but I would have preferred not to be given an ultimatum. I would have preferred to live my life by my own standards and time schedule. The choosing of a wife should not have been forced down my throat."

Walter sighed. He stood now and took a couple of steps towards his son. "This brings me back to my original question. What are you doing? She's not the sort of woman you're used to, and frankly I think that goes the same for her."

"I'm trying to do what you asked, Dad. Didn't I just say that?"

"Yes, I know. I just hope you're not using the girl to serve your purposes, Michael. I will not forgive you that."

"I don't think she would easily succumb to being used, Dad. I asked her out, she… surprisingly agreed. As far as forgiving…" Michael sighed, "if I allow myself to open up to the uncertainties of a serious relationship only to have it blow up in my face… I won't forgive *you*. Good night, Dad."

CHAPTER TEN

Michael made more frequent visits to the plant in the days that followed. He made a point of looking her way, and although Jackie tried to act unaware of his eyes upon her, her co-workers were quick to notice the direction of Michael Madison's attention.

Marjorie, however, was the only one to comment. "I think he likes you!"

"Who?"

"Oh, don't give me that! You know perfectly well! And you like him too."

Jackie just smiled and shook her head, but she couldn't fool Marjorie. She refused to admit it, but every time Jackie caught sight of Michael from the corner of her eye, strange unwanted butterflies would invade her stomach and she'd begin to fidget nervously.

Nearly two weeks had passed since their last date. He had

made no attempt to call her since then. So, naturally the sight of him would make her nervous, she tried to justify to herself. She had no idea what he was thinking. He was toying with her, playing with her life as if it were a simple board game.

That same day Jackie and her co-workers were just finishing lunch when Michael, Jerry and the productions manager entered the room. The three men each took a soda from the vending machine and sat at the end of the table with Jackie and the others.

Now what? She prayed he wouldn't speak to her. She would just die if he did! Already everyone was whispering and Jackie was becoming unnerved.

Michael, however, seemed completely unaffected by everyone's obvious curiosity. In fact he made no attempt to hide his fascination with his new employee. Until now he'd purposely stayed away, trying to determine if his eagerness to see her again was only to fulfill his ultimate plan. But two weeks had been thirteen unnecessary days too many. His plan had nothing to do with the way she felt in his arms, the way her lips had responded to his during that kiss...

Fortunately he was called to the telephone, which at least put some distance between them until the buzzer rang, marking the end of the lunch hour. She had no choice but to pass him in order to leave, and as Jackie neared him Michael put out his hand to stop her, indifferent to the attentive eyes of the other employees.

"Are you busy tonight?" he asked, shifting the receiver away from his chin.

"...No. I don't think so."

"Yes, I'm here," he said to the person on the telephone, but again he spoke to Jackie. "I'll talk to you later..." he promised, and

Jackie returned to her work.

Marjorie hurried to her side. "What did he want?"

"He... he asked if I was busy tonight."

"Oh, my gosh!"

"What?" Jackie tried to sound unaffected by the boss's interest.

"I told you he likes you! This is just like the movies!"

"Oh, please."

Michael didn't speak to her again during that afternoon, but as Jackie and Marjorie left the building at 4:00 p.m. she saw him at the end of the long driveway, standing by his car. He was speaking to someone, but as soon as he spotted her he said his goodbyes and fixed his eyes on her, and Jackie didn't know what he wanted her to do. Was she to stop – or not? Unsure of his expectations, she averted her gaze and tried to make conversation with Marjorie.

Marjorie ignored her. "Jackie, I think he's waiting for you," her friend urged, but Jackie didn't comment.

As the two women drew closer to the executive parking lot, Michael began to walk towards them. He nodded at Marjorie, but spoke to Jackie. "Can I give you a lift?" he asked, but Jackie couldn't find her voice.

Marjorie pinched her arm. "I'll see you tomorrow."

He held the car door open for her and then walked around and got in himself. "You know, it's not a crime to be seen with me," he commented as he started the powerful engine.

"Yes, but I work for you. It's a little uncomfortable with everyone staring."

"Well, if we are to go any further with this relationship we can't just drop a bomb, we have to be seen together, don't you think?"

"If that's the case, then why haven't you called?"

It was out before she could stop herself and she didn't like the pathetic way it sounded. She knew he would have fun with the remark, and he did. He turned to look at her, while Jackie forced herself to look out the window.

"Did you miss me?" he said with a smile, as he maneuvered the car out of the parking space and out onto the street.

"Hardly," she said, and realized she was lying. "But you can't expect me to put my life on hold indefinitely while you contemplate changing your mind."

"I haven't changed my mind," he said quietly. Then he changed the subject a tad. "Your mother knows of our... relationship and now so does my father. I think it would be a good idea to introduce you to him ... as my ... well, introduce you. You'll come to dinner tonight."

Introduce her as what, really? What was she? "Tonight? Can't this wait?"

Michael suddenly pulled onto the dirt shoulder beside the road. "If you'd rather stop this right now, say so. I'll take you home."

Jackie looked over to him, her eyes searching. "And then what?"

Michael averted his gaze momentarily, his heart pounding in his chest. "Back to square one, I guess."

What had she expected? Jackie turned her attention to a little boy trudging through the few snow banks left as he walked his dog. "I'm not dressed," she said quietly.

Michael exhaled. "I'll take you home first to change, if you want."

Jackie didn't answer, and he continued. "As I expected, my father saw us the other night, so I told him we'd been seeing each other. He is ecstatic about this turn of events, although he admitted that he was, shall we say, surprised to see you with me. He said that he never thought I'd go out with someone like you."

"Oh? And why is that?" She asked the question knowing full well, unfortunately, that the answer would probably bother her.

Michael looked at her now, his eyes sparkling mischievously. "You're... not my type."

And it did. She wasn't any happier about the sudden constricting feeling in her chest, either. "Whose type would I be, then?"

"I don't know, but not mine," he said bluntly, choosing to retain his usual gruff demeanour.

"Then why am I here?" she asked, feeling rejected.

"Because my type would never have been able to fool my father."

"How wonderful that my misfortune proved to be so convenient for you!" Jackie's voice was drenched with cynicism.

"I believe you're forgetting that this would be beneficial to both of us," to which Jackie just huffed in response. "He says he remembers you as a tomboy with pigtails!" Michael looked at her again. "I can't seem to be able to picture you in pigtails."

Jackie winced at the memory. "Actually... our paths did cross once upon a time..."

"Oh? Were you wearing pigtails?" he smiled.

"No. Regardless, you obviously don't remember, so..."

Michael watched her for a moment. He remembered a pretty young lady arriving with one of his father's business acquaintances... She had captured his attention – to say the least... He'd asked about her then, but his father had quickly deterred his questions and his wandering mind. She was much too young for him, he'd told him… not at all his type…

"He wants to see you," he continued, keeping his memories private. "I downplayed our relationship."

"Downplayed? Down from what?"

"Otherwise," Michael ignored her, "he'd see right through it, even if it is you I'm seeing. So, are you coming to dinner or not?"

She was about to say that she didn't have a choice, but she was tired of saying it.

"Yes."

"Try to keep your enthusiasm down, will you?" Michael shifted gears and turned the car onto the road once again.

Luckily, her mother was working that afternoon. At least one performance would be postponed. Michael waited downstairs while Jackie showered quickly and searched desperately for something suitable to wear.

Finally deciding on a plain black skirt and white blouse, she then brushed her hair loosely around her face and grimaced at her reflection in the mirror before going downstairs.

Michael was standing by the window when Jackie announced that she was ready. He looked at her, noticing her change of clothes, but again made no comment. He remained quiet during the ride to his home as well.

As they drove northward, Jackie couldn't help but wonder where he lived, but when he continued into the elite community of Woodland Acres, she smiled cynically. *Naturally*, she thought to herself.

Jackie had often driven through this neighbourhood on Sunday afternoons just to admire the beautiful homes. Once within this quiet residential area, it seemed as though nothing else existed. The properties were vast, no less than an acre. The homes were large, and in some cases, barely even seen through the large trees and elaborate landscaping.

Michael turned onto a long driveway flanked with dozens of mature trees. She recognized birch trees and maples and blue spruce. A light blanket of snow covered flowerbeds and rock gardens and a pond with a fountain, which was not yet operational. The grounds were beautiful even without the blooming flowers.

As they neared the large Tudor home, her breath caught in her throat. She'd always wondered what the insides of these mansions would be like. Now that she had her opportunity, she wished she could just turn around and go home.

Jackie hadn't realized that Michael had stopped the car and walked around to the passenger side until he opened the door and extended his hand to her.

"Coming out?" he asked, the same mocking smile on his lips, and she took his outstretched hand. "What's the matter? You look as though you're about to go to the gallows!"

Wasn't that where she was headed?

The entrance was wide and bright. The natural sandy colouring of the marble floors complemented the darker taupe walls with the subdued shade. The circular staircase was also in marble, with an elegantly worked wrought iron railing coiling down with it like a black lace ribbon. To the right, at the bottom of the stairs, an open doorway exposed the study. An antique entrance table adorned with a vase of fresh flowers sat against the opposite wall on her left. A large mirror trimmed with a golden frame hung above it, and Jackie turned away from her pale reflection. A massive chandelier covered in large teardrop crystals hung, seemingly precariously, high above their heads, completing the look of elegance. It was all very beautiful, but suddenly she felt as though she was downtown and those tall buildings were closing in around her. Was it his home – or the fact that she might have to live in it with him?

A tall, grey-haired gentleman appeared in the doorway next to the table.

"Jackie. It's wonderful to see you again!"

Jackie swallowed. "Hello, Mr. Madison. I'm sorry, I only vaguely remember you."

"That's understandable. You were no more than a young teenager when I last had the pleasure of speaking to you. I hope you don't mind my saying so, but you've grown into a beautiful young woman."

"Thank you." Jackie was a little embarrassed.

"Come in, come in." Walter gestured toward what Jackie gathered was the living room.

This room was magnificent. There were two large plum coloured sofas, marble coffee tables and large wing-backed chairs upholstered with stripes in complementary shades of plum and cream. Drapes of the same plum colour covered the two large windows, stretching from the high ceilings to the floor. There was a large marble fireplace on the far wall, and a wall unit on the opposite side to hold the entertainment centre. She was certain that the paintings on the walls were not imitations.

Walter sat in one of the chairs and motioned for Jackie to sit on the couch. Michael draped their coats onto a chair and joined her.

"I can't believe this." Walter was saying, excitedly. "This is wonderful!"

Jackie just smiled, nervously biting the inside of her lip.

"Jackie, first of all, I'd like to offer my condolences."

"Thank you."

"I was at the funeral, but you and your mother were so distraught... I didn't want to intrude."

"That's all right." She hoped that he wouldn't bring up the subject of her father. She wouldn't be able to handle that.

"You know, Jackie, if there's anything I can do..."

"No. Thank you very much, but you... you've both done quite enough, really." Jackie hoped that Walter would remain oblivious to her sarcasm, but she was certain Michael got it.

"Well, life goes on, doesn't it? It's difficult sometimes, but..." Walter raised his hands in a gesture of resignation to make his point.

"Yes, I know." *Please change the subject!*

Walter slapped his knee, and his expression changed again. "I can't tell you how happy I am about you two!"

"Dad..." Michael started, in a tone taken to warn his father not to see too much into this association.

Oh, he was good, she thought to herself. She wanted to slap him! She couldn't believe how he could be so deceitful towards his father. But was she any different?

"Michael, I'm not pressuring! But a man can hope, can't he?" Walter chuckled.

Michael smiled back at his father, shaking his head.

A middle-aged woman entered the room.

"Ah, Alice," Walter announced. "Jackie Ellis, this is our housekeeper, Mrs. Alice Delaney. Her husband Elmer is our groundskeeper, and once in a while he drives me around. Alice, Jackie is Michael's... friend."

Alice Delaney was a kind-looking woman with grey hair kept in a tidy shorter style. Her black-and-white uniform was crisp and professional.

"Oh, how wonderful to meet you! I can count on one finger the times we've been introduced to Mr. Michael's lady friends, and that's just as well, I might add," she said towards Michael, who gifted her with a knowing smile. "Welcome, Miss Ellis."

"Thank you," Jackie said shyly.

Mrs. Delaney turned to Michael, her hands clasped in front of her ample bosom. "Well, I approve of this one, Mr. Michael – not that my opinion counts for anything, but I approve."

"Now, don't you start on me!" Michael joked.

"It's time, Mr. Michael. It's time." She shook a finger at him with familiarity, giving Jackie the impression that scolding him was not an uncommon practice. "Come now, dinner is ready."

Walter stood and extended his arm to Jackie.

Michael followed.

"Alice is a wonderful cook," Walter was saying as they entered the dining room.

Michael held out her chair and walked around the table to sit facing her, and Jackie closed her eyes and prayed for strength. When she reopened them she took in the beautiful dining room furniture.

Tonight the three took up one quarter of the long rosewood

table. The chairs were covered in a heavy striped damask fabric, three different shades of taupe. The hutch was at least six feet wide, displaying expensive crystal and china through the hand-cut glass doors. The six-drawer buffet was of the same style and size and it sat on the opposite wall. Two large gold-plated candelabras adorned each end; crystal decanters full of several shades of amber liquids were arranged on a silver tray in the centre. Every piece of furniture had ornamental copper carvings on each corner, giving it a definite antique flavour. Jackie's thoughts wandered now to 'Mrs.' Madison. She obviously did not exist in this house, and Jackie wondered if she existed at all.

As Walter had promised, dinner was delicious. Jackie only wished she could have enjoyed it. She was too nervous; too afraid of Michael's next move; too afraid of making the *wrong* move!

"Won't you have a little wine, Jackie?" Walter patted her hand. She was about to answer, but his son was first to speak.

"She doesn't drink, Dad; it makes her do wild things!" Michael said suggestively.

Jackie nearly choked as she looked sharply at him. How dare he?

"You don't have to embarrass the girl!" Walter reprimanded his son, who only replied with a grin. "Don't worry, Jackie, I know how Michael exaggerates."

"Actually," She managed when she'd stopped coughing, "I'll have a sip of something if it's sweet. Otherwise, I just don't like the taste," she clarified with a shrug, trying to ignore Michael's mocking stare.

"I'll remember that," Walter promised.

Jackie felt obliged to make conversation and after searching her brain for something to say, she finally settled on a topic that she hoped would keep discussions impersonal. "You have a beautiful home. Have you always lived here?"

Walter took a sip of his Chilean Merlot. "Depends what is meant by 'always'. I didn't inherit it, that's for sure. My parents were comfortable, but this property would have been beyond their means," he said pensively. "No, I purchased this home thirty-two years ago. There have been many renovations since then, mind you… Yes, I must say I was very fortunate in business."

Oops, they were entering dreaded territory. "You said Mr. Delaney takes care of the grounds."

Walter chuckled. "Oh yes. I wouldn't know a rosebush from a pear tree!"

"I'm sure you're not *that* bad."

"Let me tell you then. The grounds were not as plush when we first moved in so I decided to try my hand at cultivating the garden." He stopped for emphasis. "I killed half the plants and two trees! So, yes, I *am* that bad!"

"I love flowers," Jackie stated simply before she finally ran out of things to say.

Michael had been watching the exchange with interest. His eyes, unusually filled with curious interest, had never left her for a moment, a fact of which Jackie had been painfully aware.

After dinner they retreated to the living room, where coffee was served. Again, Michael sat next to her. It was *he* who did wild things to her, not the wine! Only to add to her discomfort, Walter soon received a telephone call, which he decided to take in the study. This left the lovebirds alone on the sofa, a situation that needed to be rectified!

Jackie stood and walked over to the fireplace, well aware of the pair of green eyes that followed her, inspecting her every curve. She admired some of the trinkets that sat on the mantle and looked at the pictures displayed in their beautiful frames. There were pictures of Walter and Michael, Walter and fishing buddies, two young children, but no Mrs. Madison. She was becoming increasingly curious.

Without realizing it, she voiced her thoughts. "You've never mentioned your mother. Did she pass away?"

"I only wish!"

"Pardon me?" She exclaimed, turning to look at him.

Michael came to stand in front of her. "She left my father a long time ago," he offered.

"Oh, I'm sorry. She kept in touch with you, though."

"No. Never saw her again. I was about three or four." Michael seemed indifferent.

"That must have been difficult."

Michael shrugged. "It's no big deal. We did okay."

Jackie couldn't help but wonder how something like this would affect a little boy's life – a man's life.

Realizing she'd been staring at him, she turned and pretended to look at one of the pictures more closely.

"Who are these little girls?"

"My cousins. My father's sister's son's kids," he elaborated.

"They're so pretty…"

Suddenly, his hands were on her hips. "My father likes you," he said quietly against her hair.

"Just what you wanted. Well, he's very nice, but he's out of the room right now, so…" Jackie tried to move away from his touch.

"Yes, but he'll be back." Michael turned her into his arms.

"It wouldn't look right if we didn't take advantage of being left alone."

"Please don't. I told you—" Her hands pushed against his chest as his mouth descended onto hers. She tried desperately to push away, but to no avail.

"Come on..." Michael urged against her mouth, and once again she felt herself turn to jelly as she gave in to his kiss.

Her hands slid over the soft cotton of his shirt to his neck. She was drifting away. She was oblivious to everything around her except for the strength of his hard body against hers, and his mouth sending her to another world with its kisses.

"Oops! Sorry!" Walter stopped short when he re-entered the living room.

Jackie didn't know what was happening when Michael lifted his head. All she knew was that the kiss had ended and she was disappointed. Why did he have to affect her that way, she kept asking herself, but even more questionable, why did *she* have to be so transparent? Her face felt flushed and her eyes at that moment were indeed mirrors to her soul. She tried desperately to breathe steadily, welcoming Michael's arms around her, needing his support.

"Anything wrong, Dad?" Michael asked nonchalantly.

"No, no. It was Harry, in Montreal. Nothing important. I think I'll call it a night though; leave you two alone," Walter smiled.

Jackie wanted to protest, but she couldn't speak.

"I hope to see you again, Jackie!"

Jackie was only able to smile in response and Walter waved his hand and said good night.

Finally, she regained her composure and pushed away. She walked the few steps to the couch, desperate to put some space between them.

"You're a hot little devil, aren't you?" Michael whispered, as he came to stand behind her. "Are you like that with anyone, or just me?"

Jackie remained silent and Michael took this opportunity to slide his arms around her waist.

"I thought we'd agreed…" she tried again, but he began to kiss the side of her neck. "Don't…" Jackie almost pleaded.

"Don't?" he sounded incredulous and she knew he had just cause. "Don't you tell me you don't like it." He turned her around again and looked down at her.

Unknowingly, her lips parted in anticipation of his kiss. She shivered, but she was far from feeling cold.

As his lips found hers he molded her tightly to his body, making her aware of his desire. Michael released several buttons of her blouse and his fingers caressed her sensitive skin, but his actions jolted Jackie back to reality.

"Stop!" Pushing herself free, she turned from him and fumbled with the buttons.

Michael was silent for a moment. Then he picked up her coat and held it out to her. "I'll take you home."

Jackie slipped on the coat and followed him out the door.

He was angry and took out his frustrations on the stick shift. Every time he changed gears, his passenger was jolted back and forth in her seat. His anger was justified – she was very damaging to his control! Then again, he'd never had to control himself before, not where sex was concerned. There had never been any need to wait before. Perhaps in this instance, under these circumstances... he should have refrained from being so forward. She was certainly not like anyone he had ever been with. Did he dare believe she was different?

She didn't say a word. Yes, they had made an agreement, but she was giving him mixed signals. She was more to blame in this instance than he and it irritated her, to say the least.

When Michael pulled up onto her driveway, he made no attempt to step out of the car. He sat staring at the garage door in front of him.

Jackie too, sat staring ahead of her. She didn't know if she should say something or if she should wait for him to speak, but soon he turned to look at her and Jackie decided to put her thoughts into words. "I'm not sure I know what you expect from me. But as you've informed me, I'm not like the women you're used to. Our involvement was not by chance, but by an uncommonly bizarre situation. Do you honestly think I can feel comfortable with your advances? Do you think I can easily forget what you've asked me to do – what I feel forced to do?"

She half expected a snide remark, but instead he put his head back on the headrest.

"Good night," he returned, simply.

CHAPTER ELEVEN

*D*uring the following weeks, Michael would wait for her at the end of her workday and take her home. Sometimes he'd drop her off and return to work. Sometimes he'd wait for her to change and take her out and sometimes… he would stay for dinner. All along Michael had made a point to keep advances in check and Jackie refused to admit that her feelings were mixed on that particular circumstance.

Joan was so happy when he stayed for dinner. Michael made her home seem full once again. She was happy when he complimented her cooking, but proud when he learned that some of the delicious meals he raved about had actually been prepared by her daughter.

"You can cook?" Michael asked one evening, his fork suspended for a moment.

"Yes," Jackie smiled. "Why?"

"I haven't met a woman that could, that's all."

Joan raised her eyebrows. "What type of women have you been dating?"

Michael chuckled. "Obviously not the right type!" He looked at Jackie and the memory of the time he told her that she was not at all his type came back vividly.

After dinner Joan surprised her daughter with a birthday cake for her twenty-fifth year. Jackie wanted to disappear into the floorboards! "Oh, Mom!" she whined. "I'm not a baby."

"Oh, come now. You'll always be my baby. You'll see what I mean, once you have children of your own."

Jackie couldn't help a glance in Michael's direction. Surprisingly, his green eyes lowered for an instant.

"Well, blow out your candles," she told her, and Jackie made a face.

"Is she always so difficult?" Michael teased.

Jackie obeyed her mother and blew out the candles, but she didn't make a wish... she doubted that her wish was attainable. Instead, she searched through the tissue paper in the bright red bag Joan had pushed towards her. Within the crumpled tissue was a beautiful camel-coloured cashmere sweater, a sweater Jackie knew cost much more than either of them could afford.

Then, to her surprise, Michael presented her with a gift also. Their eyes locked as she slowly accepted the beautifully wrapped box.

"How did you—" she stopped herself from completing the sentence. Naturally he knew. He had a file on her; he knew everything there was to know. Still, he must have spoken to her mother at some point to synchronize their presentation of gifts. If it had been her mother's idea, he would not have been forced to agree, but he had. "You didn't have to..."

"Just open it."

Jackie's eyes widened when she looked down at the delicate gold filigree bracelet. "Oh... It's beautiful!"

"Michael, it's lovely," Joan exclaimed happily.

Jackie knew she had to thank him, it was only right, but how? Should she simply kiss his cheek? Should she give him a proper kiss?

He watched as she toyed with the idea, then suddenly she leaned towards him, pressing her lips against his in a surprising but pleasing gesture. He had waited for her to make the first move. Granted, the situation may have forced her hand, but the results were what mattered.

Dare she confess that this had been something she'd missed? Jackie found it extremely warm all of a sudden. She was beginning to welcome his company, his touch. It was becoming more and more difficult to remember that there was an ulterior motive for all of this, and *that* was dangerous.

Jackie was thinking about this two days later when Michael came to stand beside her at her busy workstation. He leaned against the high board fronting the bench, staring at her.

All eyes were on them. Jackie felt as though she were on a podium, everyone waiting for her next move.

"Hi," he said.

"Hi," she replied.

"Want to come to lunch with me?"

His presence there, looking the way he did, dissipated any doubts she may have had about this trial relationship. Right then, she accepted that she wanted to be with him.

"Like this?" Jackie looked down at her T-shirt and jeans.

"So? Come," he urged.

How could she refuse? Particularly when she didn't want to. She looked at her watch. It was nearly noon.

"Coming?"

Jackie pulled off her latex gloves. "I'll meet you outside. I just want to wash up."

"You can do that in my office."

Jackie shook her head. "I'll meet you outside."

"Okay," Michael said with a smile, and Marjorie, who worked across from Jackie and had a clear view of his profile, visibly swooned.

Jackie watched him walk away, then turned to her co-workers who were ready with their comments.

"Ooh, Jackie! The big chief, no less!" Hassan exclaimed with a mischievous smile. "What does he have that I don't have?" He stood sideways, displaying his profile.

"You have to ask?" exclaimed Marjorie.

Hassan was a nice young man, but he was at least six inches shorter than Jackie and had an extremely large nose.

Jackie giggled along with the others.

"Aside from a little more room on his face, Hassan," kidded Inga, "he has at least a few more million than you do! Besides, I thought you were spoken for!"

"Well, I'm not hitched yet, and you can't blame a guy for trying!" He shrugged helplessly and they all laughed.

It was an uncommonly warm April day. It had rained for days, but finally the sun had decided to make an appearance.

Michael was leaning against his car when he spotted her. He had shed his tie and rolled up the sleeves of his grey shirt.

He watched her so intently that Jackie was sure she'd trip over a mere pebble if she wasn't careful. He didn't move until she was directly in front of him, next to the passenger door. Still, he watched her.

Needing to say something, the first thing that popped into her head came out. "Aren't you going to be ashamed to be seen with me in broad daylight?" she said, her tone sarcastic as she looked down at her attire.

"Why is that?" Michael's voice was quiet, and his eyes melted her into silence. Jackie could only shrug.

Suddenly he reached out and pulled her against him. He kissed her hard, as if to dissipate any negative thoughts that might escape her lips. Then it softened to a sensuous, wet kiss that left her spent and yearning for more.

"I don't care what you wear." His voice was husky, his breath warm against her lips. "In fact..."

Jackie's head was spinning, her brain filling with uncertainty, overflowing with questions. Why was he kissing her? Why was he saying these things? There was no one around to see them. Was someone looking out the window?

"We'd better go," he said against her lips, "before we get arrested." He loosened his hold and guided her into her seat. Then he raised his hand towards the building, answering now inconsequential questions. Walter's smiling face was nearly pressed up against the glass of his office window, reminding her of a small child pining over a candy display.

They entered the small restaurant near the Madison offices.

This establishment was less formal, geared more to the office crowd.

Sunlight shone brightly through large windows, justifying the thick Roman blinds. The walls were painted in a pale shade of blue, and multicoloured glass light fixtures hung over each of the tables. White tablecloths stopped the excess use of colour.

People called out to Michael, saying their hellos. The men smiled at Jackie, but the women sneered. It was incredible to think that these well-established businesswomen, who looked so together, so like what Jackie had hoped to be, were actually jealous of *her*!

Well, she told herself, if she had seen Michael with another woman, she'd be just as jealous. Suddenly realizing her train of thought, she seriously began to question her sanity.

Michael watched her as she silently sipped her carbonated water. Her expression had became pensive suddenly, her brows creasing in a frown, and he was tempted to offer her a penny for her thoughts, but decided against it. "When you refused the position in the office, my father was surprised. Now he's adamant. He's upset with me for not making the offer more attractive for you." He waited for her reaction.

Jackie didn't answer immediately, smiling politely at the waitress when she placed their grilled chicken lunches in front of them. She used this delay to allow this information to register. She'd believed Frank Atkins when he'd told her that the offer to work for the Madisons had originally been Walter's. She just wasn't sure why or if Michael had agreed. Jackie raised questioning eyes to him. "Why?"

"Why not? You know the business."

"Yes, but you don't have to feel pressured into making job

offers, nor should you feel obligated to do anything to sweeten the deal. I'm content working in the plant."

"Our senior buyer has left." Michael listened, but spoke as though he hadn't heard a word. "She's having a baby and she won't be coming back for a while. You could fill her position, if you like."

Jackie shook her head and took another sip of her water. "I'm sure there's someone else that would probably expect advancement. I can't take their job."

"It's not anybody's job. I know you're overqualified for the position, but that's what's currently available."

"I wasn't fishing for an executive position – like yours," she added, and Michael tried to hide a smile. "I'd just rather not."

Michael watched her intently. "Tell me why?"

"Why would you want me to take the position? Is it because of your father? Or is it because you feel uncomfortable—"

"Where you work doesn't matter to me, nor does it matter to my father. Granted, it would be a little difficult trying to explain why you would rather work in the plant, when there's a position in the office. I—" Michael stopped himself, and sighed. "The pay's better..."

Jackie lowered her eyes. What they had discussed in Frank's office and on their second dinner date had not been repeated since then. Naturally, the subject would resurface eventually, and Jackie stiffened.

"What difference could that make to me?"

"I don't know. I would imagine you'd want to put aside some money for school or whatever."

Jackie swallowed the lump in her throat. "I'll be fine," she assured him, her voice tight. "I can't very well keep the job, so what's the point?"

After a slight pause he continued. "This question is probably becoming tiresome, but I have to ask... we are continuing with this, are we not?"

Jackie looked at him. She wished he wouldn't bring up the reason for their so-called relationship. She disliked being reminded of his real motives for being with her, especially when she wanted so much to be with *him*.

"Have *you* changed your mind?" she asked tentatively, and Michael watched her again.

"No. I haven't, have you?"

Jackie pushed the uneaten portion of her lunch around her plate. She'd lost her appetite. "I don't like this."

"The chicken?"

Jackie wanted to laugh hysterically, her nerves suddenly raw. "No, not the chicken! This... this situation."

"Do you think I do?"

The waitress reappeared to ask if they'd finished and Jackie nodded. Once the dishes were cleared, she leaned towards him. "This was your idea, not mine."

"But you put yourself in this position, and you haven't answered my question."

"Yes, I am aware of my big mouth, and yes," she said grudgingly, aware as well of the fact that she didn't want to stop seeing him – no matter the consequences, "I agree to continue."

"Look... things don't necessarily always play out the way they've been planned. No one can predict the future. I think it would be wise to live for today." He unwittingly voiced thoughts that had been plaguing his mind for a while now, thoughts that might disclose too much. He forced himself to return to business once again. He couldn't help but be suspicious of her reasons for not readily accepting the offer. "You have the know-how, why waste it? The job's yours," he concluded. "You can start whenever you want. Just let me know."

Jackie wondered what he meant about things not always turning out as planned. She wanted to ask, but couldn't.

Upon returning to the office, Michael parked his car in his reserved spot, then turned to look at her. "I have to go out of town for a couple of days."

Jackie listened quietly. She didn't know what to say. She didn't know what she was supposed to say, what he wanted her to say. "When are you leaving?" she asked finally, unable to withstand his eyes upon her for another moment.

"It was last minute; I have to fly out tonight."

"Okay."

Michael's hand reached over and Jackie's heart accelerated significantly, but he made no attempt to touch her. Instead he opened the glove compartment and drew out a large envelope.

"This... this is a copy of the contract Frank has drawn up. You should take a look at it, maybe take it to your lawyer..."

Jackie accepted the envelope. She stared at it for a moment, then folded it and shoved it into her purse. There it was... her future... in an envelope.

After a few more moments of silence, he opened his car door. "I'll walk you back."

Jackie couldn't explain what she was feeling, but it certainly couldn't be healthy for her. She was driving herself crazy. And wasn't he already doing a good enough job of that himself?

With the envelope burning a hole right through her purse, why did she want to take hold of his hand? Why did she need his arms around her? Why did she want to tell him to take her with him? When they reached the employee entrance, he held the door and motioned for her to step inside. They walked together down the corridor, and then he stopped, obliging her to do the same.

"What?" Her voice was almost a whisper.

Michael watched her for a moment, contemplating whether or not to kiss her. He wanted to. He wanted a lot of things. "...Nothing. I'll see you when I get back."

"Okay."

Michael turned right and walked through to the offices and Jackie turned left, to the plant. He hadn't made any attempt to touch her. This was bothering her far too much. This was going to get out of hand. Why had she chosen this particular time in her life to be optimistic, when in this instance pessimism would be infinitely safer?

CHAPTER TWELVE

*T*hose couple of days seemed an eternity. Jackie hadn't expected Michael to call, but it didn't make the wait any easier. Midmorning on the third day, she heard his name being paged on the intercom.

He was back.

It wasn't until the next day that Jackie found the courage to open the envelope and read the contract that if signed, would change her life forever. She contemplated bringing it to her lawyers, but decided against it. The expected clauses and stipulations were not unwarranted or unjustified given the situation. Therefore, she found no need to involve another party. Jackie wanted no one to know. *She* would rather not know about it! Well, at least she wouldn't think about it – for now.

Instead she had thought about the job offer. Jackie had to admit that the prospect of sleeping in for a couple more hours in the morning did sound appealing. The job itself was not a problem.

She had been familiar with most aspects of her father's business. And then there was Michael... her previous opinion on more frequent encounters with her employer had changed. That fact was not as easy to admit, but true nonetheless. She would accept the offer.

He had told her to let him know when she wanted to start, making her decision a perfect excuse to see him. When the buzzer rang for her area to take their break, Jackie made her way to the offices. She asked the first young lady she saw for directions to Michael's.

Susanne was the receptionist for the production department. She was an attractive brunette who seemed very happy to help. She moved the telephone slightly away from her mouth. "You know, this place is a maze. If you'll wait just one second, I'll take you to his office."

Jackie stood aside while Susanne ended her telephone conversation. Before long she was being led through the main office area, with its many stations and rooms, and through a wide doorway which led to the executive offices. The president's office, Susanne pointed out, was the last one on the right. They stopped at the vacant reception desk. There were three other desks further along the wide corridor. A man and a woman, respectively, sat at two of the desks; the third was empty.

"I just saw Nora, his secretary, in the coffee room and the receptionist for this department seems to have disappeared, so... I don't know if he's in, but go ahead and knock. I'm sure it's okay."

"All right. Thank you very much for your help."

Susanne waved her hand as Jackie turned to leave. "Oh, don't mention it."

Jackie walked to Nora's empty desk, wondering if she should wait, although she knew that if she didn't act soon she'd lose her nerve. She took the several steps to Michael's door. Her hand halted on its way to the handle.

"I don't believe you!" A woman was saying. "I thought you liked our arrangement!"

"Brenda, I—"The man stopped short, as if suddenly silenced. He sounded like Michael. It had to have been Michael.

Jackie was frozen. She wanted to leave, but she couldn't. She felt compelled to prove that what she was thinking couldn't possibly be going on.

She took the one remaining step, and peeked through the space left by the partially opened door.

It was Michael. A woman with platinum hair was all over him, kissing him, touching him – and he didn't seem to mind.

Jackie felt nauseated. She turned to make a hasty retreat, but bumped right into Jerry. "Hello there!"

"Oh, sorry Jerry."

"That's okay. Did you want to see me?"

" ... Umm, no. I had to give Mr. Atkins something."

"Okay, see yuh!"

Jackie scurried away into the employee locker room, where she stayed long after her break was over. "Let him fire me!" she said out loud.

She had foreseen that someone would be hurt. Naturally, she was correct in assuming it would be her. But it was her own fault. She'd let it happen. She was the one who continually reminded him that their arrangement was a farce; why didn't she take heed? Why didn't she keep that in mind when he 'pretended'?

When she finally returned to her station, no one made jokes. They must have noticed that something was wrong. In fact, Marjorie asked her if she was all right to which she answered with a weak smile and a nod.

Michael had made no trips to the plant that day, no attempt to speak to her. That was just fine with her, she thought. She didn't want to see him either.

But as she and Hassan waited for the appropriate bus, his familiar black car drove up next to her, the passenger door swinging open. She couldn't make a scene. She said good bye to her smiling friend and got in.

"I came to find you, but you'd already left."

"You're back," Jackie stated lamely.

Michael put the car in gear and they were on their way. He looked over to her questioningly, but Jackie kept her face averted.

"What's the matter?" he asked.

"What?"

"What's wrong?"

Jackie looked at him now, her eyebrows raised. She desperately wanted to sound disinterested. "Nothing's wrong."

"I should have come to see you earlier, but I was bombarded by meetings and telephone calls," Michael explained as he stopped for the red light.

Jackie's pride had been tested. It was time to rebound. "Is that all?"

Michael was at a loss. Had he missed something? "What?"

"You don't answer to me," she said with a cynical laugh. "What makes you think that I expected or wanted to see you? I haven't forgotten what we're doing. I'll never forget why I'm with you. And by the way, you can tell your father that I'll take that job. You're right; I *will* need the money."

He had taken her for a fool. She had fallen for all his advances, but vowed never to let that happen again. At least she had been able to stop herself from falling for him completely, she congratulated herself. She had succeeded in that, she thought proudly, albeit by only a thread.

A sudden coldness passed over Michael's face, and his expression turned to stone. While he was away he'd tried to fight feelings that plagued him for the duration of the trip. He hadn't wanted to admit that he'd missed her, but he knew he did. He enjoyed her company, not to mention how her touch could send him reeling. He had been wrong to allow himself to be affected by her. He should never have let his guard down. Obviously he hadn't learned this yet; obviously he was glutton for punishment.

The car behind them honked loudly, and suddenly his features became sardonic and mocking. Back to normal. It was better this way. At least she wouldn't forget to hate him.

The tires squealed as Michael pushed forcefully on the gas pedal. He didn't look very happy, but she didn't care. She was glad to return some of the discomfort he'd caused *her*.

Michael stopped the car in her driveway. He didn't turn off the engine; he didn't even look her way. "Report to Jim Nyland at nine a.m."

Jackie didn't respond. She left the car and winced as the tires screeched all the way down the road.

CHAPTER THIRTEEN

*L*ooking very business-like in her black tweed suit and white blouse, Jackie arrived at Madison Electronics at 8:45 that morning. She entered the spacious entrance with its black granite floors and pale gold walls. The wall behind the tall reception desk was black, with large brass letters spelling 'Madison Electronics' prominent against the dark background. Jackie smiled at another visitor, an older gentleman who appeared to be more prompt than she was, and walked directly to the receptionist.

"Ah, yes, Jackie Ellis," the young lady exclaimed. "I've been expecting you. Please have a seat. I don't think Mr. Nyland is in yet."

Actually, Mr. Nyland left Jackie waiting at the front reception for nearly forty minutes before he came to greet her. Jim Nyland, as of the previous year, had been promoted to Director of Purchasing. He was in his early thirties, a handsome young man who seemed extremely confident.

He led her through the offices, introducing her to a pretty

young woman with short auburn hair.

"Pleased to meet you, Jackie." Shawna was the purchasing secretary, whose desk was just outside his office. "If you need anything at all, just buzz me," she said, offering her hand.

Shawna, Jackie later learned, had worked for Madison Electronics for the past eight years. A devoted employee, Shawna was almost always there. The majority of her absenteeism: the birth of her two children.

The junior buyers for Madison were Alicia, Gabe, Ives, and Diane.

Alicia, a middle-aged woman with silver hair wound up in a French roll, and wire-rimmed glasses neatly perched on her smooth pale face, seemed nice, Jackie concluded, though perhaps a little too uptight.

Add twenty or so years, a white beard and a red suit, and Gabe could pass as Santa Claus. He was a happy individual with a ready smile and willingness to help her get to know the ropes.

Ives was from Montreal and thus sported a heavy accent. He was a small man with thinning hair and glasses that sat upon the bridge of a long nose. "Mademoiselle, welcome. I normally handle our French-speaking suppliers – you might have guessed why," he joked, "so if you need any help in that area, please let me know."

Jackie was allowed to thank him before she was gently pushed to the next cubicle.

"Hi, I'm Diane."

"Jackie Ellis, hi."

Jim Nyland entered as well, forcing Jackie to move aside. "Miss Ellis will be filling in for Sara for the time-being."

Diane gifted Jim with a sarcastic grin. "Yes, I'd gathered that, Jim."

Jim huffed, and Jackie and Diane exchange a smile. It seemed that there was no love lost between these two.

Diane was an inch or two shorter than Jackie and just as slender. She was a pretty brunette with large blue eyes. She seemed bright and straightforward, and Jackie guessed she was going to like working with her, if only to see the sparks fly between her and Jim!

Finally, he led Jackie to her office so they could 'discuss her duties'. The office was small, approximately ten square feet, but it had a large bookshelf on one side and another set of shelves over the desk that was pushed against the opposite wall. The size of the office didn't bother Jackie. Besides, the window behind the desk made the small room bright. One or two flowering plants would cheer up the cool grey colours quickly.

Jackie remained standing while Jim gave her a list of the numerous suppliers they dealt with, along with pricelists and other pertinent information. He suggested that she take a day or two to familiarize herself with the suppliers and their products before she actually began to handle purchase orders, and Jackie smiled wryly. "I think I'm already familiar with most of your suppliers. And as for the product—"

"—Ms. Ellis," Jim interrupted, taking on an air of importance.

She'd expected this, but Jackie was not intimidated. She crossed her arms in front of her and tilted her head to one side, waiting for what he had to say.

"This is procedure. If you can't follow procedure, then it's quite likely that you can't follow instructions and—"

"—And you'd better get back to work while you still have a job."

The low, menacing voice seemed to have come from nowhere. They both turned to see Michael standing at the doorway. Neither had seen him.

"Michael, I was trying to explain procedure to Ms. Ellis, our new buyer, and I don't think—"

"—I don't think you heard me, Nyland."

Jim seemed nervous suddenly. "… Err… no, I don't think I did."

"I'm perfectly aware of Miss Ellis' identity and the reason for her presence here. As for procedures and instructions, she could probably teach you a few things. If she needs something, she'll ask. So, if you want to keep your job, you'd better get to it and leave her to hers. Do you hear me now?" Michael asked calmly.

Jackie normally would have felt sorry for someone on the receiving end of Michael's wrath, but today it wasn't in her.

"Yes, of course. I'll be in my office…" Jim's voice trailed off, as he left the office with his tail between his legs. Jackie had to smile.

Michael turned to her now. He stood with his hands in the pockets of his slacks.

"He's a little full of himself," she commented.

"Somewhat," Michael admitted.

Jackie walked around to her desk, pulled out her chair and sat down.

Still he watched her, and she was slowly but surely becoming unnerved.

"Did you want something?" she asked crisply.

Michael walked around the desk and leaned against it as he bent towards at her. He was far too close for her peace of mind!

"You said that you'd never forget why you're here, why you're with me," he recounted, in a deadly calm voice. "See that you don't. Leave your mood swings at home. Understand?"

Jackie stared back at him, her gaze unwavering.

"I have a meeting at lunch, but you'll be leaving with me tonight," he instructed, and finally Jackie averted her eyes. "So don't disappear."

He straightened and left her office, leaving her mentally exhausted.

The day progressed well despite its beginning. Jackie had taken a couple of hours, instead of the days Jim had suggested, to familiarize herself with her new surroundings and to become reacquainted with the purchasing department. Soon she was making calls and filling her purchase orders with no problems. Walter Madison was her only visitor who, aside from welcoming her to her new position, informed her that he was leaving that afternoon on a short business trip. After what she'd witnessed in his office earlier, Jackie wasn't ready to take anything anyone said at face value. She wondered what difference his trip would make to her and then reluctantly chastised herself. He was only trying to be nice.

Diane knocked on her opened door at noon. "Hi there. How's it going?"

"Oh, not bad."

Diane took a few more steps into the office. "We have an hour for lunch, as he probably told you," she said, rolling her eyes. "I usually bring my lunch, but today I had nothing in the fridge and my husband can't meet me, so... want to go for a bite?"

Jackie welcomed the invitation. "I'd love to. I didn't bring a lunch either, and I don't have a husband to meet!" They both laughed – something that seemed to annoy Jim as he walked by the office at that moment, presumably on his way to lunch.

Diane chose a coffee shop nearby. Jackie was grateful for that, she didn't want to risk meeting her intended either.

"How long have you worked here?" Jackie asked, taking a bite of her ham and cheese on whole-wheat bagel.

"Three years."

Jackie's curiosity on the opinion of the junior buyers regarding someone other than themselves filling in for the senior buyer on maternity leave begged to be verbalized. "I have to ask you something... you and the others, I mean Alicia and Gabe and Ives... were you hoping for that position?"

"No, because Sara intends to return." Diane looked puzzled. "Jim did tell you the position was temporary, didn't he?"

"Oh, yes. I know that. I just thought they would have asked one of you to take her place while she was away."

"No. Like I said, it's temporary, so it wasn't expected," she said truthfully. "But mind you, I can only speak for myself."

"Okay. I just don't want to step on anyone's toes."

Diane waved her hand. "You're not. So, where did you work before coming here, or did you?"

"Actually I've been in school. I'm... I'm not really sure what I'm going to do with the rest of my life, so... You mentioned a husband," Jackie prompted, wanting to change the subject. "Any children?"

Diane patted her tummy. "On the way," she exclaimed excitedly. "That's the other reason for not expecting the job you have. I'll be leaving on my own maternity leave in a few months."

"Congratulations. How many months?"

Diane went on to explain that she was only two months pregnant and that so far she'd the good fortune of feeling no effects of morning sickness. She'd been married for only two years and they were ecstatic as well as a bit apprehensive at the prospect of becoming parents to twins!

Jackie wished she could be excited and happy at the prospect of being a mother, but that was something that was unlikely to happen, at least this time around.

Michael reappeared at her door at about 5:20. "Ready to go?"

Jackie tidied her desk and returned the supplier binders to the bookshelf.

"Yes." She slipped on her suit jacket and slung her purse on her shoulder as she walked towards him. Jim Nyland watched with interest as they passed his office. Michael turned and looked at him, an eyebrow raised, waiting for a comment, but Jim made himself busy.

The few employees that were still at their desks all said their good-nights, to which they responded. Jackie was certain that they all noticed Michael's hand on the small of her back as he led her outside and wondered what they must be thinking.

Neither spoke during their ride to his home. At least, that was where she gathered they were going. Either way, Jackie had called her mother earlier to tell her not to expect her for dinner.

CHAPTER FOURTEEN

*A*s it happened, their destination was the restaurant where Michael had first taken her. There they met Frank and his wife Irene, and Jackie was happy for that. She had nothing to say to Michael and she certainly didn't want to rehash the day's events. However, before they entered, he reminded her that Irene was not to know about their plans, and that only added to her annoyance.

"I'll do my best, sir," she sneered.

The maitre d' greeted them at the door as he had done before. "Good evening Miss, Mr. Madison," he bowed his head. "Your party has already arrived. Let me show you in."

Frank rose from his chair when Michael and Jackie approached their table. He extended his hand to Michael and then turned to Jackie. "Miss Ellis, nice to see you again."

"Jackie, please." Jackie shook his hand and then smiled back at the woman who had just kissed Michael's cheek and was now smiling at her. Irene obviously understood that her husband had already met Jackie.

"Jackie, this is my wife Irene. Irene…"

Irene too extended her hand. "Jackie, I'm so happy to meet you. Michael never 'double-dates'," she accused, winking at Michael. "This is a treat for us!"

Double date? Oh yes, she had to remember she was playing a part!

Their waiter arrived, and clearly knowledgeable of Michael's and perhaps Frank's tastes, proceeded to pour sparkling water into their glasses. "Campari and soda, Mr. Madison? And for the ladies?"

Irene glanced at Jackie. "I'd rather have a glass of Chardonnay, how about you Jackie?'

"No thank you. I don't like wine."

"That's perfectly all right, Jackie. I can't drink more than one glass anyway." Irene shrugged, making Jackie feel a little less uncomfortable.

Michael ordered the wine for Irene and, once again, a Cosmopolitan for Jackie.

For at least a few moments the conversation around the table consisted of the choices of dinner wines followed by entrées listed on the menu. Once everyone had ordered, Irene turned to Jackie. "So I hear you work with Michael…"

"… Yes."

"That's wonderfully convenient, don't you think?"

Jackie searched for her starry-eyed look. "I suppose…" And Michael was silent.

Irene was a beautiful woman. In fact, Frank Atkins was proud to relay to Jackie that Irene had won the Miss Trinidad and Tobago pageant a few years back.

"Frank! Don't embarrass me!" Irene slapped her husband's arm playfully and then gasped when she realized the waiter had just arrived with their appetizers and she'd nearly caused him to spill the contents of her dish onto her lap.

"That's why she stops at one glass of wine, Jackie," Frank joked.

"Frank! Make me look like a lush, why don't you!"

Jackie smiled. "Actually I think it's wonderful – I mean winning the pageant. Why shouldn't he tell anyone?"

"Oh, maybe because it's been nearly thirty years!" Irene scoffed.

"Well, I think you'd stand an excellent chance of winning if you competed today," Jackie told her truthfully.

"Oh, I *like* you!" she laughed, and Jackie decided that she liked Irene too, very much.

"Do you have children?" Jackie asked.

While they enjoyed their dinner, Irene told Jackie that she and Frank had two girls in high school, both with aspirations of becoming doctors – or fashion designers. They talked for a while about the difficulties that arise with teenagers while the men discussed the ups and downs of the stock market.

There was a lull in the conversation while they sipped their coffee, but Irene soon put an end to that. "You know, Michael. This has been a wonderful evening."

"I'm glad you enjoyed yourself, Irene." Then he turned to Frank. "You really ought to take her out more often."

Irene nodded in agreement. "Yes, he should, but that's besides the point. No, I am so happy to have met Jackie. I must tell you I feel privileged. I'm sure Frank has met your lady friends, but we've never gone out as couples."

"And so why do you feel privileged?" asked Frank laughingly.

"Oh Frank, stop it. I mean to say, that Jackie must be someone special and in turn I feel special because he's chosen to introduce her to us and share the evening together."

Frank turned towards his wife and stared at her for a moment, drawing a questioning look from Irene and a muffled giggle from Jackie. "Irene, I am making a solemn promise here and now, that I will take you out more."

Michael actually chuckled, especially when Irene told Frank she hoped he'd find the couch comfortable that night. "Irene," Michael told her, referring to her comment, "you're right on both counts."

Winking at Jackie, Irene wrinkled her nose at her husband. "Well, thank you, Michael."

The couples parted company after promising to do this again and Jackie was actually looking forward to that. Besides the fact that she genuinely liked Irene, she knew that it was much safer to spend an evening with another couple than to be alone with Michael. Naturally, it would eventually become unavoidable.

When in the privacy of Michael's car, a small silver box was extended to her. She looked down at it and then at Michael. Reverting her gaze to the box, she took it from his hand and opened it.

Her breath caught in her throat as she stared down on a magnificent diamond ring. The centre stone must have been at least two carats in weight, flanked by a smaller diamond on either side. She looked at him now.

"What's the matter?" Michael was sarcastic. "Is it too small?"

"What's this?" Jackie asked quietly.

"What does it look like?"

"It looks… like an engagement ring, an enormous engagement ring!"

"Very perceptive. Don't tell me you expected me to propose bent on one knee and all."

"But… we haven't exactly, I mean I know we agreed to continue seeing each other, but we didn't talk about… actually going through with…" Jackie stopped and smiled cynically. "Well, naturally you knew I would, right?"

"I knew all along. I didn't think that *I* could go through with this farce, but you know, I'm actually enjoying it; I love proving people wrong," Michael announced as he changed lanes.

"Good for you. At least one of us will get some pleasure out of this!"

"That's entirely up to you."

Jackie ignored his remark. "Well, I'll be sure to take good care of it," Jackie said indifferently. "I just hope I don't lose it."

"If you do, it'll be one more thing you owe me."

Jackie huffed noisily. "I can't give you any more than I'm already giving you. You'll just have to shoot me!"

"I just might!" he agreed.

Feeling as though she'd lost the battle, Jackie gave in and slowly removed the ring from the blue velvet cushioning. She slipped it on her left ring finger. It fit.

Unknowingly, she voiced her thoughts. "How could you possibly guess my size?"

"I'm clairvoyant."

Jackie sighed. "What do we do now?"

"I want to get this over with as soon as possible. We'll pick a date, tell our parents and get on with the preparations. I'll give you my credit card; buy your dress and whatever else you need. Just remember that in everyone's eyes, but Frank's and possibly John's, if I decide to tell him, we are a typical couple, planning a wedding."

"We are far from a typical couple. And who's John?"

"John's a friend."

"*You* have friends?" Jackie asked sarcastically, but he continued.

"Draft a list of guests; pick a maid of honour. Keep it small; I'd like to keep this deal under one hundred."

He was issuing orders as if arranging a business deal, not a wedding. This was about their lives − *her* life!

"Anything else?" Jackie was fuming.

"Yes." Michael paused. "I want a schedule of your... cycle."

"—I beg your pardon?"

"If our sex life is to remain solely for the conception of a child, it would be to your advantage to provide me with the dates that you perceive yourself to be most fertile."

Jackie glared at him in astonishment. "You're a real son-of-a-bitch, aren't you?"

"Yes, I am," he agreed as he stopped at the traffic light.

"I pity this poor child," she said softly, "for having the likes of you as a father! Maybe it *is* best that I leave; I couldn't bear watching you raise him to be like you!"

Jackie threw the empty ring box at him and started to open the car door, hoping to jump out and disappear, if only for tonight.

Michael's vise grip stopped her, pulling her back into her seat. "What the hell do you think you're doing? Don't ever do that again!"

"Don't give me orders!"

"Don't push me, Jackie," he threatened.

He had never used her name. Hearing him call her 'Jackie', even in anger, was like having an ice-cold bucket of water poured over her, dousing her raging fire. She shivered involuntarily and turned from his examining eyes.

Michael stepped on the gas again, but stopped soon afterwards on a darkly lit side road.

He pulled her to him roughly. "From now on you do as I say, where and when I say it! Do you understand?"

"You didn't buy me!" She wasn't going to back off – not yet!

"I bought your services, and in this case, it's the same thing!" he growled, his face only inches from hers.

When he closed the gap and kissed her, he made no secret of the extent of his anger. His mouth was hard and unyielding; his hands were rough on her body, tearing buttons and fabric, kneading her flesh as if it were dough.

Jackie tried to push away from him, but she did not succeed. Her breath came in gasps when he finally left her mouth for the soft skin at the base of her neck.

"You... didn't want to have to tell your child... that his conception was artificial," Jackie said breathlessly, desperately trying to keep her tears in check. "Is it better to tell him that you raped his mother?"

"Damn you!" Michael swore against her flesh, his voice muffed.

Suddenly he pushed her away from him. He sat motionless in his seat; his head back against the headrest.

Jackie watched him from the corner of her eye as he fought to calm himself. He had lost control, but it was not fear she had felt. He had left her confused, unsure of her emotions.

Instead it was he who'd felt fear, not anger, when she'd reached for the door handle. Fear for her safety, fear that she'd disappear into the night, never to return… Yet anger seemed to be the only emotion he ever displayed. After a moment, Michael restarted the engine and they were moving once again.

She would have preferred not to, but as he neared her home, she found it necessary to speak. "I can't go home yet; my mother will still be up for sure and you ripped my blouse, and my jacket won't cover it."

He looked down at her, noticing how she held the two sides of her blouse together. He sighed in exasperation and proceeded to make a 'U' turn.

"Where are you taking me?" Jackie started to think she shouldn't have said anything at all. Michael's look told her he'd like to throw her off a cliff.

"The only alternative is my house; there's nobody there."

"For what? So you can continue your assault in private?"

Michael glared at her. "You don't know when to quit, do you?"

"And *you're* perfect!"

"The idea was to change into one of my shirts or something. Hopefully she'll be in bed by the time you get back – and if not, you can say you soiled your blouse, and… I gave you something to wear."

"You're just full of ideas, aren't you?"

"Have you got a better one?"

"No, I don't." She only wished she had!

As soon as they entered, Michael practically dragged her upstairs to his room.

Jackie was too upset, too nervous, to notice her surroundings.

Otherwise she might have wondered who had decorated his room. The colours and fabrics were dark in shade, but had not been restricted to those usually associated with an all-male household.

"The bathroom's through there," he pointed, throwing her a white polo shirt from a dresser drawer.

Jackie followed his instructions this time. When she reappeared, she found him lying across the end of the bed. He had discarded his jacket and tie and undone several buttons. At the sight of her, he propped himself up on elbow, his head resting on his hand.

Michael's eyes drifted downward to the oversized shirt and noticed immediately that she wasn't wearing her bra.

"Trying to tease me?" His voice was quiet.

"You broke the clasp!" she hissed, throwing the bra at him.

In one swift movement, Michael sat up, grabbed hold of her and pulled her down onto the bed. He rolled over, pinning her with his weight.

Jackie hoped that if she remained passive, he would lose interest and let her go. She was wrong. He stared at her for a moment, as if waiting for her to fight him. She didn't and he proceeded.

Once again, he kissed her, roughly at first, but slowly his lips became softer, more passionate. As his lips were busy on hers, enticing her to respond, his hands were busy elsewhere.

He tugged at the shirt, pulling it free from her skirt. His touch was electrifying, sending tiny shocks throughout her body.

She shuddered uncontrollably as his lips trailed along her neck to caress her bare skin. Unaware of her actions, she arched her back to him. Her hand, a moment ago on his shoulder, half holding, half pushing, was now at his jaw line, urging him to continue.

His hand slid downwards over her hip, over her thigh, lifting her skirt as it made its way back up over the silkiness of her stockings.

Somewhere in the back of her brain, a little voice was striving to be heard. It wanted to tell her to snap out of this trance, to come back to her senses. But Jackie wasn't listening. She wanted him to kiss her, to touch her.

Without realizing it, she whispered his name, unwittingly... she caused him to stop.

"You drive me crazy!" he growled softly against her throat.

Michael tore himself from her and walked away, through the sitting area, coming to stand by the windows on the far side of the bedroom. "Get dressed," he called over his shoulder. Why hadn't he continued? She was willing. Well, at least physically... She was getting to him. He couldn't allow it.

Jackie sat up, his polo shirt falling back in place on its own. Why had he stopped? Why... was she questioning his motives for stopping?

Michael gave her a moment to tuck in the shirt, then walked past her, keeping his eyes averted, towards the door.

"Let's go."

Stuffing the torn blouse and bra into her purse, she followed him out.

What a hypocrite she was! She vowed to hate him, yet she invited him to do as he pleased! Why did he have to completely destroy her defenses?

They didn't speak until he stopped in front of her house. He faced the windshield, gazing at nothing, before breaking the silence.

"You have a contract to sign. I'll check with Frank and I'll let you know when he's ready."

"Fine," was all she could manage before opening the car door and running up the steps to the security of her home.

It was nearly midnight, and just as she'd hoped, Joan had gone to bed.

Jackie paced outside her mother's bedroom door, trying to gather the courage to tell her about the 'good news'. She didn't feel like pretending to be excited, especially since all she felt was confused! But she realized that there was no use putting it off. She had to tell her that same night – otherwise it might look as though she wasn't as happy as she should be. That would be infinitely more difficult to explain.

She opened the door and walked over to her mother's bed. She sat down next to her.

"Mummy? Mummy," Jackie shook her arm.

"What? What is it?" Joan asked, startled. "What's wrong?"

"Nothing, Mummy." Jackie smiled lovingly at her mother. "I have something to show you."

Jackie held out her trembling hand and flashed the beautiful diamond engagement ring that adorned her finger.

"Oh, Jackie!" Joan exclaimed. "Oh, I'm so happy!"

Joan embraced her daughter and cried with joy, unknowingly giving her daughter an excuse to do the same... but for other reasons.

Jackie lay awake for hours that night. Her mind was so filled with conflicting thoughts; she was certain it would soon short-circuit and she would be left with nothing but a pile of burned out wires for a brain.

CHAPTER FIFTEEN

*T*he next morning at the office, her telephone rang. Twice, intermittently, confirming the call was being made from within the Madison offices.

"Yes?"

It was Michael.

"Come to my office; Frank has the papers ready."

He hung up before she could answer and Jackie took a deep breath and made her way there.

The platinum blonde was sitting behind the large desk in the centre of the corridor of the executive offices. She now knew the identity of Michael's elusive receptionist. She was beautiful, Jackie had to admit, but she had to wonder how much of her was plastic. Susanne, the young woman who'd helped Jackie to Michael's office the day he returned from his trip, was standing next to her busily gossiping, and this particular liaison led Jackie to suspect that overhearing Michael's conversation with his receptionist had not been coincidental.

Jackie had every intention of bypassing the two of them altogether, but the woman behind the desk would not allow it.

The platinum blonde rose from her chair. "Excuse me, do you have an appointment?"

"She doesn't need an appointment, Brenda." Michael's voice startled the young woman, leaving Brenda speechless, and Susanne flipping through papers obviously trying to find an excuse for her presence there. "We're in Frank's office," he told Jackie from where he stood by the lawyer's door a little further along the corridor.

"Good morning, Jackie." Frank greeted her, then motioned for both to sit down. He took in her pale complexion and drawn features. "I have to tell you Jackie, Irene had a wonderful time. She's quite taken with you."

"Irene is very kind."

There was silence. Frank looked from one to the other.

"Frank? Do you have the papers?" Michael asked impatiently.

"Oh! Yes, yes. I have everything ready!" Again he paused. "Okay, now... there's the surrogate contract and the prenuptial agreement. First of all, let me just say that as was discussed before – about payments towards your debt – those will stop immediately. Now... naturally Jackie, under the circumstances, you are not entitled to any of Michael's assets—"

"—I know that. I don't want anything."

"Good," Michael interjected. "I think half a million is more than enough."

How he could blow hot and cold like this was beyond her! How could he kiss her and hold her as he did one minute and the next... Oh, why was she so dense? He was just claiming what he perceived to be his paid privilege. Once a jerk, always a jerk!

"I said I don't want or expect anything!" Jackie repeated coldly. "Do you want it in blood?"

"Come on, you two. You're going to give me grey hairs!" Frank tried to intervene with comic relief. "Here, if you'll sign this, Jackie, we'll put Michael's overactive mind at ease."

Jackie signed willingly.

"Now," Frank continued. "Let's get to the important matters. I'm going to put this plainly. In return for the cancellation of your family debt... these are the sums here and here." Frank pointed to the numbers. "Along with any medical expenses as a result of this agreement, you, Jackie Ellis, agree to serve as a surrogate mother for Michael Madison.

"You will be married to Michael for the sole purpose of conceiving and bearing his child. Until that time, you will live together as husband and wife – however long it takes or until Michael decides otherwise. Walter Madison is not to learn of this agreement. The marriage is to look real."

Frank took a breath and looked up at Jackie for a moment.

"If... you should become involved with another man during this time, it is Michael's right to do as he wishes with this contract. He could cancel it, which would in turn indicate that you would owe him the original amount, or he could, of course, bind you to the contract. Do you agree so far?" Frank rambled on as if he were dealing with a mere merger.

"Just when am I going to have time to become involved with anyone, while I'm so busy being happily married... to him!"

"Stranger things have happened!" Frank smiled, but he

added more seriously, "Jackie, you're a beautiful young woman; it could happen. Do you agree?"

Jackie took another deep breath and closed her eyes. Forgive me, Mummy. Forgive me, Daddy. "Yes... I agree."

Frank paused again and looked at Michael.

"Okay, now for the difficult part." Frank turned the pages. "After the child is born... it is considered to be in everyone's best interest that you, Jackie, do not see the child at all. Afterwards you are to leave, or more specifically... you are not to return to Michael's home."

"Why can't I see my baby?"

Frank looked at her pale face. He felt sorry for her.

"Jackie... could you leave once you saw the baby?"

"... No."

"Right. Divorce proceedings will be commenced a few months prior to the baby's birth, so as not to prolong things unnecessarily. You are not to sue for custody... unless Michael agrees to grant this to you, and obviously, by that I intend 'partial'."

Jackie lowered her head and rubbed her right temple with her fingers, her hand keeping Michael's face hidden.

"Of course, there is another alternative," Frank started slowly. "And this is directed to you, Michael. I mentioned it before. You... might consider remaining married to each other... for the child's sake or—"

"—No! No. I couldn't." Jackie was adamant. She even shocked Michael with her quick response. "I... disagree Mr. Atkins," she continued, her voice steady, monotone. "I think it's better that I leave. I couldn't keep this act up for years. Besides... children pick up on things quickly. I believe it's in the child's best interest *not* to remain in a loveless marriage. I agree not to sue for custody, I just…" Jackie's words trailed off.

"You just…?" asked Frank.

She would have loved to be part of her baby's life, but as she had just stated… "Nothing, never mind."

Frank exchanged glances with Michael, but Michael remained silent.

"Jackie, have you had your lawyers look at the contract?" Jackie shook her head.

"Well, perhaps you'd feel better—"

"—How? How would I feel better? No… I don't want anyone to know."

"So, you agree to the original terms, then," Frank said slowly.

Jackie's heart ached. She didn't want to do this. "Yes," Jackie agreed.

"All right. If you'll both please sign here." Frank pointed his pen to the appropriate areas. "And here." Then he made two separate piles with all the papers. "All done," he said unnecessarily. "Michael, if there are any changes… I'm sure you'll let me know."

Frank stood now and gave each of them their copies of the contract and agreement.

Michael stood and looked down at Jackie as she slowly rose to her feet.

Jackie couldn't return his stare. "I have to get back to work," she said, looking a little dazed. She turned and left the office, leaving the two men alone.

"You know… this was my bright idea, but I'm feeling a little apprehensive. Are you sure about this, Michael?"

Michael tore his eyes from the door to focus on the documents in his hands. "I have to, Frank. And not just because of my father." He looked up at his friend now and sighed. "I have a wedding to plan. I'll talk to you later." Leaving Frank to decipher the significance of his words, he returned to his office.

Jackie had a splitting headache. After spending the better part of half an hour in the ladies' room crying into toilet paper she returned to her desk, although she was in no state to accomplish anything.

Diane poked her head around the door. "Hi," she smiled. "You okay?"

Jackie looked up, startled. "Oh, hi. I just have a headache."

Diane didn't comment on Jackie's puffy red eyes. "Coffee helps my headaches, believe it or not. I can't have any now, but I'm going to the coffee room for a juice, would you like to join me?"

"Sure," Jackie agreed. She had to get her mind off the events of that morning.

They walked into the coffee/lunchroom provided for the office employees, but much to their displeasure, they would not be alone. *Jim Nyland* was there speaking to two other men.

"Morning, Brian, Leonard," greeted Diane. "Have you met Jackie? This is Jackie Ellis. She'll be filling in for Sara. Brian Khun is our vice-president. He shares the load with Walter when Michael's out of town," she explained as she chose a bottle of orange juice from the refrigerator.

"Welcome aboard, Jackie," Brian said politely, and Jackie thanked him, just as politely. Brian Khun was in his forties, tall and handsome, with dark brown hair and eyes to match.

"Leonard Kravitz is our controller." Leonard was older,

perhaps in his late fifties. What was left of his hair was grey, but attentive blue eyes shone youthfully from behind wire-rimmed bifocals. He was average in height, but a little big around the middle.

"Pleased to meet you, Jackie!" Leonard shook her hand, and then became pensive. "Ellis…" he repeated, as he turned towards the others. "Where have I heard that name before? Didn't we take over a company not so long ago? Ellis… Ellis Electronics?"

Jackie quickly made herself busy. She poured herself a cup of coffee, while her hands could still function.

"Yes," answered Jim. "How can you forget? All my contacts were buzzing about it when it came through! Apparently, the poor bastard didn't know what hit him!" he continued, laughing.

Neither Brian nor Leonard returned the laughter. Jackie's pale face had captured their attention, as well as that of another man who'd entered directly behind her, his face dark with anger.

"Nyland!" The newcomer growled.

Jackie had to leave at once, before she snapped. Excusing herself, she put down her cup and turned sharply, bumping force-fully into what felt like a brick wall. She didn't have to look up to know the wall was Michael. He put out his hands, holding her shoulders, keeping her from leaving the room as she took a few calming breaths.

No one knew what was going on, but they all had a feeling it wasn't good. Michael raised her chin with his fingers and turned her to face the others once again.

"Nyland, I'm becoming increasingly tired of you and your mouth. But then, you can't help yourself, can you? I'm sure if you had half a brain you might learn to control it. I think you need to be introduced for a second time." Michael's voice was steady; his hands remained on her shoulders.

Jackie stared into space, unable to look at anybody. Tears stung her eyes, threatening to once again flow uncontrollably. Confirming her vulnerability, however, was not a welcomed option.

Brian, Leonard and Diane looked as though they wanted to make a hasty retreat, but didn't dare move.

"This is Jackie Ellis. Jackie *Ellis*... of *Ellis* Electronics."

Jim Nyland's face seemed to have taken on a strange shade of green.

"Sam Ellis was Miss Ellis' father. The takeover of his company was not a personal vendetta. We don't take pleasure in others' distress. It was a business deal."

"Well, I didn't know... I mean, honestly, how could I possibly imagine that she would be working here—"

"*Miss Ellis* is not only a part of the Madison team... but has just recently consented to be my wife!"

The only thing that kept her tears in check was the sight of Jim's face becoming yet a deeper shade of green.

The other three looked at each other in surprise, then they grinned, showing their pleasure in hearing this news.

"Oh!" Jim exclaimed nervously. "Well, I... I'm sorry..." Jackie wanted only to put an end to all of it, yet she couldn't bring herself to excuse him.

"You know, you're actually very lucky," Michael was saying now. "My fiancée has quite a temper. She was holding a cup of hot coffee when you made that remark. You're lucky you came out of this with your family jewels intact!"

Diane giggled, but Brian and Leonard laughed out loud,

which finally eased the immense tension in the small room, at least for them.

"Congratulations, Michael." Brian and Leonard offered their hands. "And best wishes to you, Miss Ellis."

"Thank you."

"This was my fault," Leonard offered. "I'm the one that remembered your father's company. I'm so sorry."

"That's all right," she told him in a tight voice, and he nodded in acceptance and went back to work.

"Congratulations," said Diane to both of them.

"Yes, congratulations," Jim joined in, and quickly preceded Diane out of the room.

Michael's other hand finally dropped from her shoulder and Jackie felt compelled to turn around.

She looked up at him, her eyes still swollen from her reaction to their own confrontation earlier that morning, now shimmering with a new supply of unshed tears. His face was blank. "I have to get back to work," she told him, leaving him alone.

Michael bowed his head and exhaled noisily. He had felt the need to come to her rescue regardless of his anger towards her. And he was angry with her… for what reason exactly?

CHAPTER SIXTEEN

Jackie absentmindedly picked up the receiver to answer yet another inter-office call. "Yes?"

"It's me," Michael told her.

" ...Yes?"

" ...I called the church for available dates..." He paused, expecting a response, but none was forthcoming. "The second weekend in June is available."

" ... Fine."

"It took a little persuading. Apparently they're pretty adamant about their marriage classes, but when I mentioned your name he was a noticeably more receptive. I suppose it facilitates matters when the priest is a friend of the family..." No response came from Jackie and Michael continued. "Under the circumstances, I think it's best to keep the festivities to a minimum. We can hold the reception at the house; we have plenty of room."

" ... Fine." Jackie repeated.

"I called a wedding consultant. We'll stop there on the way home. We'll need invitations and so forth."

"Fine."

She heard Michael huff on the other end of the telephone. She knew she was pushing it.

"Did you tell your mother last night?"

Darn, she couldn't use the same word. " ... Yes. She was ecstatic," she recounted offhandedly as she flipped through the pages of a catalogue.

"Good. We'll tell my father tonight. He's back from his trip."

"Fine."

"Be ready to go at four. We'll leave early – and don't say 'fine'!"

Jackie actually wanted to laugh!

" ...Very well!" she said instead.

Michael hung up the phone.

It was past four o'clock when Jackie decided to walk towards Michael's office.

Again the receptionist was not at her desk. Nora, his secretary, was busy speaking to someone and Jackie didn't want to bother her. Impatiently, she paced the spacious corridor, which was flanked by three offices on either side. Finally, she sat on one of the plush chairs facing his office.

After waiting for fifteen minutes she decided to let him know she was there. She got up and walked to his door.

Again, there was a voice, the same voice.

"Married?" Brenda sounded incredulous. "You can't be serious! Why?"

"Because..." Michael answered.

"I don't get it. Did you get her pregnant?"

"No. Brenda, this is the way it is. Accept it."

"Humph! So, I suppose you have to play the faithful husband now?"

"What do you think?"

Brenda made a suggestive sound and then there was silence.

It didn't take a nuclear physicist to figure out what they were doing. Jackie smiled cynically as she made her way to Nora's desk.

She decided to introduce herself to the woman. It would be much easier to pretend when he wasn't there to listen to every word.

"Hi."

"Oh, hello. May I help you?"

"Actually, I'm just waiting for Mr. – for my – for Michael." That was smooth.

Nora's face lit up. "You must be Jackie!"

"Yes."

Nora stood and offered her hand. From a distance Nora looked like somebody's grandmother, but up close Jackie realized that although Nora was middle-aged, her kind face was not as old as she had first thought. "I'm so happy to meet you." Suddenly Nora glanced towards the empty receptionist's chair. She tucked an imaginary hair behind her ear. "Umm… was Michael expecting you?"

"We were supposed to leave together…"

"Maybe I should buzz him."

Jackie stopped her. "No, that's all right. I'll wait. It was nice meeting you."

"Oh, likewise dear," Nora said a little nervously, and sat again to tend to a phone call.

When Michael and the receptionist appeared moments later,

Jackie was sitting on one of the chairs in the small waiting area trying to look disinterested, unaffected by what they knew she had at least imagined.

Brenda looked down at her, a mocking smile on her lips. *Gee, I wonder where she learned that?*

"Ready to go?" Michael asked Jackie, the same sardonic look on his face.

Jackie asked with a sweet smile: "Are *you*?"

Michael's mocking green eyes held hers for a moment, and then he turned, forcing her to follow him. "Let's go."

As they walked through the office everyone offered their congratulations and best wishes. Naturally, the news had travelled throughout the office by now. She should search for that fake smile and sew it onto her face; she'd need it for a while!

The accounting secretary rose from her chair and rushed over to them. She gave Michael a kiss on the cheek.

"Leonard told me! I never thought I'd see the day!"

"Emma is Leonard's wife," Michael explained.

"You must be pretty special, Jackie, to be able to nab this guy! He swore to me he'd never marry!" Emma laughed.

Jackie just smiled.

"Okay, let me see!" Emma reached for Jackie's hand. "Good heavens!"

Her exclamation caused the other women in the area to muster the courage to gather around to see the ring. The expressions on their faces were priceless, but then, they should have seen hers last night, Jackie thought.

She thanked them for their compliments and good wishes. They were so nice, and she was deceiving all of them...

Jackie slid into the passenger seat of Michael's car. It was time she gifted him with an earful. "I gather the terms of that agreement don't apply to you."

He turned to look at her, unsure of her question. "Which terms?"

"I didn't agree to double standards and I won't be made to look like a fool!"

"And who's going to do that?"

"You told me that you wanted everyone to think our marriage is real, especially your father. I've caught you twice—" she blurted, causing Michael to turn sharply towards her.

"So is that what's got your knickers in a knot?" Michael smiled. Finally! Some enlightenment! He now understood the reason for the change in her since his trip.

"Are you so sure that he won't see you with her?"

"That's really none of your concern," he assured her, desperately trying to suppress the urge to sigh in relief – *relief?*

"No? You're right – not in the way you think, but don't blame me when your little plan falls apart."

"Don't worry about it, all right?"

"No, I won't worry about it, but maybe you should. I have nothing to lose at this point!" Jackie warned.

Michael looked at her again. "Is that a threat?"

"Take it any way you like."

"Look, Brenda and I were... involved, and my father was well aware of it."

"Were? Is that why Nora was so edgy?"

Michael slanted her another look. Why was this bothering her so much? "Nora is always worried about one thing or another and yes, were. If I didn't know better, I'd think you were jealous."

"That'll be the day! And by the way," she said, avoiding the innuendo, "you wanted me to supply you with my medical file. I believe I have the right to ask for the same. I don't think I want to come out of this with an incurable disease!"

"I've always used protection," he told her, chuckling.

"I don't want to know what you use or don't use! I told you what I want!"

"Fine. John's a doctor, or so he tells me. I'll have him give you a report on my health, all right?"

Michael stopped the car in front of an elegant shop.

Jackie stepped out and walked towards the store; Michael was close behind. She stopped suddenly and turned to him. "I don't want to do this. Can't you take care of it?"

"I don't know what you like."

"What does it matter? It's not exactly my dream wedding."

"I'd sooner not do it at all, but we're here now. Let's just deal with it."

The tall blonde woman greeted them as they entered.

"I called earlier..." Michael began.

"Mr. Madison?"

"Yes. This is my... fiancée," he introduced.

The word seemed to stick in his throat, as did Jackie's own 'hello.'

The woman motioned for them to sit across from her as she sat behind her glass-topped desk. "All right. As we discussed, we will take care of catering, flowers, invitations, and transportation. This is our brochure," she said sweetly. "Feel free to browse through it. We can draw up a contract at your convenience."

Jackie was so sick of the word 'contract.'

The woman picked up two large binders from the credenza behind her and plopped them down in front of Jackie. "These are samples of invitations. You might want to look at a few."

Jackie flipped through the first of the binders. She quickly came across an invitation that was simple, yet elegant. The woman saw her hesitation.

"Oh, that is one of our best!"

"We'll take it," confirmed Michael.

"Now that was easy!" the woman laughed. "I'll need all the information: names, dates, et cetera. We'll take care of that later." She jotted down the code number for the particular invitation and continued with the rest. "All right. What about flowers? You said the reception will be at your home?"

"That's correct."

The woman turned to Jackie again. "Did you have something in mind?"

Jackie returned her annoying smile. "What do *you* have in mind?"

"Oh! Well, we've supplied our other clients with a wide variety of arrangements... Here," she said, producing yet another binder with numerous photos. Aren't these just lovely!"

"Yes... But a little much for my taste." Jackie turned to her fiancé. "What do you think, *hon*?"

Michael's eyes danced. It was obvious he was amused. "I agree. We'd prefer something a little more subdued."

"Oh! Alrighty! Tell me... do you have a preference as to which types of flowers? Perhaps I can show you something more suitable."

Jackie shrugged. "I like roses, white roses. I know they're delicate. Will that be a problem?" Her tone unabashedly mimicked that of the wedding consultant.

Oblivious, the woman replied. "Hmm. White roses are very delicate, but they are lovely. Did you want other colours in the arrangements for the church or reception, or do you prefer to keep everything white, with greens of course?"

"White. I suppose I'd prefer a variety of pastel colours for the maid of honour's bouquet."

"How many bridesmaids?"

"None. Just the maid of honor."

"Okay." The woman placed yet another binder in front of Jackie. This was filled with an array of less extravagant bouquets, corsages and centerpieces. "If you choose the styles for the bouquets and other arrangements, we can always change colour or flowers."

Jackie glanced through the pages as Michael retreated to the office to speak to the woman in private.

Jackie informed the woman of her choices when they returned.

"Wonderful!" the woman exclaimed. "I'll take care of everything! Please call me as soon as a list of guests is compiled. I'll give you my card; feel free to call anytime."

Jackie wished this woman could tone down her excitement, at least a notch. She looked happier than the bride!

Soon they were driving away again, to destinations unknown.

Michael's eyes narrowed slightly and his tone seemed almost suspicious. "That didn't seem too difficult for you."

"I know what flowers I like," Jackie said absently, then realized what had just taken place at the shop. "It's just about a month away..." she added nervously.

"The consultant will take care of all the tedious matters. All you have to do is buy a dress."

"A dress?" Jackie's mind felt exhausted suddenly.

"Yes, you know... the white dress that brides wear... or does white not apply to you?"

Jackie's cynical smile did not reach her eyes when she answered him. "Virginity was not stipulated in the contract." Michael laughed and Jackie wanted to punch him. "I'm so glad you find this amusing!"

CHAPTER SEVENTEEN

Tonight Jackie had been informed that they were to meet Michael's friend John for dinner. John apparently had been made privy to the reasons for their upcoming wedding. Well, Jackie thought, at least she didn't have to pretend with him.

The maitre d' came forward to greet him.

"Mr. Madison, Madam. Welcome. Dr. Bellows has already arrived. I've seated him at your table. If you'll follow me..."

They were led to a table at the far corner of the room. A handsome, dark-haired young man sat engrossed with the menu that lay in front of him. He had a nice face, a kind face.

"Dr. Bellows," Michael greeted his friend formally.

John's head came up quickly.

"Hey! I was wondering where you'd gone!" He stood as he caught sight of Jackie. He stared as if he were surprised to see her. Jackie sat in the chair that the maitre d' held for her. She felt uncomfortable.

"What's the matter, John? Don't you approve?" Michael asked his friend sarcastically as they sat as well.

John came out of his trance, looking a little uncomfortable himself.

"I'm sorry. You must be Jackie." John held out his hand.

"Yes, I am. You must be John." Jackie shook his hand and John still looked uncomfortable.

Now he and Michael were exchanging looks and Jackie had to wonder just what her dear husband-to-be had told his good buddy! She was becoming annoyed. "Is there something wrong?"

"No! No, of course not," John assured as he repositioned himself in his chair. "It's just that... well..." John was at a loss for words. "Forgive me. I don't know why I'm surprised. I know Michael's standards."

"Oh, yes. So do I! They're double!" Jackie smiled. Michael laughed quietly into his menu and John looked confused.

"What do you say we order?" Michael signaled for the waiter, and they ordered their dinner. After a while, Michael broke the uneasy silence.

"All right, spit it out, John," he said lazily. "You have something to say; say it."

John leaned over towards Jackie. "*You* are a *beautiful* woman! Why do you want to do this?"

Jackie was caught off guard, but her fiancé was quick to answer.

"You'd be surprised what people do for money, John." His cynical smile distorted his handsome face.

"Do you mean *me* or *you*?" she asked, finding her voice.

"Touché!" Michael replied.

John shook his head vigorously. "Michael, this is crazy!"

Michael was losing his patience now. "What's your problem, John?"

"I don't have a problem, but I think you do! You're not just doing the 'surrogate' thing, something about which I already have my doubts. But this entire act... This is a very dangerous game you're playing, and someone is bound to get hurt!"

"Not if everyone does what they're supposed to do," Michael concluded.

Jackie wished they'd change the subject. They were speaking as if they'd forgotten she was present.

"You're wrong. I want that to go on the record."

"Fine. But I'm doing this anyway."

And John sighed, admitting defeat. "So, have you set a date?" He had no choice but to try and accept his friend's plan.

"June tenth. Want to be my best man?" Michael asked lightly.

"You don't waste any time."

"I don't see why we should have a long engagement. My father approves of my choice for a bride; that's all that counts."

"In that case, what can I say? Sure, I'll be your best man."

Jackie watched the two of them discuss the details. She need not have been there at all. It wouldn't be so easy with Walter.

Walter was genuinely happy. Jackie actually saw tears in his eyes, and she felt like a heel.

"I'm so happy! So very happy!" Walter hugged his future daughter-in-law. "You see, Michael, I told you this would happen! He wouldn't give me the satisfaction, but I knew!"

Neither of them commented; they simply smiled.

"Have you set a date yet?" Walter wanted to know.

After exchanging glances with Michael, Jackie decided to answer. "Yes we have... the tenth of June."

"That's wonderful! That's just around the corner! Never believed in long engagements myself!"

They sat together for a while and discussed wedding plans. Michael sat beside her, his hand periodically sneaking onto her shoulder or the base of her neck. She jumped every time, but Michael continued, just the same.

On the ride to Jackie's home, Michael was quick to comment on her nervous state. "What was with you tonight?"

"What do you mean? What did I do now?"

"Every time I touched you, you flinched! I don't think you're supposed to cringe every time your fiancé touches you. You'd better get used to it – this baby is not going to come about by immaculate conception."

Jackie shuddered. Was it disgust... or anticipation? After the way she had been reacting to his advances, she would be fooling herself if she claimed anything but the latter!

"I have to go," she said, opening the car door as soon as Michael stopped the car in her driveway.

Michael took hold of her arm. "Try to look a little more enthusiastic about this blissful event, will you?"

"Anything else?"

"Don't I get a goodnight kiss?"

"Get lost!" Jackie yanked her arm free and left the car before he could stop her again.

CHAPTER EIGHTEEN

*I*t was Michael again; she knew it! Jackie wanted to ignore the annoying ring, but it wouldn't stop.

"Yes?"

"What took you so long?" he asked impatiently, and Jackie simply sighed in response. "You'd better take the afternoon off and find yourself a dress."

"Why today?"

"Not your wedding dress; a dress for the engagement party."

"The what?"

"I couldn't talk my father out of it."

Jackie sighed again and placed a hand on her forehead. "And when is this?"

"This Saturday. He's inviting a few people to the house. Nothing big, but it'll be formal."

Great! As if the farce of the wedding wasn't enough, now she had to endure another evening of watchful eyes and inquiring minds. "Wonderful."

"I couldn't get out of it," he repeated.

"Fine." There was silence on the other end and Jackie wondered if he'd hung up.

" ...You can take my car; just come back and pick me up when you're finished."

"I don't drive standard, and besides, I wouldn't drive that thing if you paid me."

She wished she hadn't said that part. Fortunately, he didn't comment. "It won't bite; it looks more menacing than it really is."

"Unlike its owner," she commented.

"All right; take a taxi, then. I can't leave, I have a meeting."

"I'm not ashamed to take the bus."

"Take a taxi," he repeated.

"Yes, master! Anything else, master?"

Michael was silent for a few moments, but when he spoke again, there was laughter in his voice. "No, that's all."

Jackie slammed the receiver into place. She took a calming breath and then picked it up again to call a taxi.

She did as he had asked. She bought herself a dress – a very expensive dress. When she'd looked at the price tag, her eyes had rounded in astonishment, causing the salesclerk to make a face as she watched her very large commission go down the drain. But when Jackie told her she would take it, the salesclerk suddenly changed her attitude, nearly tripping over herself trying to accommodate her client's every need!

She had returned to work as soon as her shopping was done. Michael had come by her office to ask her if she'd been successful, and she'd said yes. He had not asked to see her purchase, nor had she volunteered to show it.

Michael stayed at Jackie's for dinner that night. It was nearly nine when there was a knock at the door. Joan looked concerned as she rose from her husband's chair.

"I'll get it." Michael gestured for her to sit down and opened the door. "Dad! What are you doing here?" his son asked with obvious surprise.

After an astonished look towards her mother, Jackie rose to go and greet their guest.

"Hello, Jackie." Walter gave her a kiss, and then looked past her to Joan, who had followed, but lingered behind.

"Joan..." Walter said quietly.

Jackie's brow creased. She looked from Joan to Walter and then to Michael, who was also watching attentively.

"Hello, Walter..." Joan allowed him to take her hand and hold it between both of his.

"It's been too long. It's wonderful to see you again, Joan."

Feeling their children's eyes upon them, Walter took it upon himself to explain.

"We go way back, your mother and I... "

"Really?" Jackie sounded suspicious. *Any more skeletons in the closet, Mummy?*

"Your mother worked with one of the suppliers I dealt with when I first started my business. That's where we met... but we... lost track of each other... "

"It has been a long time, Walter," Joan concluded with a kind smile, and Jackie had the feeling that her mother was anxious to stop him from continuing down memory lane. "Please, won't you come in?"

Naturally he did, but mercifully they didn't touch again on the subject of the 'old days.' It was too disturbing and Jackie didn't want to deal with it.

Walter had come to personally invite Joan to the party and to tell her that he'd send a car to bring her to his home. The two spent the better part of the evening talking about the wedding plans and even made suggestions on destinations for a honeymoon.

Michael and Jackie often exchanged curious glances, but neither voiced their opinions on their parents' suggestions or their mysterious association.

CHAPTER NINETEEN

As Walter had promised, a car arrived for Joan the following afternoon.

Jackie was nervous! She had eaten nearly half a carton of ice cream when she stopped suddenly. "What am I doing?" she said out loud, her mouth full of chocolate ripple fudge. "I won't fit into my dress!" Then, realizing the time: "My dress!"

She stashed the remaining ice cream in the freezer and threw the spoon into the sink. She ran up to her room, and shrugging off her bathrobe, Jackie unzipped the garment bag and slipped on her new dress.

It was an ankle-length copper-coloured silk chiffon. It clung to her like glue. The sleeveless gown had a boat-like neckline, and a very low back. It was impossible to wear a bra, but the flower embroidering of a darker copper camouflaged the lack of lingerie.

She had flipped her hair into a loose French roll, which gave her a more dramatic, sophisticated look. Pleased with her reflection, she took a deep breath, picked up the tiny purse that matched her sandals and made her way down the stairs.

Halfway to the bottom, she heard the doorbell ring, and she stopped in her tracks. So much for her cool appearance! Her stomach fluttered anxiously as she took the final steps to the door.

Michael was looking over his shoulder when she opened the door. He turned to look at her and actually did a double take. His heartbeat accelerated as his eyes took in the entire look: from the style of her hair to her excellent taste in dresses. She looked spectacular, but he decided to keep any comments to himself.

He didn't look so bad either, in his black suit, she thought.

"Are you ready to go?"

"Yes." Jackie picked up her keys, and Michael, taking them from her, locked the door and led her to his car.

As they neared the Madison mansion, Jackie noticed that the flowers had started to bloom and leaves had begun to adorn the many trees, giving the grounds a beautiful botanical appearance. She also noticed the white BMW parked in front of the house. It would have been difficult to miss the enormous red bow on its roof!

"What's that?" she asked, curiously.

"It's a car."

"Yes, I'd gathered that. Do you have weird friends?"

"No more weird than I."

Michael came around to her door and held out his hand. "It's yours," he explained as she stepped out.

"Mine?"

"I can't very well have my wife taking the bus, now can I?"

"Naturally… we have to keep up appearances," she smiled cynically, but there was more. The personalized license plate read:

'Jackie.' She turned to look at him. His eyes held hers for a moment, but she could read nothing.

"It… wasn't necessary… but thank you," she said, and noticing Elmer Delaney at the door, taking a coat from a recently arrived guest, she pushed herself to raise her lips to his. Michael's one hand still held hers. The other was now on her bare back as he willingly accepted her kiss.

"We should get inside," he said against her mouth.

Again, he had succeeded in bringing down her defenses.

"Jackie! You look wonderful!" Joan exclaimed as her daughter entered.

"You are a vision!" Walter agreed.

"Thank you."

"Did you see your present?" Walter's excitement matched that of a child at Christmas.

"It's a little hard to miss!" Jackie laughed nervously. "It's beautiful!"

"Just like its owner," Michael said, as his arm encircled her waist.

Her breath was suddenly stuck in her throat. This was the first time he'd ever complimented her on her looks and she didn't know how to take it.

The doorbell rang, startling her. Oh no! The guests were arriving! Michael must have felt her pulse quicken, and he gave her a little squeeze. "Relax," he whispered in her ear. "It'll be over before you know it."

Jackie had reservations, and even fears about the outcome of that evening, but as it turned out, things didn't go too badly. The Madisons' family and friends were not ogres or monsters, after all.

Jackie met Walter's sister, Annette, and her husband, Charles.

Charles and Annette were both dentists. Their son Gary was a stockbroker and his wife Debbie was presently a stay-at-home mom. Michael had told Jackie that his father suggested that Gary's two girls, Bridget and Rebecca, be included in their bridal party. Jackie didn't mind, but now it forced her to include her two cousins. She was certain that they'd be hurt if she didn't. However, it worked out perfectly: her two cousins were boys.

Jackie bent towards the two little girls and smiled. "I'm very happy to have you in my bridal party." Bridget and Rebecca giggled as Michael watched with interest.

Bridget, who was only five, smiled shyly and hid behind her older sister. Rebecca was three years older and spoke for the both of them.

"We can't wait!" Rebecca confessed with enthusiasm. "Are we going to wear white dresses or the same colour as your bridesmaids?"

"Well, I don't have bridesmaids; just a maid of honour, which makes you girls very important to our wedding." Jackie remembered just how special it was to be part of a bridal party. When she was just seven years old, Aunt Beth had asked Jackie, her favourite – her *only* little niece, to be her flower girl. She'd been a bridesmaid as well for Carol's sister, and that was a different experience. It was great fun in a different way, but her fairytale-like memories of her white tulle dress and the sparkling tiara in her dark locks were incomparable. They'd stay with her forever. It would be no different, she imagined, for these little girls. Their faces beamed! "So, in that case, I'd like *you* to choose."

"Really?" Rebecca squealed excitedly and looked at her sister, who had just poked her head out from behind her.

Debbie and Gary came to join in their conversation.

"I can't tell you how excited they are, Jackie!" Debbie told her, touching her arm.

"They're so sweet. We're happy to have them," Jackie returned.

They were all very nice people. Walter's brother-in-law joked with her about how they thought she seemed too good for the likes of Michael, and that she must be extremely special for Michael to finally decide to settle down. Walter's sister warned Michael that if he didn't behave himself, he'd have to answer to her! They made her feel welcome, and for that she felt infinitely grateful.

John arrived and he spotted Jackie immediately when he entered the room. He greeted the other guests, but his eyes seemed glued to her. When he reached her, he sighed and shook his head slowly. "Wow! You look absolutely delic—" John stopped short when Michael's hand suddenly appeared on her shoulder. "Absolutely wonderful! Doesn't she, Michael?"

"Yes... she does."

Walter appeared now, and offered her a crystal flute filled with what looked to be wine. "Jackie! I have something for you!" But Jackie wrinkled her nose at the liquid. "Now, now. I want you to try it." He extended the glass to her, and she accepted grudgingly.

However, upon her first sip, her eyebrows shot upwards. "Mmm! This is good! What is it?"

"This is ice wine. I knew you'd like it!"

"Mmm, yes, *this* I like!"

The ice wine was delicious! Although the numbness at the back of her neck was a little disturbing, Jackie continued to drink it; it was relaxing her. She found, in fact, that she was actually enjoying herself.

Michael remained close for the rest of the evening. The few times that he was forced to leave her side, he watched her from a distance. She had caught him several times.

Irene was also staying near, making sure her new friend was never alone. She confided to Jackie that everyone loved her and that she shouldn't worry about being accepted. "They should be worried about whether or not you'll accept them! And if they give you any trouble, you just call me, okay?"

Irene was a wonderful lady. She made her feel comfortable and Jackie appreciated that. "Okay, I will," Jackie promised. She wondered, however, what Irene – in fact the entire family – would think of her if they knew why she was really there.

Later in the evening, when Jackie was returning from freshening her lipstick, John stopped her in the entrance. He leaned close to her.

"I hope you know what you're doing."

"Yes, I do, but I have to do it anyway," Jackie returned with a wry smile.

"Why?"

Jackie wasn't able to answer his question, as Michael had just appeared beside her.

"My father wants to make a toast," he announced, breaking up their little meeting.

Jackie smiled apologetically towards John and took Michael's hand as they re-entered the living room.

Walter gave a wonderful speech, expressing his feelings on Michael's good sense, and his happiness that Jackie was the one he chose.

Joan wiped away her tears, as did a number of the other women.

Those were kind words, but Jackie's eyes were dryer than the Mojave Desert! Actually, Jackie had the most unnerving urge to giggle!

"Kiss! Kiss!" Everyone tapped their champagne glasses with spoons, forks, key chains, whatever they could find.

Michael gazed down at her as he gathered her into his arms. Jackie slid her hands over the front of his suit to entwine her fingers in the hair at the base of his neck. She willingly accepted his kiss, responding, enjoying it immensely. There was a strange ringing in her ears… However, much to her disappointment, the kiss was over. Only then did she realize the ringing she heard had actually been their own personal cheering section.

It was past midnight when their guests began to leave.

Walter offered to take Joan home, so that Michael and Jackie could have a few moments alone. The caterers had cleaned up the bulk of the mess; they would be back in the morning for the rest. Alice Delaney, the housekeeper, and her husband Elmer, had since retired for the evening, and now the loving couple was indeed… alone.

Michael discarded his jacket and tie and undid several shirt buttons. His voice was quiet when he took a few steps closer. "You looked beautiful tonight…"

Jackie was standing in the middle of the room, not quite sure if she should be grateful that the evening was over. She turned to look at him, but it was a while before she answered him. She was too busy studying him. He stood with his hands in his pockets, legs slightly apart. Come to think of it… he looked like the hero on the cover of a romance novel, tall and dark, and most definitely handsome, muscles straining against his shirt…

"You didn't look so bad yourself…"

Michael looked away suddenly, and curiously changed the subject. "Did you want to take your car home?"

"Well, I really don't think I should," she smiled sheepishly.

Michael half expected a snide remark, but he asked just the same. "Why not?"

"Because I think I've had a bit too much to drink," she confessed. "You?"

Jackie giggled. "Yes. That ice wine is so good! I must have finished a whole bottle on my own!" Jackie put her hand to her head. "I'm a little dizzy."

She sank down on the couch, nearly missing it altogether.

"Whoa! I'm *a lot* dizzy!" she giggled again, and Michael smiled down at her.

He sat next to her and watched her as she kicked off her shoes and put her head back, sighing in contentment.

"I had a nice time," she conceded quietly, as she closed her eyes.

Walter returned home a short time later. He stopped in the doorway. Michael was still sitting next to Jackie, his head resting against his arm, simply watching her as she slept.

"Still here?"

"She fell asleep," Michael told him.

Walter chuckled. "She had quite an evening! Well, don't wake her. I'll call her mother to tell her she fell asleep and that she'll stay here tonight."

Michael wasn't too certain that Jackie would appreciate spending the night. "Maybe I should just take her home…"

"Michael, I think that even you won't take advantage of a girl who's had too much wine!" Walter looked at his son. "On second thought, take her up to your room, and since there are no guestrooms prepared, *you* will sleep on the couch tonight!"

"Dad, these aren't the dark ages! Besides, I'm going to marry the girl," Michael laughed at his father's prudery.

"I don't want any hanky-panky while I'm just down the hall! What you do out of earshot is your business, but under my roof… and with this girl… yes, you'll be married, but I have to defend her honour until then!"

Michael shook his head and smiled. "Fine, I'll sleep on the couch."

"See that you do! Good night." Walter waved his hand and disappeared up the stairs.

Michael looked down at her once again. Sleeping with her had been at the forefront of his mind since he met her, yet he had been extremely patient. He slowly gathered her into his arms and carried her to his room. He laid her down on the bed, then sat next to her, caressing her cheek, stroking her hair away from her fluttering eyelids.

"Michael," she breathed.

Michael's lips covered hers in a gentle, tentative kiss to which she again responded freely, willingly.

Her arms wrapped themselves around his shoulders, drawing him closer. Her hands reached to the front of his shirt, tugging at the fabric, straining to feel his skin under her fingertips.

Michael obliged, discarding the shirt. Now his hands too longed for the same sensations. His fingers slid around her shoulders, slowly slipping the soft chiffon downwards, exposing her bare flesh. His hands sensually caressed her, molding and teasing her. His lips trailed along her throat and shoulders, to finally rest against her breasts, stirring endless sensations of pleasure.

Michael again searched for the lips that she offered willingly, and Jackie drew him to her, yearning to feel his bare chest on hers.

However, as he slid his hands to her hips, hoping to push the dress lower still, the telephone rang and Jackie was suddenly brought back to earth.

She pushed at his chest, and Michael sat up; bewildered.

"What are you doing?" she exclaimed, as though unaware of what had happened. Frantically, she searched for a corner of her dress with which to cover herself.

"What am *I* doing? I think you got that backwards," he said quietly.

"My God! I think I was dreaming!" she stared at him, her eyes open wide, as she noticed his bare chest.

"Must have been some dream! Just who was it you were dreaming about?"

"Not you, that's for sure!" Jackie put a hand to her head. She wondered just how much of a fool she'd made of herself!

Michael got up and slipped on his shirt. He opened his dresser drawer and threw her a T-shirt. The sardonic look was back.

"What happened?" she wanted to know.

"Nothing happened. I'll just take it as a proper thank-you for the car."

Jackie's eyes grew wider. "Take what as a proper thank-you?"

"Go to sleep."

"No, I have to get home!" Jackie swung her legs onto the floor, but the room started spinning.

"No. You're staying here. Your mother knows; my father called her."

"Take what as a proper thank-you?" she asked again, realizing he'd never answered her question.

"Go to sleep," he repeated, and closed the door behind him.

CHAPTER TWENTY

ackie heard sounds of shuffling feet, drawers opening and closing, water running, but she couldn't open her eyes. She was so comfortable against those soft sheets, in that warm bed…

It was hours later when she finally awakened. She opened one eye, then the other. She looked around, taking in her surroundings.

Suddenly she gasped, sitting up quickly. Then she stopped and listened intently for any sounds. There were none. She looked down at Michael's T-shirt and then over to the pillow next to her. It didn't look as though anyone had slept there. Had he slept there?

Jackie slowly made her way to the bathroom. She peeked inside before quickly entering and locking the door behind her.

She showered and redressed in Michael's T-shirt, and then caught her reflection in the mirror. She couldn't very well go downstairs like that! Spotting his bathrobe on the hook behind the door, she put it on. She brushed her wet hair away from her face and ventured downstairs.

"Well, good afternoon!" Walter exclaimed, and Jackie put her hands to her ears.

Walter lowered his voice to a whisper. "Oh, I'm sorry, dear. Michael's in the dining room. We just had lunch, but Alice can make you breakfast, if you like."

"Oh, no. Thank you, but I'm not very hungry."

"All right, dear," Walter laughed and went into the study, leaving her to face Michael alone.

Michael was still sitting at the table, reading the paper. He looked up when he heard her trip over the hem of the robe. Her hair was wet, she wore no make-up, and she was barely visible from beneath that oversized robe, but he realized, that no one, no matter what designer outfit they wore – or didn't wear, for that matter – ever looked more desirable...

He smiled. "Have a good rest?"

Jackie frowned. "I'm not sure."

"Why?"

"Because... I don't know why I'm here," she looked at him suspiciously. "Or what happened."

"Nothing happened," he told her innocently. "You fell asleep."

" ...And then?"

"And then... you slept!"

"That's all?"

"Yes. Are you disappointed? Would you rather I'd slept with you?"

"No. I'm just not sure if I was dreaming, but I..."

"But what?"

Jackie frowned again. "Nothing, never mind."

"I went by your house and got you a change of clothes; they're in your room."

"Thank you. *Your* room," she corrected.

"Soon to be *our* room!" Michael said suggestively, and Jackie rolled her eyes.

"Are you hungry?" he asked.

"Not particularly. I'm... going to get dressed."

"Need any help?"

"No," she said forcefully, and scurried back upstairs.

Michael stood at a window at the rear of the house as Jackie, dressed in a short denim skirt and long-sleeved cotton sweater, strolled along the spacious grounds. He watched as she walked around the large in-ground pool, peeking into the windows of the cabana. She stopped at every flowerbed trying to identify the extensive varieties of flowers that Elmer Delaney had planted.

She lingered for a while to admire the tulips more closely. There were red ones and yellow ones, pink and purple ones. They were so pretty.

She bent over the rose bushes, reading the tags, suggesting the blooms to come, and Michael watched as the middle-aged Elmer came towards her with a small bouquet of tulips of every colour. Jackie gasped in surprise and thanked him for his thoughtfulness.

Michael had never given her flowers... He turned and retreated to the study.

Jackie decided to bring her lovely bouquet inside. She entered the yellow and blue kitchen through the French doors on the far end of the patio.

"Hi, Mrs. Delaney! Your husband just gave me a gift!" she

smiled. "Do you have a vase I could put these in?"

"Well now!" Alice Delaney kidded as she reached for the vase. "Should I be jealous?"

Jackie giggled as she arranged her tulips. "Maybe! Can I help you with dinner?"

Mrs. Delaney looked surprised. "You want to help?"

"Yes, if you don't mind."

"Mind? No, of course not. I just... well, none of Mr. Michael's girlfriends stayed long enough for a conversation, let alone any meals, but I'm sure if they had they certainly wouldn't have come into the kitchen!"

"I love to cook," Jackie told her, opting not to comment on Michael's choice of 'girlfriends'.

Mrs. Delaney gestured for Jackie to join her. "I am so pleased! By all means!"

Jackie closed the doors, noticing that the lemon yellow of the walls almost exactly matched the colour of the casually styled window coverings that hung from iron rods at either side of the doors. The only difference: the little clusters of fruits scattered throughout the cotton fabric. To her right, a blue granite countertop stretched the width of the kitchen in the shape of a 'U'. A large island of the same granite floated in the centre of the room. Mrs. Delaney stood behind it chopping vegetables. Directly behind Mrs. Delaney, an industrial sized stove gleamed in stainless steel. To the right, a Sub-Zero fridge stood against the wall, and beside it, a sliding door to the pantry that hid enough dry goods to feed this small family for years. Continuing to the left, completing the 'U', two large sinks and an even larger window overlooked the garden. Despite its size, the décor made the room warm, cosy and inviting to one's culinary creativity.

Mrs. Delaney waved a hand over the vegetables and herbs that cluttered the island. "I was thinking of making chicken tonight. I haven't yet decided how."

"I see you have fresh mushrooms... I have an idea."

Placing her flowers in water, Jackie took over and started to ask a delighted Mrs. Delaney for ingredients and utensils.

Over an hour had passed when Michael, dressed in blue jeans and a T-shirt, finally walked into the kitchen. Jackie was completely involved in the preparation of dinner, and that was something that none of his other lady friends would ever contemplate. This too was different... but definitely pleasant.

"There you are," he said unnecessarily, as Jackie uncovered several pots. "I thought you'd gone down to the wine cellar for more ice wine."

A little startled, she looked at him, trying very hard not to notice the fluttering that had returned in her stomach the moment he appeared. "I don't think so."

"What are you doing?"

Mrs. Delaney put her hands together. "Ah, Mr. Michael! Dinner will be extra special tonight! Miss Jackie has been cooking!"

Michael just watched her, keeping his eyes intently on the face that Jackie kept averted.

"Go on; it's almost ready. Call your father," the housekeeper instructed.

Jackie knew that Michael enjoyed her cooking, but Walter had never tasted any of her meals. She was a little nervous.

She watched as he savoured yet another piece of her chicken Marsala, and then helped himself to yet another spoonful of sautéed asparagus, grilled onions and herb-mashed potatoes. "This is delicious!" Walter raved as Mrs. Delaney placed a pitcher of water on the table.

"Yes, I know. My husband has already had two helpings of everything! But I didn't cook. Miss Jackie did." She winked at Jackie and returned to the kitchen.

"Jackie?" Walter seemed surprised. "You're a wonderful cook!"

"I'm glad you like it."

"Oh yes!"

Then he looked at Michael. "You definitely don't deserve her."

After coffee in the living room, Walter announced that he was going to visit one of his fishing buddies, and Jackie felt uncomfortable again. Unable to remain sitting next to Michael, she stood and walked aimlessly around the room.

"I think I should go home now."

Michael watched her for a moment longer. Today had been... nice. Suddenly their cold house felt like a home. "All right. Do you want to take your car home?"

"My car? Oh! I don't know. I guess..."

"Okay."

Jackie started towards the door and Michael followed. She stopped and turned. "I... need the keys," she said quietly.

Michael pulled out a set of keys from his pocket and dropped them into her extended hand.

He followed her outside and held the car door open as she took a seat behind the wheel. He then asked her to insert the key so that he could show her where all the instruments were situated on the dash. Closing the door now and leaning his arms on it, he examined her through the open window. She looked up at him, unsure of her next move.

"Are you coming in to work tomorrow?" Michael too, was searching his brain for something to say.

"Yes."

"All right. I'll see you tomorrow."

Michael straightened and took a few steps away from the car. Once again, he had not made any attempt to kiss or touch her.

Jackie didn't say another word as she pulled out of the driveway and turned onto the street that would take her home.

CHAPTER TWENTY-ONE

She had contemplated keeping Carol out of this extremely complicated and outrageous situation. However, if she had not chosen her best friend as maid of honour, her mother would have known something was not right.

Jackie had spoken to Carol several times since she'd been forced to leave school, but she hadn't discussed the particulars of the events that had changed her life so drastically.

Now she was calling to ask her to stand by her as her maid of honour. Naturally Carol was honoured by Jackie's request, but she was surprised – shocked to hear of her upcoming nuptials. She wanted to know everything! But Jackie couldn't bring herself to explain, at least not over the telephone. Although, she knew full well that speaking to Carol face-to-face would be even more difficult. She wasn't certain that she'd be able to pretend with her best friend.

The following weekend was Mother's Day, and since Carol

was due to arrive at her parents' by then, Jackie decided it would be the perfect opportunity for the bridal party to shop for gowns.

Jackie invited Irene to accompany them. They had arranged to meet in front of the exclusive bridal salon that Irene herself had suggested. This was also one of the few boutiques capable of providing the service they needed with such short notice.

All the bridal gowns were beautiful. Jackie tried on so many she was afraid she wouldn't be able to choose! But as it happened, it wasn't too difficult after all; Jackie's eyes kept returning to the first gown.

"It's always like that, you know!" Irene said laughingly. "They say you never forget your first lover, either! It's a good thing mine was Frank!" Debbie placed her hands over Bridget's ears and rolled her rounded eyes at Irene.

Jackie made herself busy, unable to laugh along with everyone else. The comment was not one she wanted to hear. Jackie was counting on forgetting Michael after this ordeal was over. She wouldn't be able to go on otherwise.

She slipped on the first gown again. "It's beautiful, Jackie," everyone agreed.

The beauty was in its simplicity. The gown was entirely in silk. The full skirt flowed to the floor like water, forming a puddle of silk on the floor behind her. The sleeveless bodice was equally simple, form-fitted with a wide 'V' neckline. It was stunning.

Yes, this was the one. It was extremely expensive, but Jackie shrugged her shoulders as she slipped off the soft fabric. Her husband-to-be could afford it.

The saleswoman produced several little dresses for Bridget and Rebecca. They had decided to wear white. One style in particular was similar to the bride's gown, and naturally the girls were quick to choose that one. The girls were having a wonderful time and would have loved to stay, but they were late for dance lessons and therefore once their gowns were chosen, Debbie rushed out, thanking Jackie as she waved goodbye.

Jackie intended to make certain that the mother of the bride looked magnificent, and *that* she would in the taupe chiffon that Joan chose. Carol's gown, pale blue silk, in simple straight-cut lines, complemented her strawberry blonde hair and fair complexion. Irene was successful as well, having chosen a gown that was of a matted gold with flowering vines embroidered down one side. It was very exotic and perfect for her.

All their gowns were wonderful; *they* looked wonderful. After the seamstress documented everyone's proper measurements and promised a fitting by the end of the week, the saleswoman was only too happy to ring up their deposits. Despite Irene's protests, all their purchases were placed on Michael Madison's platinum card. It had been his request.

Later that afternoon, Jackie and Carol sat on her bed and talked. After a while, Carol took hold of her friend's hand and lowered her voice. "Something's not right here," she concluded knowingly.

Jackie tried to sound flip. "What do you mean?"

"Jackie, I know you. And I was watching you back at the shop. You should be just a little happier about this wedding. Instead you look… I don't know… strained, preoccupied."

Jackie lowered her eyes. Keeping this secret from her mother was not only terrible, but very difficult as well. Keeping the secret from Carol, whom she'd known since childhood and with whom she'd shared every event in her life, was going to be virtually impossible. She *had* foreseen this line of questioning.

"What's going on?" Carol pressed.

"You won't believe what a mess I've gotten myself into."

"What are you talking about? Are you pregnant?"

Jackie's lips turned in a cynical smile. "No, not yet."

Carol's face suddenly paled and the few freckles on her small upturned nose were immediately more prominent. "What's that supposed to mean?"

Jackie recounted to her friend the reason for her lack of enthusiasm and sudden decision to marry Michael Madison.

"I don't believe it!"

"See? I told you."

"But Jackie... how could you go through with it? I mean, how could you give up your child?"

"Carol... I got myself into this... extremely deep pothole – me and my big mouth! I'm responsible for everything. I have to do this. I don't know what else to do. Just don't hate me, okay?"

"I don't hate you. I just... wish there was some other way..."

"Not unless you have a few hundred thousand to lend me," Jackie tried to joke.

"Right." Carol sighed. "But your baby, Jackie."

"It was actually suggested that I have some sort of visitation rights or even custody..."

"And?"

"And I refused. I thought it best for the baby."

"You're a stronger person than I could ever be. And besides... how could you marry someone you don't love?"

It was a rhetorical question. Jackie lowered her eyes and Carol sensed there might be more to this.

"Jackie?" Carol asked tentatively, bringing her friend's eyes back to her. "Are you in love with him?"

"No! Of course not!" Jackie was adamant.

"Well then, how could you sleep with this man?"

Jackie shrugged her shoulders. She couldn't tell her friend that the prospect of that event did not exactly disgust her.

"Will I meet him?"

"Actually, no; he's away this weekend."

Carol gave her a wry smile. "How convenient. Let me guess, he's three-foot-nothing, weighs four hundred pounds and bears a striking resemblance to Quasimodo!"

Jackie laughed. "No... not quite." But she didn't elaborate.

"Hmm," mused her friend.

Jackie had visited her old friends Marjorie, Hassan, and Inga occasionally since she'd accepted the office job, so she didn't perceive it as odd when on her last afternoon before the wedding, Jackie was summoned to the plant. The office was unusually quiet, and everyone seemed to have disappeared, but she'd thought nothing of it, until Michael met her in the small corridor.

"I was called too. It must be something to do with our wedding. Put on your smile!" Michael instructed as he opened the door to the plant.

As he had guessed, all the employees were there, with the exception of Brenda.

Jackie was a little taken aback and welcomed Michael's supporting arm around her.

Jerry and Brian, the vice presidents, were chosen to speak.

"We know that you don't really need anything," Brian began. "Besides, now you have each other; that's all you'll ever need!"

Oh, if only they knew!

"But," Jerry added, "we all got together and decided to book the bridal suite at the Plaza for your wedding night!"

Everyone started to cheer and clap. Jackie wanted to find a corner and die! Naturally, she had to stay there with her husband-to-be, looking and acting as though she was happy and looking forward to that night!

She was grateful that it was Michael who decided to speak first. He thanked everyone for their thoughtfulness and generosity. Jackie forced herself to thank everyone as well, and let shyness be taken as the excuse for her short speech.

Walter then reminded his employees that a luncheon had been provided for everyone. The food was being served in the lunchroom and everyone was to take an extra hour for lunch, in celebration of his son's wedding. Everyone cheered once again – and Jackie couldn't wait for the day to be over.

CHAPTER TWENTY-TWO

*J*ackie had told Michael that she needed a few days off for any last minute preparations, but in actuality, the wedding consultant had taken care of everything; she only had to give the okay whenever and wherever needed. Besides shopping with Irene for a new wardrobe, there was not much she had to do. Still, Jackie needed the time to think, to pray for an alternative – or a miracle! Neither came.

Time did come; it had caught up to her. It was Friday. Tomorrow she'd become Mrs. Michael Madison.

Carol arrived early that morning and together they packed her suitcases. Holding a yellow floral sundress against her body, she whirled around the room. "Hey, do you get to keep these clothes?" she asked her, a grin on her pretty face.

Jackie threw a hat at her in response, and they both laughed. It was a nervous laugh. There was far too much tension, too much happening…

After the giggling subsided, Carol looked seriously at her friend. Their gowns had been delivered and now hung in the doorway of her nearly emptied closet. The bride hadn't even looked inside the garment bag.

"Jackie... are you sure?"

Jackie nodded and gave a strained smile, and Carol hugged her, hoping to give some comfort; that was all she could do.

Jackie's mother broke up their moment, summoning her to greet her guests. Joan's sister and her family had just arrived from Ottawa for the wedding.

Jackie had called her uncle a few weeks prior. She'd had a very important request to make. Jackie had asked Uncle Jonathan to walk her down the aisle, and after a pause, during which Jackie was certain he had swallowed back tears, he'd told her that he'd be honoured. The two boys were also happy to be part of their cousin's wedding and to wear their first tuxedos.

Uncle Jonathan and Aunt Beth were so glad to be back for a happy occasion this time. "We're so happy for you, darling!" they exclaimed, each of them giving her a hug.

Her aunt gave Jackie yet another hug. "You look wonderful dear, but you really should put some weight on those pretty bones of yours!"

Aunt Beth believed that if there were more of you then there'd be more to love. Aunt Beth was not excessively overweight, but she was plump and proud of it. Uncle Jonathan didn't mind either, although he was much thinner than his wife. Her mother's younger sister by twelve years, Aunt Beth was still an eye-catching woman at 43. She kept up with all the current styles, from hair to clothes, and always looked her best. Five years her senior,

Beth's husband was more reserved, but Jackie's father always joked that accountants usually were.

Their two boys, Jason, 9, and Matthew, 11, were car lovers. Naturally, since Jackie had mentioned to them on the telephone the type of car that Michael drove, they couldn't wait to meet him – and his car! They were outside now, waiting on the front step.

It wasn't too much later when Michael arrived, and Jason and Matthew ran to meet him.

"Hi! You're Michael aren't you?"

Michael smiled down at the boys. "Yes, I'm Michael. Let me guess, *you* are Jackie's cousins."

"Yes. I'm Matthew and this is Jason."

"Well, it's very nice to meet you." Michael shook their hands.

"I love your car!" Jason exclaimed excitedly.

"It's a Dino Fiat, isn't it?" Matthew elaborated.

"Yes, it is," Michael confirmed, surprised at their knowledge of this rare vehicle. "How did you know? There aren't very many of these around."

"I know," said Matthew.

"We have books on Ferraris," Jason explained. "We love Ferraris!"

"They call this 'The Other Dino'," Matthew continued. "Because just like the Dino Ferrari, this one is also named after Dino, Mr. Ferrari's son. He died when he was young. It's got the same engine as the Dino Ferrari, but a Fiat chassis, and Fiat built it." Matthew rambled on, proud to show Michael how much he knew.

"What year is this – '69, '70?" asked Jason.

"It's a '70. And very good; I'm impressed."

Jackie's cousins were so proud. They smiled from ear to ear.

Joan and Carol were in the study when they heard the boys

come in. Joan was the first to reach Michael, and promptly gave him a kiss hello.

"Aunt Joan, may we have some iced tea?" Matthew and Jason asked.

"Of course! Come!" Then she disappeared into the kitchen with the boys to fetch their drinks and call the rest of her family so that they too could come and meet Michael.

"Hi," Jackie arrived on the scene and greeted him obligingly, and Michael replied, kissing her.

He looked over to Carol, who was standing next to Jackie staring in awe.

"This… this is my best friend, Carol Lankowsky. Carol this is my… this is… Michael," Jackie introduced with difficulty.

Carol's lips turned upward into a wry smile, and Michael looked from one to the other as he extended his hand.

"Miss Lankowsky… is something wrong?"

"Oh, no! It's just, well, I wondered how Jackie, who's always been so very stable and sensible, could marry someone whom she's only just met. And call me Carol, please."

Suspicious eyes shot over to Jackie. "And?" Michael turned to Carol once again.

"And I understand now… how Jackie could fall head over heels."

"Careful… you're going to make me blush," he smiled.

The subject was dropped as Jackie's family hurried towards them to meet the wonder man who had captured their Jackie's heart.

Walter arrived moments later, along with his sister and her family. Following close behind was John, the best man. After cool drinks for everyone, they headed for St. Mary's Parish for rehearsals.

Jackie felt that the real deal was going to be difficult enough – why repeat it; but Father O'Malley wouldn't hear of it. He'd already waived all marriage classes and agreed to such a quick ceremony for the daughter of his good friend Sam.

All present and accounted for, Father O'Malley directed everyone to stand in their appropriate spots. Walter extended his arm to Joan and they were first to start the procession. Bridget and Rebecca giggled as they walked together with the boys, and Debbie cried. Carol made her way to the altar and stood across from John and Michael. Jackie's turn. After several unsteady breaths, Jackie took Uncle Jonathan's arm and allowed him to lead her towards the groom-to-be. He placed her ice-cold hand in Michael's, kissed her forehead and went to stand by his wife, and Beth cried…

"Wonderful! Wonderful!" Father O'Malley exclaimed, clasping his hands. "You people are perfect!" He congratulated everyone. Then he turned to glare at Michael and Jackie. "I hope you two look happier tomorrow. This is your wedding, remember?"

Thank God for Carol! "Jackie has a headache, Father."

"Oh, I'm sorry dear. Make sure you get plenty of rest tonight. Make that headache go away, okay?" And Jackie nodded. "What's *your* excuse?" He squinted his eyes towards Michael now, who actually broke into a smile.

Father O'Malley read the vows, which in turn were repeated by Jackie and Michael. The words 'love, honour and cherish you all the days of our lives' stuck in both their throats.

"Now that wasn't so bad, was it? Okay everyone, tomorrow

it counts!"

Back at the Ellis home Michael was being perfectly charming and polite, though this must have been very difficult for him. Jackie didn't think he was much on family gatherings, especially under these circumstances.

However, Michael and his clan seemed to be getting along well with her uncle. Well, why not, she thought proudly. Uncle Jonathan may not have had millions in his bank account, but he was intelligent and personable.

Joan had invited Father O'Malley and he had readily accepted. He was a pleasant addition to the group who provided the comic relief.

After Joan's elaborate dinner – consisting of rack of lamb, veal medallions in white wine, and a multitude of vegetables: baked, steamed and grilled – everyone agreed to wait until later, much later, for dessert. In the interim Michael offered to take the boys for a ride in his car. Jason and Matthew nearly exploded with excitement! Jackie thought it was a kind gesture, but then again, perhaps he just wanted to get out.

Carol took this opportunity to take her friend aside. "Okay. I'd sleep with him too!" Carol confessed. "I don't think I could go through with the whole deal, but I'd certainly sleep with him!"

"Carol!"

"Well, at least his looks will make it more bearable," she giggled, but soon became serious. "Jackie?" Carol touched her friend's arm, forcing her to turn towards her. "Are you sure you're not in love with this guy?"

"No, of course not!"

"Frankly, that would explain everything. 'Cause I still can't believe you'd do this."

"I told you why, Carol – and I am not in love with him."

"Okay, okay. But that would at least change things."

"How? He doesn't believe in that emotion. He sees women only as sex objects and as means to an end."

Carol watched Jackie intently. She was about to speak again, but decided against it. She knew her friend very well. Michael Madison had pushed her into a corner. If she had any feelings for him, she wouldn't readily admit it.

When Michael and the boys returned, their parents shooed them off to bed, and Debbie and Gary and their two girls also decided it was time to leave.

After more coffee and desserts were offered, Michael took her hand. "Let's go outside."

Once outside, in the cool spring air, he let go of her hand and walked to his car. He reached into the glove compartment and pulled out a rectangular leather box. He came back to stand in front of her, handing it to her.

Jackie's eyes silently questioned him.

"Your wedding gift."

She slowly took the box and looked up at him once again. "Couldn't you get out of this, either?" she asked, with a wry smile.

"No."

Jackie looked down at the box again, and with her heart pounding a touch quicker than normal, she slowly opened it.

"Oh my!" she breathed.

It was a necklace, a single strand of diamonds. The centre stone was at least one carat in weight. Smaller diamonds scaled down on either side. Accompanying it was a similar bracelet and earrings.

They were so simple, but so breathtakingly beautiful – and much, much too expensive a gift for her to accept, even if it were only for the duration of their marriage.

"I… I can't accept. I mean, I… can't wear these."

"Why not?"

"They're just… too much! What if… what if I lose them? I'll owe you for the rest of my life!"

"They're insured, so it really doesn't matter," Michael said offhandedly.

"Well, naturally they're insured, but still—"

"—Don't worry about it, okay?" he sighed, as if tired with the conversation. Then, suddenly, he bent and kissed her on the lips.

Startled, she looked up at him.

"I needed some lipstick to wipe off," he shrugged. "Naturally, you would have at least kissed me for your gift."

Jackie couldn't think of a smart reply.

Michael was already heading for the door, when she took hold of his arm. "Michael…" she started quietly, and Michael turned to look at her. "I… I know that this is all a farce, but… sometimes…" Jackie sighed. "Sometimes you can be so different – like tonight. Is it all an act? Is any of it real?"

Michael remained silent, and Jackie sighed again.

"Sometimes… I actually think that you… that you really mean some of the things you say; that you may actually care… Sometimes, I wish…"

"Jackie…"

"Jackie! Michael!" Joan called from inside. "Come on, you lovebirds. Come have some cake. It's nearly midnight; Michael has to leave!"

"We'd better get back," he decided, opting to leave what he was about to say unsaid, and Jackie concluded it was for the best; she was afraid of things she didn't want to hear.

Michael didn't try to speak to her again that evening. He was still reluctant to admit feelings that were becoming too strong to ignore. The fear of ultimate rejection prohibited disclosure. When he left, he had told her not to walk him out, just to simply go to bed.

CHAPTER TWENTY-THREE

"Jackie!" Joan called as she entered her daughter's room. "The photographer is waiting for you! He's becoming quite edgy; not to mention the girls!"

Suddenly she stopped and looked at her daughter.

Jackie was still in her bathrobe. She had been sitting quietly at her dressing table, staring blindly at her reflection, her fingers absently playing with the diamond necklace.

Carol sat on Jackie's bed. She too remained quiet, giving her friend the time she needed to get on with the day's events.

"Jackie... is something wrong?" Joan looked concerned.

Yes, something was wrong! She just couldn't tell her!

Last night, she had allowed herself to admit that her feelings for Michael had changed. Last night... she had allowed herself to imply that to Michael. Unfortunately, it had made no difference to him. Now she was going to become his wife... in bed only, and even this was for the sole purpose of giving him a child.

"Jackie?" Joan called her name again. "Are you all right?"

"I... I just wish Daddy was here," Jackie said finally.

Tears sprang to her mother's eyes. "I know honey, so do I. But I also know that he is here with you... in spirit."

Jackie closed her eyes. She wanted to scream. *No, Mom! That's not what I mean! I don't want him here to share my 'happy day'! I don't want him here to walk me down the aisle!* She took a calming breath and stared again at the mirror. If he *were* here, she thought miserably, *she* wouldn't be; she'd be in school, and none of this would have happened.

Her friend came to stand behind her, her hands on her shoulders.

"Jack... do you want to dress now?" Carol asked quietly, and Jackie nodded.

Carol helped the bride with her wedding gown while Joan secured the embroidered headpiece in Jackie's freshly coiffed hair.

She looked beautiful.

Carol gave her hand a little squeeze, and, after stealing another glance at the mirror, Jackie gathered her full skirt and made her way downstairs to put on that infamous smile for the photographer.

John looked suspiciously to his friend, who stood quietly, leaning against a wall in the church rectory. "What's the matter, Michael?"

"What?" Michael asked absently.

"I said, what's the matter? Are you having second thoughts or something?"

Michael looked at him, somewhat annoyed. "No. Why would I have second thoughts?"

"Oh, I don't know... maybe because this entire plan is ludicrous?"

"John, give it a rest, okay?"

"You know, I was watching you last night. I know you were out of your element… but you actually seemed to be enjoying yourself. You looked… happy. If you would have allowed yourself to feel as a normal human being does, you might have surprised yourself."

"Really? How's that?" Michael's tone was cynical.

"You might have fallen in love with her. It would have been for real, and you wouldn't be worrying about whether or not you could pull this off."

"I don't 'fall in love'."

John flashed him a wry smile. "You think you can remain indifferent to her?"

"Why? Do *you* think otherwise? She's no different—"

"—Oh yes she is, and you know it."

Michael was about to speak when Walter entered the room.

"Let's go, boys! The bride has arrived!" he announced happily.

John gave his friend a knowing look before extending his arm, allowing Michael to precede him.

Sunlight shone through the glorious multicoloured stained-glass windows, shedding an almost iridescent glow over the gleaming wood of the pews and the wonderfully ornate altar, the focal point of the old cathedral.

Jason and Matthew were already standing by the first pews.

The wedding march began and the two men directed their attention to the great doors at the end of the church.

Along came Bridget and Rebecca, who were joined by Jason and Matthew. Everyone smiled and chuckled as they watched little Bridget scatter her petals in bunches as she walked slowly down the aisle.

Carol appeared. Gracefully she made her way towards them. The music played on, but there was no sign of the bride. The doors that had been opened for the maid of honour were closed once again.

Michael took a deep breath, preparing himself to be left standing at the altar.

Carol reached her place opposite the men and still no Jackie. The organist started the wedding march for the second time.

Finally the heavy doors opened, and there she stood.

The hush amongst the guests turned immediately to gasps of breath as the beauty and elegance that was now drifting down the aisle dazzled every last one of them.

"She's beautiful!" John exclaimed quietly, which earned him a strange look from Michael.

As her uncle placed her right hand in the hand of the waiting groom, Jackie looked up at him. A muscle twitched nervously at Michael's jaw, but he said nothing.

The ceremony seemed to be over before it began.

Jackie wasn't really there. She was there in body only as, she was certain, was Michael. How ironic, she thought cynically.

They exchanged their vows and the groom kissed his bride. They walked together down the aisle as husband and wife, amidst the warm applause of their invited guests, and through all this Jackie felt she was elsewhere. She had gone through the motions, but didn't really experience them.

They posed for pictures in the gardens of the Madisons' home – now her home also. Friends and family offered their congratulations and best wishes, but Jackie could only smile in response. In fact, her face ached from all the forced smiles. She searched Michael's eyes desperately, trying to see at least an ounce of sympathy, a touch of tenderness, but nothing – not today, not when she needed it most.

The wedding reception was a success, or so it seemed. Their guests enjoyed the lavishly prepared food and expensive champagne. They danced to the music played by the six-piece band. Then the bride tossed her bouquet, and both husband and wife disappeared into the waiting limo while everyone cheered and waved goodbye.

The evening was over, but her new and complicated life was only beginning. She stole a glance towards Michael who sat quietly across from her in the ample interior of the stretch limousine. He had drunk excessively that evening, and now he poured himself yet another glass of liquor. He offered a glass to Jackie, but she refused. She didn't think alcohol would diminish the raging migraine that threatened her sanity.

The bellboy opened the door to the bridal suite and motioned for the newlyweds to enter. Michael tipped him and closed the door.

Jackie looked around the beautifully decorated room, but saw nothing. She waited nervously for her husband's next move.

Michael threw the plastic access card onto the hand-painted wooden entrance table, startling her. "Need any help with that?" he asked.

"With what?" Jackie was feeling somewhat dazed.

Michael pointed to her gown. "That."

"Oh. Yes, I guess so…"

Jackie turned, giving him access to the little silk-covered

buttons that stretched down the back of the bodice, but when his hands slid over her bare back she took a step forward, moving away from his touch.

"Thank you," she managed, and after slipping out of her dress in private, she disappeared into the bathroom.

Wearing only the pants of his black silk pajamas, Michael stood beside the satin-shrouded king-sized bed. On the dresser next to him was a nearly empty bottle of champagne and two goblets. One of these he filled as Jackie re-entered the room.

"Champagne?" he offered, as his eyes scanned the beautiful white lace negligee, a gift from Irene for her wedding night.

Jackie simply shook her head in response. She was too nervous. She wasn't sure what his intentions were. She had supplied him with the schedule for her cycle, as he had requested, but they had not discussed the wedding night. Something told her, however, that this unresolved point would not have made a difference.

Michael walked slowly to her.

"What took you so long? Were you hoping I'd be asleep?" Michael's words slurred slightly.

She didn't dare tell him that he was right! Instead she stood motionless, staring into his bloodshot eyes as he unfastened the sash of her matching robe and removed it.

"You're drunk," Jackie stated, but it didn't seem to deter him.

Michael swayed towards her. "I don't know why you bothered with all this stuff; you knew I'd take it off. Are you just trying to prolong the inevitable?"

"Can't this wait?"

"No."

Realizing that nothing would change the course of tonight's events, she stopped trying. "Will you turn out the light?" she whispered.

"Turn out the light? No way. I want to take a good look at what I've paid for."

He was certainly drunk, but his state of inebriation did not excuse him. He was being downright nasty, and Jackie shut her eyes momentarily, the thought of jumping from the balcony actually crossing her mind.

He proceeded to slip the straps of the nightgown from her shoulders, allowing it to slide from her body and onto the floor. He laughed when he noticed her panties. "Anything else under there?"

Jackie wanted to tell him she'd recently purchased a chastity belt and had somehow lost the key, but instead opted not to answer. She looked him square in the eye, her chin raised, the thought of fighting or pleading leaving her mind as quickly as it had appeared.

He slid his hands down her hips, removing the last bit of clothing along with whatever dignity she had left.

He looked her over like a side of beef. Then he pushed her slightly, forcing her to take a couple of steps backwards. He reached down and switched off the lamp on the nightstand, instantly dimming the entire room.

He undid the drawstring on the waistband of his pajamas and let them drop. Still Jackie remained as motionless as before he pulled her to him. She felt no pleasure as he pressed himself against her.

Jackie tried desperately to disassociate her mind from her body. She was able to achieve it for at least a while, especially since his point of concentration was not her face.

His strong hands were like vises on her soft flesh, bruising and hurting. She wanted to lash out; to hit him, but she didn't; she couldn't...

To Jackie it seemed an eternity, but in reality, only minutes had elapsed since his weight had descended onto her and the pain she felt from the start suddenly intensified. Although it was anticipated, she couldn't stop from making her discomfort known. She gasped instinctively, pushing against his shoulders hoping to lift him from her, but the effort was futile.

Finally it was over. He rolled away from her.

It took all the strength she could muster to turn from him. She tasted blood and realized that she'd been biting her lip. She buried her face in her pillow and cried.

"You could have told me," he said accusingly.

She didn't answer him. What difference would it have made if she had told him that he had married a bride who indeed deserved to wear white? That was such a rarity in this day and age that she was certain he wouldn't have believed her anyway.

Drunk or not, she would not forgive him this!

Michael was still asleep when Jackie was awakened by their early wake-up call the next morning. Their hotel stay was only for one night. The private flight that would take them to the French Riviera was leaving in just a couple of hours. Praying he wouldn't wake, she quietly slid out of bed and slipped into the bathroom for a shower.

He was still asleep when she returned to the bedroom to dress. She watched him for a moment, knowing full well that if he didn't wake soon they would be late for their flight, although she was also well aware that the jet would not leave without them. Jackie left the room, closing the door behind her.

Michael couldn't understand why someone was pounding his head with a sledgehammer. He tried to speak, to tell whomever it was to stop before he went completely mad – but he couldn't. He buried his face deeper into the soft pillow, hoping it would subside.

Finally he opened one eye, then the other. The events of the previous evening flooded his mind. His recollection was extremely fuzzy yet definitely disturbing. "Oh God..." he whispered.

Slowly he turned on his side, hoping not to wake his wife, but the bed was empty. Immediately thoughts of mutiny crossed his partially coherent mind. Had she abandoned ship? Finding his discarded pajama pants on the floor next to her negligee, he quickly dressed and began the hunt.

After an unsuccessful search of the bathroom, Michael ventured out into the remainder of the suite. Unknowingly, he sighed in relief.

Jackie had ordered coffee and was enjoying her second cup of the calming liquid when he entered the room. She looked up at him briefly, then returned to switching between the vast amount of channels on the television set.

He didn't speak. Neither did she.

Michael showered and dressed and was now placing the overnight bag on the floor next to their other luggage. The gown and tuxedo would be picked up later by Elmer Delaney.

"Are you ready?" he said in her direction. His voice was monotone, but not cold. He knew to be wary of his tone, as well as to keep his distance this morning.

Jackie tossed the remote onto the table and picked up her purse. Obviously he had called for the bellboy, who now stood at the door collecting their belongings.

The trip to the airport, the seven hours onboard the airplane, and the final ride to their hotel were absolutely silent. They might as well have been travelling apart.

However, even her anger could not cloud the beauty that surrounded her. The evening breeze was warm and the air was fresh. She could smell and taste the salt from the ocean.

Their Mediterranean-style Chateau Hotel resembled a fairy-tale castle situated high on a hill overlooking the gulf of St. Tropez and the seven beaches of Pampelonne. Set amidst 25 acres of pine forests, vineyards and the hotel's own gardens, the hotel provided a magical setting. An enormous pool, they were told, overlooked the sea and the gulf. It was a haven of peace and tranquility – a perfect honeymoon setting. Too bad theirs would be nothing of the sort...

Jackie walked through their elegant room cheerfully decorated in orange and yellows. Her fingers absently touched the ceramic candelabra on the table, the plush yellow pillow on the couch... She ventured across the spacious room to the French doors on the far wall opposite the entrance and, opening them, walked out onto the large terrace adorned with different types of plants and potted flowers. A glass vase filled with fresh cut flowers sat on a small wrought iron table; two chairs flanked its sides. The private terrace was ideal for sunbathing or perhaps intimate breakfasts...

Their terrace also provided a breathtaking view of the

incredibly blue sea in the distance. To her right, villages appeared to have been carved into the rocks of the distant hills and greenery of the peninsula that protruded into the sea.

Yes, St. Tropez was absolutely breathtaking.

"Would you like to go down for a late dinner?" Michael's voice startled her out of her trance. He stood at the doors.

Jackie would rather not go anywhere with him, but she had to admit she was hungry; she hadn't eaten on the plane. She turned and brushed past him, and he, assuming her answer to be 'yes', led her downstairs.

Michael chose to dine outdoors. This was what Jackie had hoped, but would never have asked. She didn't want to speak to him, let alone give him the impression she liked being there – with him!

Dinner was as wonderfully delicious as she had imagined. But they both remained silent; the only words spoken were directed to their waiter.

Afterwards they sipped their espressos as Jackie continued to admire her surroundings. The sun had all but disappeared now and thousands of shimmering lights had taken its place to illuminate the extensive patios.

"I thought we might head to the beach tomorrow morning – the hotel provides a shuttle. It only takes a minute or so to get down to the beach... Maybe we can go into town in the evening..." No answer. Michael tried again. "If there's something in particular you'd like to see or do..." But Jackie held her ground and the silence had taken its toll on his patience.

"Do you intend on giving me the silent treatment for the duration of our marriage?" he said in a low, steady voice.

Jackie's lips turned slightly to form a cynical smile and Michael sighed heavily.

" … I had too much to drink last night," he offered. "I… don't remember much, but I obviously behaved like an ass. I apologize. It won't happen again."

Jackie's eyes filled with tears and she quickly returned her gaze to the yacht anchored in the middle of the bay. She hadn't expected an apology, although the reference to the previous evening only intensified her obstinacy.

"Unfortunately, I've come to know the extent of your pride. You'll hold it against me forever or, even if you do forgive me, you'll never let it be known," Michael concluded knowingly.

Knowing also that Jackie would not reply to this comment either, he stood and announced that they should call it a night.

As she stood in the marble bathroom, changing into her nightgown, she hoped and prayed that there would not be a repeat of last night. She glared at her pale reflection in the large golden-framed mirror and sighed. If there was, she thought miserably, she would do exactly what she'd done before – nothing.

There were two bathrooms in their suite. Michael had already showered and was lying in bed flipping channels when Jackie walked into the bedroom.

She lay down on her side and waited with loathing for him to claim her body.

Michael turned off the TV and then the lamp. Jackie closed her eyes tightly and held her breath.

"You can relax, I'm not going to touch you."

Her eyes shot open and stared through the darkness. Had she

heard correctly? Had it been her silent prayers that allowed for tonight's pardon? Yet, not until Michael turned onto his side away from her was Jackie able to exhale the breath she'd been holding.

Late the next morning Jackie came out of the bathroom wearing a black two-piece bathing suit. She was about to walk past him to reach for her wrap when the gentle touch of Michael's fingers on her arm stopped her.

He looked down at her arms, her chest and hips. He noticed the small, but obvious bruises that were beginning to darken in colour.

Michael's brow creased into a frown. "Did I do that?" he asked quietly.

Jackie looked at him now, but held her silent ground. She deemed it unnecessary to confirm that fact. He knew full well that only he could have been the cause of those marks on her body.

"I'm sorry," he told her, apologizing for the second time. Jackie blinked, her stare faltering momentarily. She tied her black and pink chiffon wrap around her waist and walked ahead of him to the door.

CHAPTER TWENTY-FOUR

During the next several days, Michael became as quiet as she had been. His eyes sometimes wandered to the bruises on her body, but he said nothing more on the subject. His only words to her were questions regarding where to dine or where to go. Meanwhile, her vocabulary consisted mainly of three clipped responses: 'no', 'thank you' and 'fine'. Jackie was aware that he regretted his excessive force and realized it had not been intentional, but her husband had guessed correctly: she was not going to let him off the hook that easily.

They sat by the hotel pools, walked along the beautiful beaches, and took evening strolls in the village. He often entered the exclusive shops, obligating Jackie to follow, where he invited her to purchase some of the exquisite trinkets or designer clothing, and still she remained limited to her stock answers, applying whichever she considered appropriate. The days passed without him ever intentionally touching her, and Jackie knew this had to come to an end.

On the third day of her most fertile time, Michael finally voiced his thoughts. "Look…" he started, "the sooner we get this over with, the better."

"I agree."

Michael looked at her sharply, surprised that she'd spoken to him and surprised at her reply.

"You do?"

"I know why I'm here. Just don't expect anything from me."

Michael sighed. "I told you… I had too much to drink."

"Don't expect anything from me," Jackie repeated, matter-of-factly.

"I wouldn't dream of it," he told her, sarcasm returning to his tone.

That night, Jackie stood on their balcony. The cool evening breeze fanned against her silk nightgown, causing it to flutter softly against her legs.

She looked out to the St. Tropez bay, where several brightly lit yachts cruised along towards another port. She wondered if maybe she could hitch a ride…

Michael came to stand directly behind her, and Jackie stopped breathing.

His hands were on her hips, holding her against him. He buried his face in the curve of her neck, scattering kisses on her bare skin. He turned her towards him, lowering his head towards her, but she averted her face from his descending lips.

She couldn't let him kiss her. That was too personal. It would be an invitation to intimacy and she didn't want that – not now. Jackie was also quite aware of the effect that his kisses had on her senses and stamina, and she wasn't ready for that either.

Michael held her loosely against him. Then he exhaled his breath against her temple, realizing there would be no cooperation. His hands fell away from her body. Surprised, Jackie turned her eyes towards him. Michael held her gaze for just a moment.

"Go to bed," he said quietly, and Jackie, her brain filled with questions and her insides in turmoil, silently obliged.

The third and last week of their honeymoon was to be spent in Cannes. They packed their bags and were driven by the hotel limo to their next destination.

The scenery was just as spectacular.

The coastal road, with its tortuous bends, provided a breathtaking view of the gorgeous red rocks of the mountainside as they tumbled into the aquamarine sea. The sun shone brightly in a blue sky that was free of a single cloud. The reflection of the sea made the rocks appear to shimmer with a luminous glow. The hillsides were golden, the mimosa filling the air with its intoxicating fragrance.

It was magnificent, and Jackie placed yet another memory stick in her digital camera.

While shopping in Cannes one evening, Michael was approached by an attractive brunette.

"Cheri!" The young woman latched onto him, embracing him, kissing him. "I thought I was not going to see you this year!" She pursed her full, red lips. "Why did you not call me? You are angry with Margot?"

Outwardly, Jackie watched with a lazy interest, but in fact she was extremely intrigued and… perhaps a little annoyed.

Michael untangled Margot's arms from around his neck. "Margot…" he said, looking at Jackie's cynical expression. "I'd like you to meet my wife."

"Your wife?" Margot exclaimed, her laugh incredulous. But when Michael did not return her laughter, her amused expression soon disappeared. "You are joking, *mais oui?*"

"No, I'm not. Actually, we are here on our honeymoon." Michael put an arm around Jackie's stiff shoulders. "This is Jackie."

She had to search for that fake smile again.

"Margot is an old friend," he explained.

"Yes… an old friend," Margot purred. She glared at Jackie, her eyes taking in her simple beauty, her elegance. "What can I say?" Margot shrugged, indifferently. "Congratulations! You are a very lucky woman, Jackie. Just remember, though, if you do not keep Michael happy, he knows where to find me! *C'est vrai, cheri?*" The voluptuous brunette kissed him once again, oblivious to the fact that his wife was witnessing this exchange. *"Au revoir!"* she waved.

Michael stared after her; Jackie stared at *him*. This meeting confirmed the difference between her and his previous 'girlfriends'.

When he turned towards Jackie, he watched her in silence for a moment. "I've been vacationing here for years."

"Did I ask?" Jackie returned rudely, unable to resist.

"No, you didn't," he smiled wryly.

After a delicious dinner at a quaint little French bistro they walked the cobblestone streets of the village and came upon a vendor standing beside a small cart filled with beautiful flowers.

The old woman extended a rose to Michael. *"Une rose pour*

ta belle cheri?"

Jackie smiled at the woman and would have walked on by, but Michael stopped and spoke to the old woman in her own language. Then she gathered the entire container of white roses and wrapped them in lilac tissue paper. Michael paid the woman, who thanked him repeatedly for his generosity, and then he turned and offered the bouquet to Jackie.

This was an unexpected surprise. It was... a romantic gesture... perhaps one that held yet another apology, and regardless of her vow to be unforgiving, she couldn't find it in her heart to be rude in front of the old woman. She smiled at her and accepted the roses from Michael.

"You didn't have to do that," she said curtly, to which he did not reply.

Michael wished the old woman a good night and they continued to walk down the path to their hotel.

The remainder of their stay was more or less the same. However, although their vacation was nowhere near a real honeymoon, Jackie was not looking forward to returning home.

At home, she would have to pretend to be happy; she would have to act as though nothing was out of the ordinary. At home she would have to eventually leave her precious child to a father seemingly only interested in his own inheritance.

Nevertheless, home was where they were now headed.

CHAPTER TWENTY-FIVE

T he massive front door opened even before their limo came to a stop in front of the Madison home. Walter stood at the doorstep, a wide smile adorning his weathered face.

"Welcome home! Welcome home, newlyweds!" And Jackie accepted her father-in-law's embrace.

The driver brought the luggage to the door while Michael hugged his father hello. Then he turned to his wife. Without warning he scooped her into his arms, shocking her but delighting his father, who quickly walked inside, allowing the newlyweds their private moment.

"Put me down," Jackie demanded through clenched teeth.

"I can't. It's tradition. I have to carry my bride over the threshold." Michael's eyes were guarded when he looked down at her.

"Nothing about us is traditional," she retorted.

Jackie had just been placed back on her feet when Walter

appeared once again. This time, he was not alone.

"Look who's here to welcome you home!"

"Mom!" Jackie exclaimed nervously. She was not in the mood for this. She wished she could tell her mother everything. She wished she could go back in time and take back what she'd said to Michael. She wished... she wished a lot of things, but none were about to come true... not in this lifetime.

The evening was awkward to say the least. Jackie had spoken so little during her honeymoon that she felt as though she had forgotten how to speak at all. Her mother asked her repeatedly to explain the places she had visited, but Jackie resorted to showing pictures instead.

Before long, she stifled a second yawn and Joan decided it was time to leave the newlyweds alone.

"Oh dear. You must be so tired after your trip. You should get to bed."

"No, I'm fine," Jackie protested. Going to bed was not exactly what she wanted to do. But Walter concurred with her mother's request and took Joan home, leaving them alone... again.

"You don't have to come in tomorrow; you could sleep in," Michael offered, and her shoulders raised a fraction in a shrug. He stared at her for a moment longer. "Coming up?"

She didn't answer. She simply turned and began to mount the stairs.

Jackie looked around the newly decorated room. The dark, subdued colours had been replaced by softer shades of matte golds and creams. She liked the change, but couldn't help but wonder whose idea it had been to redecorate. Naturally, she had no intention of commenting, either.

She showered and changed for bed. When she was finished, he did the same.

Her fertile days had come and gone, so she need not worry about his advances. Yet, she couldn't stop the nervous fluttering in her stomach when he came to lie down beside her.

She turned to her side and stared across the room, unknowingly holding her breath. She was becoming an expert at it.

"Good night," he told her.

Jackie closed her eyes tightly; she didn't reply.

When she awakened the next morning, her eyes immediately scanned the room, familiarizing herself with her surroundings, then finally focussed on the figure of her husband.

Michael stood at the foot of their bed watching her as he slid his belt through the loops of the waistband of his slacks.

She swung her legs out from under the covers and smoothed her nightgown over her thighs.

He reached for his tie. "You don't have to come in."

"I'd rather," she replied, brushing past him to the bathroom.

Downstairs, Jackie accepted coffee and toast from Mrs. Delaney, and Michael's offer to ride together to the office. She wasn't feeling up to driving this morning.

Everyone welcomed the newlyweds, and naturally she was bombarded by questions about the honeymoon. Jackie did her best to answer everyone, returning to her trusty pictures for help. She took a moment to visit the plant and gave her old co-workers the little souvenirs she had brought for them. They were happy to see her and were amazed with all the beautiful pictures, and Jackie realized she missed working with them. But her 'place' was elsewhere now; in the office, by her husband, and that's where she now headed.

Her first day was uneventful, as were the days that followed. The nights were just as uneventful, while Michael was forced to wait until her 'time' was right. Only during the evenings, in front of his father, did she have to tolerate his hand on her shoulder or her waist while he played the part of the loving husband and she the loving wife.

However, although Jackie was reluctant to admit it – in fact she had been deeply perturbed by this fact – she had enjoyed his touch before they were married. Their wedding night had changed that; her pride forbade her from allowing the pleasure back in. The tension, in the meantime, grew with every passing hour… she wondered if she'd be fortunate enough to eventually leave with her sanity…

When the time finally arrived, Michael tried again to gather her into his arms. No response. It was no use, he decided. It was best to continue with the 'business arrangement'. He had to resign himself to the knowledge that nothing more would come of this association.

Jackie acknowledged that she was there to perform a task. Regardless of her determination to maintain detached, she had signed a contract, she had agreed. There was no turning back.

Therefore, there was a job to be done. Michael was gentle and her body was tempted, but her brain still said no. So, unfortunately, her lack of participation and her determination to stay impassive made her extremely tense which in turn caused her pain. Thus, the act they performed was only an act.

One morning, weeks later, Jackie informed her husband that she'd be taking her own car to the office; she had a few errands to run during her lunch hour.

"Everything all right?" Michael asked upon her return later that afternoon.

Jackie hadn't noticed that he had come to stand at her doorway, taking in her pale complexion and somber mood.

"What?"

"I said, is everything all right?"

"Yes. Why wouldn't it be?" she snapped defensively.

Michael walked slowly towards her desk and leaned towards her.

"You don't let up," he accused in a quiet voice. "Whether it's me or PMS, I told you before to deal with your mood swings; especially here."

Jackie sighed. She had every right to be edgy, but she should avoid exposing her temper in public.

"Yes sir, boss," Jackie saluted defiantly.

Michael had refrained from any advances during the last few days. That evening, however, he stood before her, a hand stopping her from getting into bed.

Jackie lowered her eyes as he tried to gather her limp body into his arms.

His hands gently molded her to his body as he desperately tried to encourage her to accept his kiss. He hated the current state in which they found themselves, and he knew he was to blame, but his wife was not the only one with an overabundance of pride.

His lips were but an inch from hers, when she sprang the news.

"I'm pregnant," she blurted.

Michael immediately drew his head back, unsuccessfully trying to make eye contact with her.

"What?" he breathed.

"I'm pregnant."

"Oh." Michael's hands fell away from her body. It was what he'd wanted. It was the reason for all of this. Yet the 'good news' did not elate him as it should have done. His gut reaction was far too confusing, too complicated, and something on which he did not want to speculate. "That's… that's good."

"Good for *you*," she sneered and walked around him to slide into bed.

Jackie didn't sleep a wink that night. As if in consolation… neither did Michael.

She gathered he was contemplating the best way to explain things to his father once he was rid of her. *She* could only think that in eight months the child that was growing inside her would be born. It would never know its mother, and she would never know her child.

Tears sprang to her eyes and she let them flow freely. She was about to provide him with her part of this disgusting deal. At least, she told herself, the farce would be over…

Michael heard the change in her breathing and knew she was crying. A pang of guilt constricted his chest. He turned towards her, his hand poised above her shoulder, hoping to comfort her, wanting to tell her… But he withdrew his hand. He doubted she would be receptive to anything he had to say.

CHAPTER TWENTY-SIX

*I*t was almost becoming a ritual.

Jackie began her mornings kneeling on the bathroom floor, hugging the cold porcelain of the toilet. Upon many of these occasions, Michael would join her and hold her forehead as her body revolted against absolutely nothing.

"Would you like a glass of water?" he'd ask.

Jackie would nod, and Michael would fetch a glass, only to have it end up in the toilet as well.

It was no use. She couldn't seem to hold anything down until after midday. Jackie had done this for two months. She didn't know how much more her body could withstand.

"Why don't you stay home?" Michael suggested this morning.

Walter was not to be told about her pregnancy until at least after her first trimester so as to make certain that everything would be all right. She was also hoping it would give her time to think of a way to keep her mother in the dark for the next few months.

"Then your father will certainly know something's wrong. We'd have to tell him and we haven't yet decided what we're going to do about my mother. Have you come up with one of your famous plans yet?"

"No."

"Well then?" Refusing his help, Jackie rose to her feet and ducked into the shower.

As the warm water pounded against her skin, she chastised herself for being so stubborn. But Jackie believed it was better this way. If she allowed herself to be taken in by his caring act, she might believe it was actually real. At that point she would have fallen too far and too hard and would only be more devastated when, in the end, she'd realize that it was indeed just an act — and nothing more.

Walter decided to give the newly married couple a bit of privacy, and therefore a fishing trip was in order. He and his friend Marty made arrangements to travel to Northern Ontario for a few weeks. A trip was long overdue, and in this case it would serve two purposes.

This development was one that Jackie welcomed. With Walter gone, Michael didn't have reason to touch her and she in turn had no reason not to avoid it. They didn't touch. In fact, they barely spoke. Instead, she often helped Mrs. Delaney in the kitchen. Jackie was certain the elderly woman was aware of the strain between the newlyweds, but if the loyal employee had any suspicions she would keep them to herself.

As the days turned into weeks, Michael's mood became a

little darker and Jackie suspected that the lack of physical contact was beginning to rattle his brain.

Many a morning, Jackie would wake to find Michael's arm draped across her midriff, his face snuggled in the curve of her neck. She would turn from him, causing him to do the same, whether asleep or awake. However, as time passed, so did her resistance. She didn't invite him to touch her, but she didn't flinch or turn away from him either. She missed him, but wouldn't dare tell him so.

Walter returned home and his presence justified closeness, but Michael's mood didn't change.

Her telephone rang.

"Yes?"

"I'm going to be staying late."

"So?"

Michael sighed. "So… my father will take you home." Her queasy state had forced her to accept Michael's ride these mornings.

"Fine."

Michael hung up and Jackie replaced the receiver, banging it several times.

Her nerves were so unravelled! She was fit to be tied! She wanted to yell out, to cry, to wring someone's neck! She settled on breaking a few pencils.

"Oh my! What's got you so upset?" Walter startled her, stopping her from breaking the eighth pencil.

Jackie sighed and gave him a wry smile. "Nothing. I just feel very edgy. The poor pencils got the brunt of my mood."

"Better the pencils than some poor unsuspecting soul, I

guess!" Walter chuckled. "Are you ready to go, dear?"

"Yes." Then she paused suddenly, changing her mind. "Actually, I wouldn't mind staying a while longer. I have a few orders to place and the time differences are just about right."

"I'll wait for you then."

"No, no. You go on. I'll come home with Michael if he doesn't stay too late."

"All right then. Perhaps if you're here, he won't. Good night."

Diane appeared at her door moments later, startling her. "Diane! I didn't know you were still here."

"I haven't been at my desk. I was helping Shawna with a manual this afternoon. My husband's picking me up, and in fact he's outside; he just called. You're still here," she stated.

Jackie motioned to the order sheets on her desk. "Yes. I had a few calls to make."

"I see. You going home with Michael?" she asked, to which Jackie nodded. "Okay. I'll see you tomorrow."

Jackie waited until the best time then placed her orders with the companies in varied time zones. Nearly two hours had passed since her last call was completed. She decided it was time to check on her husband. Her stomach had started growling. She was hungry and tired and wanted to go home.

She walked through to the now darkened area of the executive offices and suddenly wondered if Michael had already left. The place seemed deserted; everyone had gone home.

Then she did something tremendously stupid. Without thinking, without knocking, Jackie turned the handle to Michael's office door and opened it. Unwillingly, she gasped in surprise. Her heart was jolted from its pocket and now floated in some unknown place, elsewhere in her body. She felt nauseated, and it was definitely not morning sickness!

Michael sat in his chair behind his desk. Brenda sat straddled on his lap. His shirt was unbuttoned, her blouse flapping open. She was *not* taking dictation.

Startled by the interruption, both turned towards her, but neither spoke.

Jackie didn't speak either. She didn't really know what to say. Her lips curled in a knowing, cynical smile. She took a step back and closed the door.

Stiffly, Jackie walked back to her office. She picked up her purse and left the building.

She walked quickly, periodically looking over her shoulder for any sign of Michael's car.

Reaching a coffee shop, Jackie sat in the shadows as she waited for a taxi. She didn't go straight home, however. In fact, she had the driver roam the city for hours before finally giving him her address. Home was not sanctuary for her, especially not tonight.

Her husband's car was in the driveway when Jackie arrived home, but it was Walter who appeared from the study as she entered. "Hello there. How is your mother?"

"My mother?"

"Yes, Michael said you'd gone to visit – did I misunderstand?"

"No, no, you didn't misunderstand. She's fine, thank you. I'm... I'm going straight to bed. I have a bit of a headache."

"Yes, of course, dear. You go on. Michael's just having a bite to eat. I'll tell him you've come home."

It was only moments later when Michael entered their bedroom and walked over to the couch where she sat pretending to read.

She looked up at him, arching an eyebrow.

He stood in a lazy stance, his hands in the pockets of his slacks, his eyes guarded.

"Where've you been?"

"You told your father I was at my mother's," Jackie said calmly.

"Why did you take off?"

Jackie's smile was incredulous. "Did you want me to join in?"

Michael seemed to ponder that possibility. "I wasn't cut out to be a monk," he told her finally.

"So?"

"So… this is your doing." Michael's voice was steady.

"What?"

"I know full well that you were not exactly revolted by my touch before. Yet, you haven't given me the time of day since… our wedding. I've apologized for that night, but we both know that's meaningless to you. Your lack of… participation and/or enjoyment since then has been entirely your choice. You've made certain this remained a business deal."

Jackie was determined to show indifference. "At what point did this become anything *but* a business deal? Our sex life was for the sole purpose of conceiving a child, was it not? We've achieved your goal. I'm pregnant, remember? Did I say at any time that I was disconcerted by your… extramarital activities?"

"You didn't have to; you're acting like a jealous wife."

"Well, I hate to disagree with you, but I'm not at all jealous. As far as being your wife…" Jackie shrugged. "Don't turn this around. This *was* a business deal derived from your greediness. What did you want from me? Did you expect me to fall head over heels in love with you and your ultimatums?"

"I am fully aware of your feelings for me. Now stop sulking and come down to eat."

"I'm not hungry."

"Aren't you supposed to be eating for two?"

"Ah! Naturally your concern is for your child. Don't worry, your heir won't starve, he'll be fine. Too bad I can't be just as sure about the rest of his life!"

"Well, you won't have to fret about that, now will you?" he snapped. He turned and left the room.

CHAPTER TWENTY-SEVEN

*J*ackie was so hungry, but she absolutely did not want to go downstairs. She didn't feel like acting for his father's benefit and she absolutely did not want to face Michael again.

She feigned sleep when, long after midnight, Michael finally came to bed. She waited until the slow, even rhythm of his breathing told her he was asleep, then quietly rose out of bed. She slipped on her robe and ventured out into the dark hallway. She didn't turn on the lights so as not to draw any attention to herself.

Jackie was fine in the dark until she reached the stairs. Then somehow her foot caught the belt of her robe, which had looped itself around the hem. She tripped and reached for the railing, but in the darkness she missed. All she could do was let out a horrified scream before tumbling down the long marble staircase.

Everyone was awake now. Within seconds they were by her side. Michael called her name frantically, but Jackie didn't hear the fear in his voice as he looked in horror at her bloodstained face. She was bleeding profusely from a gash over her eyebrow and she was unconscious.

"Good heavens! Elmer!" Walter hollered. "Call an ambulance!"

Mrs. Delaney held a towel to Jackie's forehead, panicking as it became discoloured with more blood.

"Oh, Mr. Michael, this is a deep cut!" Mrs. Delaney cried.

"Jackie, wake up!" Michael ordered his wife.

Jackie opened her eyes for just a moment. "The baby…" she breathed.

"Baby!" Walter exclaimed. "Baby?"

"We didn't want to say anything just yet, Dad," Michael explained to his father, who now paced aimlessly across the foyer.

While everyone attended to Jackie, Michael dressed quickly so that he was ready to ride with her when the ambulance arrived. He told his father to stay home; he'd call him with any news.

The hospital had notified Jackie's obstetrician. Dr. Francis was there when she arrived and quickly instructed the ambulance attendants to wheel her into the maternity area.

"Michael?" A familiar voice swung Michael around to face his friend. "Michael, what happened? Is it Walter?" John asked anxiously. He was on call for the ER that evening.

"No. Jackie fell down the stairs," he said, as he took up pacing.

"She fell down the stairs? How?"

"That's what I'd like to know!"

"What's that supposed to mean?" John asked, but Michael did not reply. "Is she all right?"

"I don't know. Dr. Francis is in with her."

"Dr. Francis? You mean…"

"Yes, John, she's pregnant – or at least – she was."

"Buddy, you are one cold son-of-a-bitch."

Michael was about to rebut, but stopped when Dr. Francis and another doctor, who looked as though he'd just graduated med school yesterday, finally appeared from Jackie's examining room.

Michael wanted to walk towards him, but was unable to do so. He seemed stuck to the floor beneath him. "How is she?" he managed as the doctors neared him.

"Mr. Madison? I'm Dr. Kline." The young doctor extended his hand to Michael. "Aside from the cut on her forehead, which earned her six stitches, and severe bruises over most of her body, there are surprisingly no broken bones. She does have a mild concussion, but that's not the worry right now."

"What is?" Michael asked slowly, mentally predicting the answer.

Dr. Francis was nearing retirement, but still one of the best in his field. Michael remembered how Jackie had thought he resembled the old actor Jimmy Stewart...

Dr. Francis did not extend his hand. It was apparent that greetings were not necessary at the moment. Michael looked as though he was going to pass out and the news he was about to relay would surely worsen his current state.

"I'm afraid it's the baby, Mr. Madison."

"Damn!" Michael cursed, raking angry fingers through his hair.

"She's bleeding. A part of the placenta has detached itself from the walls of the uterus. This places both mother and child at risk. There's only a slight chance for the fetus. We might have to abort."

He was going to lose his child... He didn't want to lose either of them.

"We'll wait as long as possible, but I can't make any promises."

"I want to see her."

"Well, she's asleep right now; she needs to rest. You should go on home. I'll have you called if there is any change." Dr. Francis patted Michael's shoulder and both he and Dr. Kline disappeared into the doctor's lounge.

"So," John began, "you going home?"

"No, I'm not going home!" Michael growled, and ignoring the doctor's advice, he made his way to the examining room.

Michael stood at her bedside for a few minutes, looking down at her, taking in her pale face, the ugly cut that would forever scar her forehead. He was experiencing a multitude of emotions. His wife's life was at risk, their child's life hung by a thread, he was afraid, but at that moment the strongest feeling of all was rage. He sat down in the armchair next to her bed and stayed there until the early hours of the morning.

Michael was awakened by the sound of shuffling feet. The curtain was drawn around Jackie's bed. A faint moan could be heard as the two nurses pushed back the curtain and left the room.

The doctor and nurses had been in and out all morning. Jackie too had drifted in and out of a tortured sleep. Her condition remained the same.

She opened her eyes to find Michael standing beside her. She was unaware of his disheveled appearance, his unshaven face, and bloodshot eyes.

"Michael… the baby…" Jackie's voice was but a whisper as she drifted off to sleep once again.

"I thought I told you to go home," Dr. Francis scolded when he saw Michael's tired body slouched in a chair, but Michael didn't comment and the doctor pulled the curtains around Jackie's bed.

When the doctor appeared once again, he turned to Michael. Michael's voice was anxious. "Well?"

Dr. Francis shook his head. "The longer we wait the more at risk we place your wife."

Michael swallowed and closed his eyes tightly against the pain in his chest, the fear that threatened his sanity. "Then take the baby," he said quietly.

Dr. Francis came to sit in a chair next to Michael. He placed a hand on his shoulder. "I understand what you're going through. We'll wait just a little while longer. Perhaps by some miracle..."

"Take the baby... she can't die."

The doctor nodded. "I won't let that happen. We'll wait just a little while longer," he repeated, and left the room.

A short time later, John came in.

Michael sat up. "John! I forgot to call my father."

"Yes, I know, he's called every hour on the hour. I've spoken to him myself. Don't worry." John glanced at the monitors that flanked Jackie's bed. "How's she doing?"

Michael simply shrugged.

"Hey, I know it's almost lunch, but how about some breakfast?" John suggested. "We'll have to go to the cafeteria; I'm still on duty."

Michael shook his head in response.

"I'll even pay," his friend joked, but again Michael shook his head. "Okay, I know when to quit. I'm going to stick around after my shift, so I'll check in on you later," he said, and left the room.

After pacing endlessly for the last hour, Michael started to feel claustrophobic. He had to leave that room if only for a moment. He had to think of something else if only for a second. Slanting a look towards his sleeping wife, he left the room to fetch a candy bar from the vending machine. He was just approaching Jackie's room when he heard her cries of pain.

Michael burst into the room only to run back out to call for the doctor.

Dr. Francis arrived immediately and shooed Michael outside. Only a moment later, Jackie's bed was wheeled out into the corridor.

Jackie's knees were raised as she held her belly in obvious pain. She was crying, her face wet with perspiration.

"What's wrong?" Michael wanted to know, as he hurried along beside her.

"I'm sorry, Mr. Madison. She's hemorrhaging. We have to extract the fetus now. I'm sorry." The doctor shook his head apologetically as the labour room door closed behind him.

Michael was left standing in the middle of the corridor, the unwrapped candy bar still in his hand.

He waited what seemed like a lifetime when Jackie was taken to recovery, and then without even a glance towards her or a question about her, he left the hospital.

Michael returned several hours later, bringing an overnight bag for his wife. Jackie had been admitted and taken to a private room upstairs. He was informed that she had awakened earlier and was asking for him, but not to worry. Jackie was asleep now, and she would be all right.

He paced the floor like a caged animal. Every so often he would steal a glance towards her, but he kept his distance.

"Michael..." Jackie's voice was barely audible. "The baby..."

Michael came to stand by her bed. "You lost it," Michael blurted coldly.

Jackie closed her eyes as the tears rolled down her cheeks.

Unfortunately, the anger Michael felt was voiced towards the most innocent of parties. "Why did you do it?" he demanded to know.

Jackie stared blindly at him.

"Why did you do it?" he repeated.

Jackie began to whimper softly. "What did I do?" Jackie begged to know.

"Why were you going downstairs?"

"Downstairs? I... I was hungry."

"If you had eaten when I came to call you, you wouldn't have been hungry in the middle of the night, would you? But you were too busy sulking! Why didn't you turn on the lights?"

"I... I didn't want to wake anyone. Why are you doing this? Do you think I planned to fall?"

"Didn't you?"

Jackie stared at him in horror! How could he be so cruel? Suddenly, she thrashed out at him, but she didn't have the strength to reach him.

"I hate you, I hate you!" she cried hysterically.

Caught off guard, Michael didn't know what to do. He tried holding her still, but she only screamed louder.

"Get out! I hate you! I hate you!"

The nurses heard her screams and burst into the room. John was there too.

"What the hell's going on? What did you say to her?" John demanded as he tried to hold Jackie down. "Get out, damn it! You've done enough!"

John instructed the nurse to prepare a sedative, which he quickly administered. It wasn't long before Jackie calmed down and was once again drifting off to sleep. He asked one of the nurses to stay with her and went looking for Michael. As it happened, he didn't have to look too far.

Michael stood just outside her room, leaning against the wall, his head bowed. John took hold of his arm and forced him to follow. He closed the door to the nurses' lounge and Michael resumed his previous stance.

John was disgusted. "You make me sick. I am ashamed to call you my friend."

Michael was about to leave, but John pushed him back against the wall.

"What did you say to her?" John wanted to know.

"This is none of your business."

"You're wrong. It became my business the day you told me about this cockamamie plan of yours. I told you someone would get hurt, and somehow I knew it would be her."

"Her? She lost my kid!"

"She didn't just decide to fly down the stairs on purpose!"

"Really? You're so sure?"

"I can't believe you! She could have died! Michael, she's a good person. You backed her into a corner so you could take advantage of her! She's done what you've asked. This was an accident. How could you put the blame on her?"

"You're in love with her, aren't you?" Michael was behaving irrationally. "I've seen the way you look at her. Well, tell you what. Once she's *delivered*—" Michael smiled at his pun, "then, you're more than welcome to her. How's that for a deal?"

"I'll pay you what she owes you," John said quietly. "Let her go."

Michael stared at him, a cynical smile curling his lips.

"You *are* in love with her," Michael concluded. "Sorry, you'll have to wait until I'm done with her."

With that he left the room, practically taking the door with him.

Someone was standing by her bed. She blinked, then blinked again.

"Michael… " Jackie's voice was but a whisper.

"No. It's me, John."

Jackie rubbed her eyes. "Oh. Hello."

"Jackie, I'm very sorry."

Jackie sighed.

"I wish there was something I could do." John tried to console her. "You just don't deserve this."

"I guess I do in a way. I made my bed and now I have to sleep in it… literally," she said quietly, and John remained quiet. "My baby's gone, John, how could he think I caused this?"

"I think you should ask *him*."

"I don't want to talk to him."

"I don't blame you, but unfortunately there is a reason for this assumption."

"You're saying he was justified in accusing me?"

"No, not at all. But…"

Just then her mother, accompanied by Walter, poked her head around the door. With the baby gone, Joan had finally been told.

"I really didn't want to see anybody," Jackie whispered to John.

"I'll tell them they can't stay long," he promised, squeezing her hand.

Michael didn't show up again until the next morning.

Jackie was sitting in a chair looking out the window when he entered. She didn't turn to look at him and she did not greet him.

He came to stand in front of her, forcing her to raise her eyes to him. He leaned against the wall and looked down at her, the harsh expression gone from his face.

"I'm… sorry… about what I said," he offered.

The apology was unexpected, but Jackie sneered at him. "What do you want from me?"

Michael lowered his eyes and sighed. "What you walked in on… I was just so frustrated. I… could tell you it didn't mean anything, but somehow I doubt that makes a difference to you," he said, searching her eyes. "Anyway, your fall was my fault; I shouldn't have blamed you."

Jackie was speechless. She couldn't believe he was accepting responsibility. Her eyes narrowed, suspicion overtaking her anger. "Then why did you? How could you think that I would purposely fall down the stairs, purposely harm my baby?"

"Because… it's happened before. I mean… not exactly the same – just the same results…"

"What? What are you talking about?" Jackie just then remembered what John had said – or rather – had not said.

Michael slowly sat down in the chair facing her, watching her for a moment longer before speaking. "I was married before."

Jackie listened in silence, trying desperately not to show interest in his story.

"I was young – barely out of university. She was a model. I think," he said, shrugging, "that I mistook infatuation for love. I didn't know what being in love was supposed to feel like." Michael watched her intently as he spoke, but Jackie forced her expression to remain blank, and he continued. "Anyway, we were married. She was very content with the lifestyle. The travelling, the money... these were extremely attractive to her. She didn't want for anything. I thought everything was perfect until I mistakenly picked up a message on her machine. It was the abortion clinic confirming her follow-up visit."

Jackie lowered her eyes. She actually felt sorry for him.

"The marriage was annulled," he said, answering the question that brewed in her mind.

"I didn't have an abortion; I fell."

"I know that." Michael bowed his head. "What happened to me before shouldn't have had any bearing... I was wrong to judge you."

"If I'd wanted to harm your child, I would not have chosen to tumble down the stairs. If I wanted to harm myself, I would have done that instead of agreeing to your idiotic proposition." Jackie shook her head slowly. "You must think that because I'm only impersonally providing you with an heir, that disconnects me from any feelings I may have towards this child, but you're wrong. I realize that this baby was conceived not out of love but out of greed, or at least a means to an end, but it was part of me nevertheless."

"I know that."

"Besides all that... I told you before; I know what I have to do. Why would I want to prolong the inevitable?"

Michael leaned forward, resting his arms on his knees, his eyes downcast. Absently, he twirled his wedding band around his finger.

"You don't have to."

"I don't have to what?"

He looked up at her now. Their wedding night, Brenda, the

fall... Michael felt horrible, he felt responsible, and he had to make it up to her. "You don't have to do this anymore. I'll let you out of the contract."

Jackie was taken aback and suddenly she shivered. What was he saying? "I have no other way to pay you back," she said slowly, finding it difficult to breathe, and *why* was that? Why was she questioning him? Is this not what she wanted? Why did she not jump for joy at his offer? Why, she thought miserably, did the prospect of leaving suddenly fill her with panic?

"We'll think of something," he said quietly.

Jackie watched him for a moment, and then, almost without a second thought, without giving her husband the opportunity to tell her anything, she answered him, shocking him as well as herself. "I made a deal, I'll stick to it."

It was Michael's turn for disbelief. "But I—"

"—Don't push it. I know I'll regret it, but a deal's a deal."

CHAPTER TWENTY-EIGHT

*T*he garden was so beautiful, so peaceful in the early morning. The flowers were still in bloom, although some of the leaves of the maple trees had already begun their yearly passage through deep green to the more vibrant oranges and golds and reds as they approached the imminent fall. Water flowed softly over the rock garden and the only other sounds were the chirping of birds and a dog barking in the distance…

It had been two weeks since the miscarriage. Dr. Francis had ordered her to stay off work and take it easy. Poor Mrs. Delaney waited on her hand and foot. Jackie assured her that she felt fine, but Alice wouldn't hear of it. But then, neither would Elmer or Walter, nor of course, would her mother.

Joan, along with Irene, came to visit often during her recovery, and with everyone fussing over her, Jackie was beginning to feel suffocated.

She breathed in the fresh morning air and sighed as her fingers traced the flowers on her cotton dress.

Michael too, had been attentive. He had been very different, but Jackie persisted in remaining aloof.

"You all right?" Michael's voice brought her back from her thoughts. She hadn't seen him approach her.

"Yes. I'm fine," she answered off-handedly, stopping the rotating movement of her hand on her flat belly.

"Are you in pain?"

"What is there to cause me pain? I'm empty."

"I know. I'm sorry. I... wonder sometimes..."

"Don't do that," she snapped. She wasn't in the mood to talk about what happened, and he knew better.

Michael changed the subject. "I didn't hear you get up."

Jackie just shrugged, and Michael sat down in the chair across from her. "Are you planning to come back to work when you're feeling better?"

"Why?"

"You don't have to – I'm just wondering."

"Well, if you haven't hired someone else... I'd rather be productive. Pardon the pun."

"She's gone," Michael blurted.

Jackie tried to sound disinterested. "Who's gone?"

"Brenda."

"So? Is that supposed to make a difference to me?"

Her husband sighed. "I'm just informing you that she is no longer employed by us."

"That must have been some severance pay."

Michael just looked at her.

"Poor boy. What are you going to do now without the

convenience of having your girlfriend so close?"

"She was not my girlfriend, and… I'll just have to learn to be patient."

"You heard the doctor – you have a long wait ahead of you – at least three months."

"I've come to the realization that some things are worth waiting for."

What had he meant by that? Was he referring to her? Jackie wasn't sure and she couldn't ask, but she decided to at least bring down the stone wall she had erected and replace it with perhaps a simple link fence.

"Really? Oh, I see," she said knowingly, a slight smile tugging at the corners of her mouth. "You've lost your little black book."

"No," he smiled sheepishly. "But I think they've heard by now, that I'm… happily married."

"I hate rumours, don't you?" It was a sarcastic remark, but her tone was gentle.

"Sometimes rumors—"

"Michael!" Walter called from the kitchen door, stopping his son from continuing. "Sorry to interrupt, but it's Brian. He says it's urgent."

Michael faced her once again, and rose from the chair.

"I have to go," he sighed.

Then he bent towards her, but Jackie instinctively turned her head a fraction, allowing him only to brush his lips across her cheek.

"I'll see you later," he told her.

Jackie was outside again later that afternoon when she

received yet another visitor.

"Hello there!"

"Hi John," Jackie greeted, walking towards him.

"How you feeling?"

"I'm okay. I'm hoping to get back to work next week. I need to get my mind off of things."

"I know. I'm so sorry, Jackie."

Jackie put up her hand to stop him from continuing. "John, please…"

"Sure," he nodded in understanding. "Well, take your time. Don't push yourself."

John motioned for her to join him under the shade of the gazebo. He watched her, a look of sadness clouding his eyes.

"I have to tell you… after what happened I thought that you would have told him to shove his contract."

"And then what?"

"I would have helped you." John sat forward in his chair. "In fact, why don't you back out? I'll deal with Michael."

"John…"

"I don't expect anything in return. I just… I just hate this! Let me take you away from here."

"John," she said again, "I decided to stay."

"What do you mean?"

"He offered to dissolve the contract."

John's eyes widened. "And you didn't accept?"

"No."

John looked at her in astonishment. "You're in love with him."

"Of course not! Who said anything about being in love with anybody?"

"The lady doth protest too much," John stated, and Jackie just shook her head. "I guess that's par for the course. I never thought he'd offer to let you out of the deal. I'm curious to know what he would have done if you'd agreed," he told her, and she had to admit she'd wondered that herself. She may have discovered that if she'd just learn to wait before speaking her mind.

John nodded, a wry smile tugging at the corners of his mouth. "Did you know... that when the doctor informed him that your life was at risk if they didn't abort... he told him to go ahead – to not risk your life further?" John asked quietly, and Jackie looked at him, realizing that he'd relayed this piece of information grudgingly.

Had Michael really been concerned for her life, or was he only avoiding the possibility of guilt if she had actually died because of his indecision? She felt a strange constriction in her heart, but she could not, would not, allow herself to see more into this action than basically a belief that it would have been the right thing to do.

She shrugged. "No, I didn't."

CHAPTER TWENTY-NINE

*J*ackie returned to the office nearly one month after the miscarriage. The fact that her husband's lover was no longer there did make the decision to return to work more appealing. In fact, she was happy to be back.

They often would drive in together and leave together. Michael continued to be attentive and even affectionate, not restricting his actions to when they were in public. She, in turn, did not recoil when he pretended to brush a hair from her cheek or when he didn't let go of her hand after helping her out of the car. Jackie's anger towards him had begun to cool and Michael had noticed. He surprised her with a Christmas tree one Saturday morning and actually helped her decorate it with boxes and boxes full of brand new ornaments, lights and trinkets. They had spent the day together and although the conversation was kept at a minimum and closeness was non-existent, they'd been civil with one another. It had been... nice.

The week before the Christmas break, Michael had worked late every night. She didn't doubt his whereabouts. This time, Jackie knew he was working. There were meetings until all hours. There was something happening, but Jackie couldn't bring herself to ask.

Late one evening, Jackie was sitting at home on the couch flipping through a magazine when Michael finally returned from the office. "Hi… Why you still up?" She didn't answer, and he posed another question. "Is Dad asleep?"

He looked tired and she actually wished she could tell him so. "No, he's in the study," she replied instead.

Jackie watched in silence as he walked towards her, then sat on the coffee table in front of her. She waited for him to speak.

"I have to go out of town," he began, placing his hands on her knees.

"Okay." Jackie didn't know what else to say. She actually admitted to herself that this information bothered her somewhat and that his touch was as electrifying as she remembered.

"I might not be back for Christmas."

"Okay." She had recently learned to use a new word.

In his usual way, Michael bowed his head. He took a breath and spoke again. "I'd take you with me," he said quietly, "but you'd most likely be stuck in a hotel room all alone anyway."

Jackie remained silent.

"There's a problem at the Montreal office. Someone's been embezzling funds; I have to go."

Still she said nothing.

"Has your mother decided to go to your aunt's for the holidays?"

"Yes."

"Will you go with her, then?"

"I suppose so."

Michael nodded. "Have you finished your shopping?"

"Pretty much."

"I'm going to try to rectify this mess as soon as possible. Maybe I could get back for New Year's. I could meet you at your aunt's."

What was he doing? "Okay…"

"I'm sorry…" Michael was saying now.

"Sorry you're leaving, or sorry you might be back for New Year's?"

Jackie didn't know why she'd said that. Perhaps it was because she was unsure of his motives, unsure of her own feelings, or just plain confused by the whole situation. *Or* as it was customary for her, because she spoke before giving him a chance to continue… Nevertheless, she'd said it and couldn't take it back.

Michael's eyes suddenly darkened angrily as he leaned towards her, his hands falling away from her.

"You just don't let up, do you?" he said in a very low voice, and Jackie was immobilized. She couldn't move; she couldn't speak. "One of these days that pride of yours is going to get you in deep water. I hope for your sake that someone will be around to help you out – it might not be me!"

With that, Michael got up and left the room, leaving Jackie with a tremendous lump in her throat and a pain in her heart.

Jackie wanted to apologize, but naturally her pride would not allow her. The days that followed were awkward; her big mouth had made certain of that – again.

Her Christmas shopping completed, she wrapped each gift in

brightly coloured festive paper. All but one – Michael's.

She presented Mr. and Mrs. Delaney with their gifts. They were off to spend the holidays with their son and his family who lived a couple of hours away.

Walter had decided to accompany Jackie and her mother to Aunt Beth's. This was unexpected, but it pleased her to know that he felt comfortable with her family. He would receive his gift along with everyone else.

This left Michael's gift. Shopping for him had been a tad difficult. She didn't want to buy anything too personal, but if her gift were too vague, too *im*personal, it wouldn't look right. She had thought of a watch, but he owned several. He didn't wear tie clips and he didn't smoke. He had golfed a few times during the summer, but she didn't think golfing accessories were appropriate for Christmas. Finally, after several trips to various malls in the miserable subzero weather, she decided on a leather jacket. True, he had three already, but this one was a little different from the others. She liked it and hoped that he would also. The only problem had been when or where to give it to him. Now she had run out of time.

Michael was placing another shirt in his suitcase when she entered their bedroom. He looked up, but didn't speak. Jackie walked over to her closet and pulled out the expensive jacket, still in the shop's garment bag. When she laid it on the bed, he looked at her again, silently questioning her.

"This is your Christmas gift. I wasn't sure when to give it to you. If you don't like it, you could exchange it or return it altogether. The sales clerk promised it wouldn't be a problem."

Michael finished zipping his suitcase and took the jacket out of the bag. He slipped it on. It looked wonderful; Jackie had expected no less.

"No, I'll keep it," he said, admiring himself in the mirror. "I'll wear it."

"Good." Jackie turned to leave.

"Jackie…" he called, stopping her at the door.

As always, the rare occasions that he used her name would cause her to tingle all over. She turned to look at him, hoping to appear unaffected.

Michael took a small, elegantly packaged box from his dresser and brought it to her.

"Here, open it. See if it fits," he instructed.

"You know, you don't have to keep buying gifts."

"You just did, didn't you? It's Christmas. Just open it."

Her eyes focused on the exquisite emerald, flanked by smaller, triangular diamonds, and once again, Jackie was caught off guard.

"It's… beautiful," she breathed, and catching herself, she added, "but really, you needn't—"

"—You're welcome," he said, cutting her off, then walked back to the bed to fetch the suitcases.

Jackie had returned her gaze to the ring in the black velvet box and hadn't noticed that he had brought the suitcases to the door until he was standing directly in front of her.

"I asked you to see if it fit," he said reaching for her right hand. "If it needs to be sized, I'll have my father bring it to the jeweller's before you leave tomorrow. I wouldn't want your family to think your husband not only leaves you on our first Christmas, but doesn't even buy you a gift."

"It wouldn't even cross their minds."

Michael slipped the ring on her finger and admired it. Naturally, it fit. He held her hand for far longer than necessary and Jackie slowly slipped it away. He had wanted to apologize for snapping at her that night, but he decided against it. He wanted to take her into his arms, but he decided against that too. He couldn't handle another rejection.

Michael picked up the suitcase and shoulder bag and walked out the door. Jackie followed.

The airport limo arrived as they reached the bottom of the stairs.

"Will you ask him to take the bags? I'm going to find Dad," he told her, disappearing down the corridor.

Jackie hoped that Walter would not follow his son to the door. If he did, what would Michael do? Would he try to kiss her? In that case what would she do? Unfortunately, she was about to find out.

" … And don't worry about Jackie," Walter assured his son. "At least she'll be with her family, and I'll do my best to keep her company."

Michael smiled at his father. "I know," he told him. "I'll call and give you an update as soon as I can."

"Yes, yes. You do that." Walter patted his son's back and went to speak to the limo driver, who had just returned to the door.

Now Michael turned to her. His father was just a few feet away. They were not alone, which presented a window of opportunity… and he would take it.

Jackie's heart started to pound in her chest and she was having difficulty breathing normally, not to mention holding his gaze.

"I'll try not to be too long, okay?" he said finally.

"Sure," she answered for her father-in-law's benefit. Her

heart was beating so loudly in her ears that she barely heard him anyway.

Michael took another step and closed the small gap between them. He slid his hands around her waist and held her against him.

"Are you going to let me kiss you?" he whispered, and Jackie felt as though her legs would soon give away.

When his lips finally closed over hers, Jackie exhaled the breath that she'd unknowingly been holding for the past few months. She hadn't allowed him to kiss her since their wedding night. Nevertheless she had often remembered the effects of his kisses and now she was experiencing that intoxicating effect all over again.

Her hands slid over the soft leather of his new jacket to wrap around his neck as he molded her closer still.

But just when she had forgotten everything and everyone around her, he ended the kiss, leaving her breathless and unsettled.

"I have to go." His voice was husky. "I'll call you."

Jackie was silent as she tried to avoid eye contact.

"Bye," he said against her lips and gave her another little kiss.

Michael withdrew his supporting arms from around her, and Jackie felt suddenly drained and somewhat unsteady. All she could do was watch after him as he disappeared out the door.

CHAPTER THIRTY

Christmas Eve at the Ellis home had always been a very joyous event. It was the same at Aunt Beth and Uncle Jonathan's. Whether it was spent with family members, friends, or both, everyone always had plenty to eat and a wonderful time.

Dinner was deliciously elaborate, but Jackie barely touched it and certainly didn't taste it. Her thoughts kept returning to Michael.

She had wanted him to kiss her; she knew that. But the fact that she had responded to that kiss had invited the intimacy of which she was so afraid, and that unnerved her immensely. The more intimate their so-called relationship, the more difficult it would be for her in the end – and there would be an end.

It was nearly eleven o'clock. Soon they would leave for midnight mass and Michael had not yet called.

"Don't worry, Jackie," Matthew assured her. He'd noticed how she jumped every time the telephone rang. "He's probably tried to call, but the circuits are busy."

"He could use his cellular phone," interjected Jason, which earned him a stern look from his brother. "But maybe it's not working either," he added quickly.

"Thanks." Jackie appreciated their concern. "I'm not worried," she told them.

They had been there for three days and Jackie had not yet spoken to him. Apparently he'd called on the first day, but she'd been out. Walter had spoken to him and told her that Michael would call her later, but he hadn't. Jackie was worried, and to add to her stress, the national news had reported that Montreal and the surrounding area had been hit with a blizzard and conditions were unsafe.

They were ready to leave for church when the phone rang and again Jackie nearly jumped out of her skin.

Matthew ran to answer it. "Oh, hi!" he was saying. "I'm fine. I knew it was you." And Jackie's heart was beating to the rhythm of a hundred tribal drums.

"Yes," her cousin continued, "I was telling Jackie that you probably couldn't get through. Oh! That's what Jason said! Okay, I'll get her. Merry Christmas!"

"You go on without me. I'll go tomorrow." Jackie shooed everyone to the door, as she took the receiver from Matthew.

"Hello?" she said tentatively.

"Hi," Michael answered.

" ... Hi."

"How's your visit?"

"Good. How's everything there?"

"Not good, but I'm getting it straightened out."

Jackie was silent, and he too paused for a moment.

" ... I would have called sooner, but every time I had the chance to, I couldn't get through. Then, I forgot the charger for my cell at the office, so I had to send someone to buy me another one, but I had to wait till the weather cleared."

"Oh. That's okay. I heard about the storm. Is it very bad?"

"Yeah. The city's snowed in. They can't seem to plow fast enough. Hopefully it'll stop snowing... How's the weather there?"

"It's snowing – heavy packing snow, you know? But it's not bad."

"That's good." Michael paused. " ...Your cousin sounded as though you'd been worried. Were you?"

Jackie took too long to answer and she heard Michael sighing in exasperation.

"Yes," she said finally. "I was a little worried – we all were."

There was silence again, but this time, she thought he'd hung up.

"Michael?"

"What."

" ... Nothing... I just thought you'd... that the phone cut out."

"No." There was still another pause. Now he was suspicious. "Where are you?"

"What do you mean?" she asked innocently. "I'm here, at my aunt's. Where do you think you were calling?"

"I mean... is everyone around you or are you alone?"

Jackie knew what he meant. "Oh. No, everyone left for church."

"How much wine did you have at dinner?"

"You know I don't drink."

"Well, I just can't believe that you admitted concern for me without reason. Are you sure you're alone?"

"Yes... I'm alone."

"Incredible," he said quietly. Then he added, "I don't suppose you miss me, do you?"

Jackie closed her eyes tightly. Why was he doing this, and how was she supposed to respond?

"Do *you?*" she returned, finally, deciding to put the ball in his court.

"Oh, I see," he started, sounding amused. "All right. Yes… as a matter of fact, I do. In fact, I can't wait to get out of here. I need you…"

Jackie placed the palm of her hand over the receiver, as if afraid that he might hear the difference in her breathing, as if afraid that she might instinctively make a verbal response that she was not yet ready to make. Then an ugly picture came to mind.

"Couldn't you find someone to entertain you for Christmas?"

"I hadn't looked," he snapped, "but thanks for the idea. Have a Merry Christmas!" Michael flipped the phone shut on her ear.

"Michael?" Jackie called out. But he was gone.

She could kick herself! If it were at all possible, she would have; she certainly deserved it! He had admitted being with Brenda had been a mistake. He had hired a new receptionist. Now, admitting his desire for her led her to believe that he had been faithful in these last few months. Why did she have to throw the past back in his face?

Michael didn't call again, and she couldn't call him. She would not be given a chance to make amends until he returned home.

Walter sat, slouched in his big chair, and read his paper. Jackie lay curled up on the couch watching TV. It was late when Michael walked in the front door a week later.

His father sprang upright and hurried to the door to greet his son. It took Jackie a little longer to find the courage. She walked slowly to the foyer, but remained in the doorway.

As if sensing her presence, Michael turned weary eyes towards her. He looked tired, but so very handsome. He had a week's worth of stubble on his face and she had to fight back the undeniable feelings he stirred within her.

"We'll talk tomorrow, Michael. Good night dear," Walter said to Jackie.

Jackie wanted to say something, anything, but it was as though she had suddenly contracted laryngitis. She couldn't speak. She just stood there, looking like a lost puppy.

"I'm going up," Michael said simply. He picked up his suitcase and went upstairs, leaving her alone.

Michael had already started to undress when Jackie entered their bedroom. He was removing his shirt now.

She walked slowly towards him, stopping at the foot of the bed. "Michael…" she began hesitantly.

He looked annoyed when he looked down at her choice of attire. "What's with the flannel PJs?"

" … I was cold," she defended herself.

"I'm taking a shower. Want to join me?" he asked, almost as a dare.

Jackie stared at him, round-eyed and speechless. She blinked, opened her mouth, but nothing came out.

"Right! That'll be the day!" he mumbled as he turned from her.

Jackie watched him close the bathroom door behind him. She heard the water being turned on and sighed heavily. She walked to the bathroom door and turned the knob. It wasn't locked.

"Well, it's now or never," she said out loud. Besides, she chastised herself, she'd long since forgiven him for their wedding night. She'd even forgiven his cutting words at the hospital. It was time to swallow that pride of hers. It had caused her such trouble, so much pain. What purpose did pride serve now? Jackie knew he wanted her; Michael had told her so, and she'd simply be lying to herself if she didn't admit that she too longed for him to kiss her again, to hold her, to make love to her...

Leaving her pajamas in a pile on the floor, Jackie entered the bathroom. Slowly, she made her way to the shower. She opened the glass door and stepped inside.

This action startled, even shocked, Michael beyond words. He passed his hands over his face as if trying to clear his view, as if he thought he was only imagining her there.

Silently, he reached for her, drawing her to him. His hands molded her against him as his lips found hers.

Jackie responded freely, finally allowing herself to accept his touch and allowing herself to be aroused by his advances. She trembled, as did he, with the desire that had been kept suppressed for so long.

Michael carried her to bed and lay down beside her. Gently he caressed her, stirring her senses, bringing desire to a peak. Still insecure of her future, Jackie was hesitant to show him the extent of her feelings for him. Yet Michael unselfishly made certain that her desires were satisfied, allowing her body to achieve its goal with ease, shuddering with insurmountable pleasure.

"Oh God, Jackie..." Michael whispered, his voice muffled in the curve of her neck as he experienced a pleasure far better than ever before. Sex with the other women in his life had been just that. This was different… it meant something… Monogamy wouldn't be so bad after all.

Afterwards he remained beside her, an arm wrapped possessively around her waist. Sleepily, she turned onto her side but she didn't move away. Instead, her hand on his invited him to continue to hold her.

She felt him kiss her shoulder. "Did I hurt you?" he asked her softly.

Jackie shook her head into the pillow. Satisfied, he gave her a little squeeze, and they were soon both asleep.

Fingers gently caressed her bare shoulders. Jackie shivered, her eyes fluttering open. Michael was watching her; his head propped up on a raised elbow.

"Morning," he whispered.

Jackie could only manage a little smile.

"How do you feel about an early morning rendezvous in the shower?" Michael asked, suggestively.

Jackie stretched, feeling deliciously contented. "Run the water," she replied quietly.

CHAPTER THIRTY-ONE

Jackie sat in her office several weeks later, flipping through the pages of a supplier's pricelist.

She smiled suddenly as she allowed herself to become engrossed in her thoughts. This was too good to be true. She would actually pinch herself every so often, to make sure she was not dreaming.

Michael had become so different. Their marriage seemed almost real. He no longer waited for an audience to make advances. He kissed her hello and kissed her goodbye. He sat next to her, holding her and caressing her regardless of the fact that his father was not always in the room. They drove to work together nearly every morning and returned home together. They even went out to lunch when his busy schedule permitted. They dined with Frank and Irene on several occasions, but mostly alone. On Valentine's Day he filled their room with roses and surprised her with sexy lingerie! They enjoyed each other' company… they talked, they laughed… and they made love… regardless of her fertile times.

Neither had voiced what they felt in their hearts, as though afraid to ruin the newly found harmony of their relationship, but Jackie couldn't have been happier. This business arrangement had somehow become a marriage. Michael seemed happy and content to be with her. What she had secretly hoped had manifested itself into reality. She hadn't become pregnant yet, but Jackie was in no hurry and since Michael hadn't mentioned it, Jackie understood that neither was he. When they finally did conceive, their child would not be raised without a mother, she was certain of that.

Jackie sighed, and focussed once again on the pamphlet in front of her. The item that she was pondering was a relatively new product called a plasma screen, used extensively by their video-imaging department. This screen could be used for computers or touch screens, which were a large part of their manufacturing. The plasma screen was a new technology, replacing tubes, and could soon replace LCDs. New technology is always very expensive, and this was no exception.

But something didn't look right.

Jackie had, on several occasions, questioned her superior about the price of the screen being purchased from AFF Electronics. Jim had always told her that the price quoted to them was the best possible for the quality of the product, and he refused to go else-where. However, the plasma screen pictured in the pamphlet before her was the same, with one exception – the price. Bradford & Sons offered their product for far less than the price of AFF.

Jackie smelled a rat!

Within the next few days, Jackie arranged a meeting with Mr. Bradford himself.

Carl Bradford had been surprised when he'd received a phone

call from Jackie Madison of Madison Electronics! The older gentleman had told Jackie that he would look forward to meeting her and helping her in any way that he could.

The greying Mr. Bradford was a stocky man in his late fifties. Despite his deep gruff voice, he seemed to have a kind disposition and a gentle way about him. He did not strike her as a forceful individual, which could explain why Madison Electronics was not buying from his company.

Carl Bradford showed her the screen along with many other components that were also being purchased from AFF at an exaggerated cost.

"I'll have to speak to Michael, but I appreciate your time, Mr. Bradford."

"Oh, it's my pleasure Jackie, but I don't think this visit of yours is going to make any difference to your husband."

"Why do you say that?"

"Well," Carl chuckled, shaking his head. "I've tried to sell to them for the past five years, but they won't give me the time of day. As far as these screens are concerned, well... I know the volume they do; that's why I also know I could give them the best price."

"You've spoken to Michael before?"

"No, not Michael and not Walter either. I don't normally speak with the owners when I'm dealing with such a large company. I've always spoken to Jim Nyland – that is – when he's granted me two minutes of his precious time!" he shrugged, chuckling once again.

"I see. Well, like I said, I'll speak to Michael about this." Jackie walked to the door, and shook Carl's outstretched hand. "Thank you very much. This meeting has been extremely interesting. I'll get back to you, Mr. Bradford."

Jackie was determined to get to the bottom of this.

Early the next morning, she went to Frank. She asked him to run a check on AFF Electronics. She was not at all surprised with his findings.

Moments later Jackie rang her husband's office.

"Yes?" Michael answered sharply.

"It's me."

"Hi." Michael's voice became almost seductive. "What's up?"

"Nothing…"

"No?"

Jackie smiled into the receiver. "I wanted to talk to you about one of our – your suppliers. Can you spare a minute?"

"Maybe even two. Come now."

Jackie hung up and made her way to Michael's office.

He was waiting for her by his door as she approached. He pulled her inside and shut the door behind them, asking Nora to hold his calls.

Trapping her against the wall he pressed himself against her and began to kiss her as he unbuttoned her blouse.

"Michael…" Jackie tried to speak against his lips. "Someone might come in!"

"They wouldn't dare," he breathed, and doused her fears by locking his door.

Much later, lying in each other's arms, Jackie forced her voice though her lips.

"I had come to see you about something," she said pensively.

Michael looked down at her. "Are you disappointed?"

Jackie met his gaze and smiled. "No," she admitted truthfully, and Michael's arms tightened around her.

"So, what was it?" he asked after they'd zipped and buttoned everything back together.

"What was what?"

"What you wanted to talk to me about."

"Oh! Yes, well… I was curious about AFF Electronics," Jackie began.

Michael took hold of her hand and pulled her down to sit next to him on the couch they'd just vacated. He continued to play with her fingers as she spoke.

"We buy plasma screens from AFF, right?" Michael asked the rhetorical question.

"Yes. Is there a particular reason we only buy from AFF?"

"What do you mean?"

"I… well… maybe I shouldn't have taken it upon myself," Jackie said slowly, "but I've met with Bradford & Sons. They sell the same part at a significantly lower price than AFF."

"So, why don't we buy from Bradford?"

"That was my question. Mr. Bradford told me that he's tried to meet with Jim, but he's always given him the brush off."

"What?"

Jackie was almost afraid to continue. "I'm afraid I took a step further," she began, and Michael's brow formed a curious frown. "I asked Frank to run a check on AFF. It seems that Jim Nyland has interests in that company. It seems that… that may be the reason why we keep buying from AFF at such an inflated price."

Michael stared at her in astonishment, and Jackie wasn't quite sure how was taking the news.

"Are you upset with me?" she asked finally.

Michael smiled. "With you? Why should I be upset with you? I just... I didn't think that working here..." Michael seemed to be having difficulty voicing his thoughts. He sighed. "I'm glad that you're taking an interest in the company. And... I'm impressed with your legwork," he added, and Jackie felt pride in her work once again.

By the end of the week, Michael had in his possession all the pertinent information he needed to confront Jim Nyland. Jackie was with Michael when he called Jim into his office.

"Michael, you wanted to see me?" Jim hovered at Michael's doorway.

"Come in. Close the door," Michael instructed.

Jim Nyland looked from one to the other. He was beginning to look nervous.

"Jim, Jackie has brought something to my attention."

"Oh? What's that?"

"Would you care to explain why we have been purchasing plasma screens from AFF at fifteen thousand dollars apiece, when Bradford offers the same product for nearly three thousand less?"

"Simple. It's an inferior product." Nyland appeared confident.

"Really? All right." Michael now produced two screens that appeared to be exactly the same. "Perhaps you can tell me which product is which?"

"They may appear to be the same, but once tested you will see that the Bradford product is inferior," Jim maintained.

"No, I installed and tested them myself; there is absolutely no difference. They are both manufactured to standard."

"Hey, maybe they've adjusted their previous problems. If you want to buy from Bradford, we'll buy from Bradford. It makes no difference to me."

"Doesn't it?" Michael picked up the file on his desk and held it out to Jim. "Looks to me like you may have a vested interest in this after all."

Jim Nyland's face grew pale as he reached for the file that Michael extended to him. He opened the file, but he didn't have to go further than the first page. He knew that his secret was now public knowledge.

"What are you going to do?" Jim asked quietly.

"I think that it would be in everyone's best interests, especially yours Jim, that you devote all of your time to the company in which you have invested so much effort. Under the circumstances you will agree that neither notice, nor severance pay come into play." Jim remained silent. "I expect you to clear your desk and leave the building within the hour."

"But I—"

"The alternative, Jim, is that I press charges. Take your pick."

"Charges? Charges for what?" Jim was indignant.

"Conspiracy, fraud..."

"You'll never make it stick."

"No? Maybe no, maybe yes. Would you care to take odds?"

Jim Nyland once again looked towards Jackie. His face was flushed and his eyes were cold. An ugly sneer distorted his mouth.

She felt the invisible daggers being thrown in her direction, but said nothing.

Jim turned and left the office.

Michael pulled his wife into his arms and kissed her. "The Delaneys are away for the weekend – so is my father. Let's go home…" And Jackie wanted nothing more.

This development was like icing on the cake.

Their relationship seemed more solid now, as though her findings had shown her dedication and devotion to him and to the family business. Jackie was content, and she told Carol so when her friend called to tell her that her boyfriend had finally proposed and that her future in-laws were throwing the two an engagement party.

"Congratulations! It's about time, Carol! I'm sorry I haven't called... I've lost track of time," Jackie confessed to her friend.

"I'm sure you have, Jackie!" Carol exclaimed.

Jackie smiled to herself.

"So? When's the party?"

"In two weeks. I don't suppose you might like to attend? I mean... as my matron of honour, I would like you to come..."

"Oh Carol! Thank you. I'm honoured! And yes, I'll be there; I wouldn't miss it for the world! Just give me the particulars."

The two friends talked for a while about Carol's engagement and how the actual 'question' had come about, but Carol became serious suddenly.

"So… Jackie... how are things, really?"

"Things are incredibly wonderful. I mean, he's been so… different. Carol, I'm happy and I think he is too."

Carol was quiet for a moment. "Are you sure, Jack?"

"Pretty sure. But for the time being, I'm going to hold on to that, you know?"

"Yes, I know. Well, I hope everything works out for you. I swear if he does anything to hurt you, he'll have to answer to me! You can tell him that!" Carol laughed.

Jackie told Michael that she had spoken to her friend, omitting their discussion about him.

"Really? That's nice. Would you like me to come with you?"

Jackie stared in surprise. "You would come?"

"Yes… if you'd like me to."

"That would be nice."

"When is it?"

"In two weeks."

"Good, I'll be back by then."

Jackie's heart sank. "You're going away again?"

"Yes. Chicago," Michael confirmed, reaching for her. "Just for a few days."

He held her against him, looking down at her upturned face. "Why don't you come with me?"

Jackie contemplated the offer. "No, that's okay. Just do what you have to do. Maybe you can take a couple of extra days when we go to Carol's party."

"Deal," he said against her lips.

Later that evening Jackie made herself ready for bed and went back down to see what was keeping her husband. Michael was engrossed in a game of chess with his father when Jackie came to stand behind him, putting her hands on his shoulders.

Michael took hold of one of her hands and kissed it. "Go on up," he told her. "We're almost finished. I think I've got him stumped."

"Think again, my boy!" Walter exclaimed as he made a calculated move.

"I think I'll just watch some TV," she laughed. Jackie stretched out on the soft couch and switched on the television. Not much later, she fell asleep.

Jackie felt herself being lifted into the air. She awakened, startled.

"Shh," Michael whispered as he carried her upstairs. "Go back to sleep."

Jackie sighed and wrapped her arms around his neck. She snuggled her face in his shoulder.

Michael laid her on their bed and sat down beside her, an arm around her, and Jackie stretched and yawned, one hand coming to rest on his as it held her hip.

"Are you going back down?" she asked quietly.

"Do you want me to?"

"No…"

"What *do* you want?" he asked, his voice husky.

Jackie wrapped her hand around his and pulled herself upright to face him. Michael sat motionless as her hands slid slowly up to his shoulders, holding him.

Still, he waited as she pressed her lips to his. Finally his hands came up over her hips, holding her tightly against him, eagerly responding to her kiss. His hands came around to the front of her robe and untied the sash. He pulled the terrycloth away from her body, exposing the soft silk of her short nightgown.

For the first time, Jackie's hand came down over the front of his jeans. She had wanted to pull on the zipper, but Michael held her hand in place, reveling in the display of her longing.

She tugged on his sweater and he obliged by pulling it off in one swift movement. His jeans were shed as well and then he lifted the silky nightgown over her head. He caressed her, his lips leaving a burning trail over every inch of her body. Then, after once again bringing her more pleasures than she'd ever dreamed of, he lay behind her and held her close.

"I love you," he whispered.

Jackie's eyes shot open. What? What did he say? Had she imagined it? Had he said what she thought he'd said? Should she ask him? Should she wait? Maybe he would repeat it... Maybe he never said it at all...

Jackie awakened the next morning to find herself alone. Grabbing her robe, she bolted from the bed. She ran to the bathroom and nearly ran into Michael as he opened the door.

"I... thought you'd left," she said breathlessly.

"No. It's early; go back to bed," he smiled.

Jackie's heart settled back into place.

"No," she sighed. "I'm up now. I'll take a shower."

When Jackie re-entered the room, Michael was already dressed.

She wrapped her robe around her bare body and lay down on his side of the bed as she watched him knot his tie.

Michael pulled down on his shirt collar and came to sit beside her. He watched her for a moment. "I wish I didn't have to go."

"Then don't," she said, surprising even herself.

Michael leaned towards her and accepted her obvious invitation. Soon his clothes were in a pile on the floor, along with her robe.

"I am so late!" he told her afterwards. "You're bad for business," he said against her lips.

Jackie could only smile mischievously as she watched him dress for the second time.

CHAPTER THIRTY-TWO

*J*ackie was feeling especially happy this morning. It was a beautiful May morning and her spirits matched the brightness outside. She was walking on air and nothing could bring her down. Placing yet another plant upon the large windowsill of her new office, she admired the vibrant green leaves, noticing how it'd grown so well in just a few weeks…

Upon Jim's departure Michael suggested that she move into the vacant office, as well as taking on his duties. Sara had decided not to return to work, preferring to stay home with her newborn for a while longer. Therefore Gabe had taken over Jackie's position and another two junior buyers were hired: one permanently and one temporarily to fill in for Diane who had given birth to two beautiful little boys.

She was just pouring a cup of water into the soil when her telephone rang.

"Jackie speaking," she said cheerfully into the receiver.

"Well hello there," answered the familiar voice on the other end.

Jackie rolled her eyes and sighed in annoyance. "What do you want, Jim?"

"Actually, I'd like to see you. I have some information that you might find interesting."

"Jim, I doubt you have anything that I might find remotely interesting. I would advise you not to call again." She would have hung up on her ex-boss, but he hadn't finished infuriating her yet. With exasperating smugness, Jim Nyland sang the next sentence. "It's about your husband…"

Jackie was silent.

"See, I knew I'd get your attention."

"What do you want?"

"I told you. I want to see you. Meet me at the corner coffee shop in half an hour," he instructed, and before she could answer, he hung up.

Jackie paced the floor of the office once occupied by Nyland. What could he possibly have to say to her? What information did he have about her husband? Well, she told herself, there was only one way to find out.

Sitting in the coffee shop, sipping a cup of herbal tea, she waited impatiently until Jim Nyland appeared before her.

He laughed at her punctuality. "My, aren't we anxious!"

"What do you want, Nyland?" Jackie demanded through clenched teeth.

"How have you been?"

"Spit it out!"

"All right. I'm here to burst your bubble," he told her matter-of-factly.

Jackie tried to sound calm and disinterested. "And what bubble is that?"

"You've got a great set-up here, Miss Ellis."

"*Mrs. Madison*, remember?"

Jim laughed. "Oh, right! *Mrs. Madison*. Well, at least until you give birth to the much longed for 'baby Madison'!"

Jackie felt something turn in the pit of her stomach.

"What?"

Jim leaned towards her. "I know about your little deal," he told her in a loud whisper.

"I don't know what you're talking about."

"Don't you? Let me refresh your memory. I'm talking about the deal you made with Madison… the one about supplying him with an heir…"

Jackie swallowed. "And what difference could that possibly make to you, even if it were true?"

"Oh, it's true, and you're right. It makes no difference to me; however, its development might make a difference to *you*."

"You think?"

"Well, let's see… I understand that Frank Atkins came to you with a proposition. Am I 'on the money' so far?" Jim sneered, but Jackie didn't reply. "In actuality, it was the big cheese himself who suggested that you be approached. What do you think about them apples?"

Jackie's mind was now in fifth gear. Michael had seemed so surprised and upset when he'd found her in Jerry's office with Frank. Could Jim be telling the truth? Had the proposition been Michael's idea all along? In any case, if it were true, did it really make a difference now? Things had turned out so well; she couldn't – wouldn't – let this news ruin everything. She would speak to Michael; he would explain… wouldn't he?

She was beginning to feel extremely warm, but she was determined to remain cool on the surface. "So?" she shrugged.

"So, that doesn't bother you?"

"No, it doesn't. My bubble remains intact, so if you don't mind…" Jackie began to rise from her chair, "I have work to do."

"Oh, please don't go," he begged sweetly, trying to reach for her hand. "I have something to show you."

Jackie jolted away from his touch and would have turned to leave, but Jim produced a booklet and was now sliding it across the table.

"Do you recognize this?"

Jackie stared at it for a moment, beginning to feel a little faint. Unable to restrain herself, she touched it. Sitting once again, she turned a page, and then another.

"Where did you get this?" Jackie's voice was but a whisper.

"That's not important right now. Do you recognize it?"

"It's my father's schematic for his computer chip. It's in his handwriting."

The smug look on Jim Nyland's face was enough to send anyone off the deep end, but Jackie composed herself quickly.

"I don't know how you got your grubby little hands on my father's papers, but whatever you're thinking, think again. This chip was defective."

"Oh? Well then… take a look at this."

He pushed yet another booklet towards her. This one was professionally bound and held an unmistaken familiarity. It was black. The gold writing read 'MADISON ELECTRONICS.'

Curiosity getting the best of her, Jackie flipped through the pages. The booklet contained the schematics for a computer chip – her father's chip.

Her heart pounded in her chest and her hands trembled… and Jim Nyland smiled.

"Why are you showing me this?" Jackie tried to regain her composure. "I mean… you know you picked the wrong party to blackmail, don't you?"

"I am perfectly aware that Michael would have paid *big bucks* in order to keep this under wraps, especially now that things are so lovey-dovey between you. But you see, although he may be an arrogant son-of-a-bitch, I never had a problem with Michael until you came along. You have been nothing but trouble since you came into the picture. I had a good thing going, and you ruined it."

"I've been trouble? I merely found out about your company and exposed you. What you were doing was wrong!"

"I wasn't hurting anyone. They've got enough money. I was only trying to make a living."

"Is that what you call it? You were dishonest and underhanded! In fact, what would you call what you're doing now? I think the authorities might call it extortion!"

"Extortion, my dear, is illegal, and I have no intention of going to jail. If I were willing to risk that then I would have gone for the money. I'll settle for the pleasure of seeing your world crumble. I think that in itself is reward enough!"

He had succeeded.

Jackie sat quietly, dumfounded by the information that screamed up at her from the pages of that booklet. Her eagerness to market the chip was not the source of their problems. The chip had not been defective. The Madisons – Michael – had been the cause of her father's destruction. They had sabotaged her father's hard work, forced his company into the ground, for the sole purpose of stealing the chip and calling it their own!

"By the way," Nyland said suddenly, bringing her out of her thoughts. "My sister says hello!"

Jackie looked sharply at him. "Pardon?"

"You remember Brenda, don't you? She wants you to know that she bears no hard feelings towards you, because although things may not be as convenient as they were, she is certainly doing a lot more travelling now. In fact, I think she's in Chicago this week. I have her hotel number." He slipped a piece of paper towards her. "Why don't you give her a call; say hello…"

Unable to restrain herself, she glanced at the number scribbled on the piece of paper. It was Michael's telephone number at the hotel. Reason would have told her that the number didn't prove an affair, but reason was not forefront in her mind just then. Jackie had a disgustingly sour taste in her mouth; she couldn't say another word.

Nyland, however, was hell-bent on proving his allegation. Before she could stop him he turned the telephone towards her and punched in Michael's hotel number, making certain she saw the numbers. He pushed it closer towards her, and admittedly unable to resist, Jackie heard the unmistakably whiny voice of her husband's former lover. That was it. It was over.

"Well, I must say, this was a productive morning! You have a good day now, *Mrs. Madison!*"

Jackie waited until she was certain her legs would carry her.

Then she gathered the booklets and left the coffee shop.

She wandered around for hours. She didn't know what to do. Jim Nyland had indeed been successful. Her world *had* crumbled – in a matter of moments. Today of all days... That morning she had learned that she was carrying Michael's child.

Jackie contemplated telling her mother, but decided against it. She didn't think her mother could bear to learn this piece of information. Her poor mother had been so happy; she couldn't burst her bubble as Jim had done to her.

Frank was sure to have known about all the gritty details. She couldn't speak to him and, although she no longer cared about keeping her secret from Irene, she didn't want to involve her in this sordid ordeal.

John Bellows was the only one she could turn to now. Jackie was aware of John's feelings for her. She also knew how much he had disliked Michael's plan for producing an heir. John couldn't help her, but at least she could confide in him before she lost her mind altogether.

"I can't believe that," John shook his head sadly. "We've been friends for a long time, and although we hardly ever discuss our work, I can't believe he could be so ruthless!"

"Believe it!" Jackie told him, adamantly.

"But that's so cold, so calculating."

"Yes, well, he's a great actor. I fell for his act – more than once. He actually had me believing that he had feelings for me." She laughed suddenly. "Silly me! All this time he's been having his secret rendezvous with his blonde bombshell! He's taken me for a fool repeatedly, but enough is enough!"

"Jackie," John said quietly, taking in her distraught expression. "What are you going to do?"

"I want to make him pay!"

"But how?"

"I don't know, but he will pay!"

CHAPTER THIRTY-THREE

Michael called several times while he was away on his business trip, and Jackie always spoke to him as though nothing was wrong.

Two can play at this game, she told herself.

That weekend, Walter decided to take another fishing trip. Jackie gave Mr. and Mrs. Delaney the weekend off, and this gave Jackie full run of the house *and* the telephone. Her husband continued to call, but now she refused to answer.

She was sitting by the pool staring at the telephone when John came to visit.

"Aren't you going to answer that?" John asked after the fifth ring.

Jackie poured him an iced tea and sat back against the plush pillows of the lawn chair. "No."

John reached for his glass and then came to sit beside her on her chair.

He looked down at her, noticing just how pretty she looked

in her yellow sundress. Her hair was pushed back away from her face, held in place by the sunglasses propped on top of her head. But her pretty face had dark circles under her eyes and strained lines around her mouth, a blatant reminder of the stress she'd had to endure.

"Have you thought about what you're going to do?" he asked.

"No."

"I know I've said this before, but… why don't you just leave? That would at least bug him, don't you think? I mean, if all he wanted from you was a child…"

"I'm pregnant, John," she confided.

"I see," he sighed, lowering his eyes, but after a moment he looked up at her as if an idea had just occurred to him. "If you leave, you never have to tell him you're pregnant. You know I'd do anything—"

"—John…" Jackie started, but something caught her eye. She sat up suddenly and kissed him, shocking him.

John was surprised, but wanted nothing more. He welcomed the kiss, until he understood the reason behind it.

"What the hell is going on?" Michael demanded to know.

John pushed himself away from Jackie. He turned towards his friend, but he was at a loss for words. "Michael! I… I… we were just… enjoying a bit of spring sun—"

"—Looks to me like you were enjoying a lot more than that! I think you should leave, while you still have legs to stand on!"

John began to rise from the chair, but Jackie took hold of his arm and pulled him back down.

"No. I don't think so," Jackie said in a steady voice.

Michael's eyes turned to her, the questions burning in his

eyes. But it was not pain, she assured herself.

"It's no use hiding it any longer, John," Jackie said to his friend, who now looked at her in panic. "John and I... well, we've been seeing each other for a while."

Michael's entire being stiffened into stone. In fact, he felt as cold as marble. His mouth dropped as he stared incredulously. But then, John had the same reaction!

"I don't believe you," Michael breathed.

"Sorry," she shrugged.

Deciding to take her cue and help her with whatever plan she had brewing, John interjected.

"Michael, you know how I feel about Jackie—"

"—And it doesn't faze you to know that she's in my bed every night? Are you doing her too? Or perhaps I should ask: for how long?"

"You don't have to be so vulgar," John reprimanded.

"Vulgar? I'm vulgar?" Michael returned with an incredulous laugh, as he finally found the strength to take a few steps towards them. "Vulgar is the way she can jump from one to the other and make it believable! Vulgar is the way you can be so passive knowing that I'm going to keep her until she gets pregnant! And by God she will, if I have to tie her to my bed and screw her morning, noon and night!"

With that he turned and disappeared into the house.

Jackie looked up at John. "I'm sorry," she offered.

"I understand why you said what you did, but what did you gain by it? What had you expected him to do?"

"I expected nothing. It wasn't planned. I just saw an opportunity and took it."

"But Jackie... why not simply confront him with this? Your so-called contract could very well be, under the circumstances, null and void!"

"I know that John, but right now, he thinks I've been sleeping with both of you. When I tell him I'm pregnant... he'll have to wonder for the next seven months whether or not this child is his. I have the upper hand now, and I'm going to take it to the limit!"

"Jackie, he'll ask for a paternity test."

"I won't agree to it. John, if you want out, I'll understand."

"No. I'll play along, if that's what you want."

"I'd appreciate it."

John shrugged. "Whatever you want..."

Inside, Michael headed blindly for his study. He closed the door and leaned heavily against it while his brain unsuccessfully tried to figure out exactly what just happened. Abruptly, he straightened and nearly sprang forward to open and close the cupboards of his credenza until he found the still-boxed bottle of very expensive cognac. Trembling fingers ripped open the flap, extracted the crystal bottle from within, then unwilling to leave the privacy of his study for a glass, he guzzled down a good portion of the contents. The fiery liquid burned his throat and chest, sending out an involuntary gasp, but it didn't diminish or compare with the pain he felt in his heart.

Michael clutched his chest as angry tears welled up in his eyes. How could he have been such a fool? He had let himself believe that things had changed between them. He had been so sure of her feelings that he'd actually voiced what he'd known to be true for a long time. He had told her he loved her. True, she had not answered, but it had not mattered. He realized that she might be reluctant to do so until she was certain the feelings were truly reciprocated. He was sure...

It hurt. It had hurt when his first wife had aborted their child. It had hurt when Jackie miscarried, but this... this left him devastated, drained, empty...

Michael did not resurface until the following evening. When Jackie came out of the bathroom, in their bedroom, Michael was there, waiting for her.

He stood in front of her, stopping her from walking past him.

"Did you sleep with him today?" Michael asked boldly.

"Do you want details?"

"You know, you're pretty good. You had me going for a while."

"I learned from the best – the master of illusion!"

Michael's lip curled into a cynical smile. "I was right after all," he said simply. He turned down the covers and slipped into bed. *You're just like the rest,* he told her in his mind.

Michael was up and gone before she awakened the next morning. This left her to drive herself to the office.

John called shortly after she arrived and told her that he would come to take her to lunch. His first stop, however, was to see his best friend.

Michael was standing at the window, a drink in his hand, when John walked into his office. He hadn't slept in days and it showed.

"I thought you'd given up that habit," John called out, startling his friend.

"I've decided to take it up again – what's it to you?"

"Nothing, nothing. Drink, by all means!"

"Thank you," Michael said sarcastically, and taking another gulp of his drink, returned to stare out the window.

"Look Michael, about Jackie—"

"—What about her?" he snapped.

"I just want you to know that I... well... I knew that this was just a business arrangement, and you told me yourself that you didn't have any real feelings for her..."

"So?"

"So, you look a little upset, and I just hope that I wasn't mistaken."

"You weren't."

"Oh. Well, good."

Michael's tone remained the same. "Anything else?"

"You're sure you're not jealous?"

Michael laughed now. "Don't be ridiculous! I told you a long time ago that you could have her, John, although I said when I was finished with her. I am definitely not jealous!"

"Just making sure," John smiled, raising his hands.

"How considerate."

"She's a great girl, Michael. I don't know how you could help falling in love with her."

"I forced myself," he said offhandedly. "I just have one question." Michael turned to look at him now; his eyes squinted, as if daring his friend to lie. "How long has this been going on?"

"Oh! Umm, for a while—"

"—How long?"

"Several months."

"Ahh… Well! You *know* that she is here to give me a child."

"How could I forget!" It was John's turn to be sarcastic.

"And this fact doesn't bother you?"

"Yes Michael, it bothers me, it bothers me a great deal! In fact, why don't you let her out of the contract? I told you before I'll pay you what she owes you."

Michael smiled. "Forget it. She had her chance. I can't for the life of me understand why she didn't take it. Now she's in for the long haul! Too bad!"

"You're a bastard."

"Yeah, I know," Michael confirmed, and John left his office.

Jackie was upstairs when Michael returned from work that evening. Walter was back so she decided to go and play the devoted wife and run down and say hello. She was almost at the bottom of the stairs, when suddenly the room began to spin. Feeling herself weaken, she sank down onto the step and proceeded to faint.

Michael ran to her side, calling her name, but Jackie wasn't responsive. He picked her up and carried her back upstairs, and fetching a damp towel from the bathroom, he laid it across her forehead.

"Jackie. Damn it, wake up!" he commanded, sitting next to her.

Slowly, Jackie started to regain consciousness. She put a hand to her head.

Michael's expression returned to one of stone and his tone was ice cold. "What happened?"

"I got dizzy."

"I gathered that. Why?"

It was time to tell him. "I'm pregnant."

He had been waiting, almost as if he knew what she was going to say, and when she finally answered, he was ready with his reply.

"Is it mine?" he asked accusingly, rising from the bed.

Jackie couldn't help the sneer that crossed her face. "Wouldn't it be ironic," she said, slowly lifting herself to a sitting position, "if it weren't?"

"I want a paternity test done right away."

"Really? Read your contract, honey. Nowhere does it state that any type of testing be done before the baby is born."

"You're not using your marbles. Aside from the money that you will owe me, is it not to your advantage to know?"

"Not particularly. You've put me through enough hell. I'm happy to say… it's payback time," Jackie told him sweetly. "And I'm even willing to remain married to you for the duration of this pregnancy, just to watch you squirm!"

CHAPTER THIRTY-FOUR

N eedless to say, Michael did not accompany her to Carol's ceremony.

Her friend, as she had expected, was quick to notice something was awry.

"Jackie… you have all the papers! Why don't you press charges?" Carol said after she'd been filled in.

"Don't worry, I won't let him get away with it. All in due time," Jackie promised.

"What about your mom?"

"That's the problem. I don't know what this will do to her."

"I know… Are you sure you won't tell her about the baby?"

"I can't, not yet. I'm not sure yet how this mess is going to unravel. I have to wait."

Carol agreed that, perhaps for the time being, it would be best to keep her mother in the dark.

Jackie did come up with one plan. However, she had to

involve yet another person.

"Hi, Aunt Beth," Jackie greeted her aunt, when she called her a few days later.

"Jackie! How nice to hear from you! Thanks for the postcards from the Riviera, they were lovely!"

"Oh, you're welcome."

After several moments of small talk, Jackie became serious. "Aunt Beth, I need your help with something."

"My help? Is everything okay?"

"Yes. Well, it's about Daddy. I may have found out a few things about his company. There may have been some wrongdoings—"

"—Wrongdoings? Jackie, your father was the most honest man—"

"—No, no! Daddy was not doing anything wrong. He may have been sabotaged."

"Oh my goodness! Does Joanie know?"

"No. I don't want to say anything yet, in case my information is wrong."

"Yes, you're right. You said you needed my help. What can I do?"

"It's simple really. I need her out of the way for a few months so that I can get to the bottom of this."

"I understand. Would you like me to invite her to come stay here for a while? I can ask her to help me with my flower shop."

"That was the idea."

"Well, that's no problem for me. But will she come?"

"I've been thinking about it. I thought that maybe after you call and make the suggestion, I would tell her that I'll be taking an extended vacation and so for my own piece of mind, I'd rather know that she was staying with you."

"Not bad!" Aunt Beth laughed. "I think that might just work!"

And it did.

Jackie had gone to see her mother the next day and told her of her plans.

"Oh, how wonderful! Michael's right to do this, you know. Once you start a family, it'll be more difficult to simply pick up and go – especially on such a lengthy vacation! So tell me, has he told you where you're going?"

Jackie felt like a heel. All these lies! She was sure to go to hell, she thought to herself. But it was unavoidable; she needed some time to digest what she'd learned, perhaps uncover more details – if any existed…

"Well… we'll be going… to Los Angeles first, then Hawaii, and… and then Australia…"

"Australia! Goodness, that's so far away!"

"Yes, it is, but you know I've always wanted to go there."

"I know, I know. I think it's wonderful of him to do this. He loves you so much, Jackie."

Jackie smiled, but she couldn't hold her mother's gaze. "Hmm… I know…"

"Well, this works out perfectly!" Joan exclaimed. "Beth called last night, asking me to go and stay with her for a while. She needs a little help at the shop, you know. I'm sure Mrs. Rose at the bakery won't mind."

"That's great! So, you'll go?"

"Yes, I'll go now that I know you won't be around for a few months. To tell you the truth, I look forward to spending some time with my sister. You will call me, won't you?"

"Of course, Mom. I'll call you!"

Walter was so happy about the baby. So was everyone at work, and she was finding it increasingly difficult to continue to pretend. Her current lie was the one about her mother's knowledge of the pregnancy. Jackie didn't want Walter to know that her mother was being kept in the dark. All that he was told was that she was away, but would naturally be back before the baby was born.

When June tenth sneaked up on her, Jackie was not mentally prepared.

Michael had already left for the office when two-dozen white roses were delivered to her door. The card read: 'Happy Anniversary, I know that next year can only be better! Michael.' Only *she* knew what he meant.

John came by the house often, and then Michael would disappear. When Walter was out, John would take Jackie out for dinner and sometimes they wouldn't return until quite late.

On one occasion, Walter was home before Jackie. Michael was in the study, the place where he spent most of his time when at home. Walter knocked on the doorframe and waited for his son to invite him in, and when he did, he entered and closed the door behind him.

Michael should have felt apprehensive, perhaps even nervous, but he felt nothing.

"What's going on?" Walter asked quietly.

Michael barely looked up from the papers he was pretending to read. "What do you mean?"

"Something's happened between you and your wife. A person would have to be deaf, dumb and blind not to notice."

"It's nothing, Dad. Don't worry about it."

"How can I not worry? You have a baby on the way and you barely look at each other. You don't speak — not even for my benefit, and she's always out. Where does she go? Her mother's still away, is she not?"

"Yes she is, and don't you dare call her with your overactive imagination."

"My imagination is not overactive. Something happened. What is it?"

"Dad... we're not the first married couple to run into problems. It'll work itself out. But this is between me and my wife and I would appreciate if you would just leave us to work out our own difficulties."

"I am only concerned, Michael. I didn't mean to meddle."

"I hope not."

Michael was already in bed when she entered their bedroom that evening.

Quietly, she ducked into the bathroom and into the shower. She worried that the sound of the water would wake him, but it had been an especially warm and humid evening, and given her present state, she felt even warmer, and she needed to cool off.

She slipped under the covers and thought she'd managed to go unnoticed, but she was wrong.

Michael turned towards her, his head propped up.

"I would appreciate it," he told her calmly, "if you would be more discreet with your affair. My father was asking where you were tonight."

"You mean I should be as discreet as you? I'm trying," she

said sweetly.

"How does he do it?"

"Do what?"

"How can he make love to a woman who may be carrying someone else's child?"

"I'll ask, if you'd like."

"You're sick," he told her, and turned his back to her once again.

Michael drank heavily. It was the only thing that seemed to lessen his ability to think about, if not diminish, the torment he felt. This left him to be a little less productive at the office. Walter had not been himself either these last few weeks, which left the work-load heavily on Brian's shoulders. Brian, as well as everyone else, noticed that something was terribly wrong, but no one had the nerve to ask what it was.

Michael watched her as her belly grew, as her face began to glow, enhancing her beauty. He wanted so much to touch her, to feel the baby kicking inside her, but he knew she would not want that – not even for his father's benefit. Several times, however, as she lay asleep beside him, he did place a gentle hand on her and on two separate occasions he was gifted with a kick from within. He had been so elated that he'd gasped in delight, awakening her, forcing him to feign sleep once again. She was torturing him, and on a more rational day, Michael had to concede that he needed to share the blame.

As she neared the end of her second trimester, Jackie decided it was time to speak to her husband. She knocked on the study door, and refusing to wait for an invitation, opened it and walked in.

Michael had been sitting in his chair staring across the room, but at the sight of her he quickly became busy picking up papers, shifting them around...

Jackie closed the door behind her. "I'd like a moment of your time."

"What do you want?"

"I have a couple of demands."

"What?"

"You heard me." Jackie was no longer afraid of repercussions. She was the one with the upper hand now.

Unaware of her findings, Michael couldn't believe her tenacity. "You're in no position to demand anything!"

"And you're in no position to deny me."

"Is that right? And how did you arrive at this conclusion?"

"I know that it was your idea to proposition me for your ingenious plan, not Frank's."

Michael's guarded eyes shifted momentarily, taking her words in. "So?"

"So? That's all you have to say?"

"Yes. Do you honestly think that this piece of information gives you the right to make demands?"

"Yes," she shrugged, "I suppose you're right. That information has become meaningless, even to me. However, I have come to acquire something far more interesting, and damaging." Jackie threw the two booklets on the desk.

Michael looked curiously at the booklets. Then he picked up the smaller of the two, her father's booklet. "What's this?" Michael asked offhandedly.

"Stupidity does not become you, sweetheart. You know

perfectly well what that is."

"I don't, so perhaps you could enlighten me!"

"I know all about the sabotage to my father's microchip."

"The what?" Michael's tone was incredulous, but Jackie remained undaunted.

"You installed a virus into the production chips, which caused them to malfunction once they were purchased and installed by unsuspecting clients. You sat back like a vulture, watching my father's business crumble; his life destroyed as each client demanded compensation. Then you proceeded to play the philanthropist and come to his aid by paying his debts. Finally, you so very easily moved in for the kill; you took over the company altogether. All this, to get your hands on that chip. You've made millions with it! Didn't you have enough? Couldn't you allow another to succeed?" she hissed.

Michael stared at her. "And how did you learn about this?"

"Remember Jim Nyland – Brenda's *brother*?" she said smugly, and Michael's eyes narrowed slightly. "As much as I disliked the guy, he's proven to be quite helpful to me."

"In what way?" Michael remained calm.

"He's the one who spilled the beans. Think about it! As it stands, it seems to me that everything that happened to my father and his business was caused by you and your greed. My father would not have been in any sort of financial woes, if not for you. Aside from your obvious quest for complete Ellis domination, there was no reason for me to render my 'services', as you called it. My father, my family, in fact, *I*... owe you *nothing*!"

Michael sighed. "When did he give you this?"

Jackie watched him for a moment, trying to read his mind.

"What does it matter when? I was with John long before Nyland came to me. This has simply made it impossible to pretend any longer."

Michael watched her in silence, a muscle twitching at his jaw.

"What do you want?" he asked finally.

"Well, don't worry, I don't want your money!" An incredulous laugh escaped Jackie's lips. "Your wallet is probably what is in your chest in place of a heart, but I'm not in the habit of resorting to illegal activities to attain what is rightfully mine. No... *I* personally want nothing from you. I've had my fill. But my mother lost her husband and has been caused a great deal of pain and hardship because of your greed; your underhanded dealings. I want compensation for that – for my mother. I think it's only right," Jackie said steadily. "I want it to be known that the microchip you stole was in fact an invention of Sam Ellis. I want all profit derived from the use of the microchip deferred to my mother. She deserves this. I don't care how you do it, as long as you do."

Michael shook his head in disbelief. "All you have is this schematic. What the hell do you think it proves?"

"It proves plenty; don't you worry."

"What about the baby?" he asked her suddenly.

Jackie swallowed hard and took a calming breath. "I want nothing more to do with you once this is over."

"What about the baby?" he repeated.

"You mean, if it's yours?"

Michael's face turned almost ashen in colour. He sighed again and lowered his eyes. "Naturally."

"That would be my greatest misfortune. In that event," she told him, her voice cold and steady, "I will expect full custody; I might give you visitation – if I decide to be generous."

"And if I don't see fit to agree to your demands?"

"You mean aside from never seeing your child again?" Jackie asked sweetly, but Michael didn't reply. "Well, I'm holding another card, and it's an ace. Along with the schematic, I also have the original software codes that my father developed. I know now why he told me to keep them in a safe place. I am prepared to give them to your competitor. Who is it that is just marginally behind you in market share?" Jackie said pensively. "Is it Feldman's? I'll start with that. Then, I'll slap you with a class action suit from all the companies that were originally affected by your sabotage. And finally, I'll go to the media, and bring you down in front of your colleagues and the rest of the country. Oh! Did I forget to say: *'I'll tell your father?'* It's your call."

"I don't understand. I thought you said you don't want to pretend anymore."

"I did."

"You just threatened to tell my father. Are you or are you not telling him?"

"What I meant is that I will no longer pretend with you. I feel sorry for your father, therefore, I won't give him the strain of having to wonder whether or not you will finally give him an heir. I won't say a word until the baby comes – as long as you continue keeping your distance. You'll have to deal with him then." Then after a slight pause, she added, "Unless you want me to tell him…"

Michael's lips curled into a cynical smile. "No, I don't. What did you tell your mother?"

"She's still at her sister's. She knows nothing yet."

"If you had the intention of keeping me from my child, or

better yet, if it's not mine, and you plan to ride off into the sunset with John, why not tell her you're pregnant? Why not tell her everything?"

"Because I wasn't sure yet what I wanted to do. I planned to tell her... when I was ready. Actually," she added as an afterthought, "I think I'm ready now. I think I'm going to call her tonight and ask her to come home. The Christmas season is approaching fast and I'd like to spend it with my mother; with those I love." Jackie raised her eyebrow. "Well?"

The olive green colour of his eyes clouded, losing its richness, leaving his expression cold and aloof.

"All right," he conceded, "I'll talk to Frank."

The dull pain in her chest suddenly intensified. "So you admit it. You admit that you destroyed my father?"

"I said, I'll talk to Frank."

Jackie didn't press further. This was admission enough. "Fine. By the way, when you see Frank, be sure to remind him to begin the divorce proceedings. John has asked me to marry him, and I'd like to be able to give him a clue as to when that might be."

Michael watched her in silence for a moment longer, taking in her determination, her defiance, her large, round belly that protruded in front of her, the belly that might be carrying his child...

"Anything else?" he asked.

"Nope!" Jackie turned and walked out the door.

Michael picked up the receiver and punched in the numbers for Frank's home telephone.

"Michael! Hi, what's up?"

"Plenty."

"Okay… what?"

"It's over, Frank."

"What's over?"

"This whole disgusting farce. It's over."

He was silent as he absorbed this disturbing news as well as all of Jackie's demands. Frank had not expected this outcome, not at all.

"But Michael, if this is true… It's obvious what happened here, let me—"

"—No. Leave it alone."

"Michael, I'm so sorry. I should have realized…"

"Yeah, well. It's my fault in the end. I involved her… I shouldn't have…"

"But Michael, you should explain."

"What for?"

"What do you mean, what for? It could change everything!"

"Frank, have you been listening to me? How could my explanations change the fact that she's with John? How could it change the fact that the baby she's carrying might not be mine? I've made a big enough fool of myself, Frank. That's just about enough for one lifetime."

Again Frank was silent. "I know, Michael. That's the part I'm having difficulty understanding. I thought you two had finally made amends. You looked happy, you both did."

"Yeah well, things aren't always as they seem, are they?"

"No, I suppose not. Michael, is there anything I can do?"

"Yes. Everything she wants."

CHAPTER THIRTY-FIVE

*J*ackie had retired to bed early this particular evening. For some reason, dinner had not agreed with her. She was experiencing stomach cramps and decided to go lie down. Michael remained downstairs.

Daily life at the Madison home had become strained, to say the least. Walter kept his distance, Alice and Elmer Delaney were careful in choosing the right words whenever they spoke, and Michael – well, Jackie barely saw Michael, but that's exactly how she wanted it!

Christmas would arrive without the trimmings this year. Alice had offered to help her with the decorations and Elmer had volunteered to go out and purchase a tree, but Jackie had refused both. She simply was not in a festive mood. Her baby would be born before Christmas and by that time they'd both be out of the Madison home.

It was just before midnight when Jackie was awakened by

sharp, familiar pains.

"Oh no," she said out loud.

She instinctively turned to look towards Michael's side of the bed, but it was empty. It had been empty for the last three months.

Managing to swing her legs off the bed, she pushed the button on the telephone that read 'study'. There was no answer.

She pushed 'living room', and still no answer.

"Michael!" she hollered. "Michael!"

Within moments Michael came storming into the room. "What the hell's the matter?" he started angrily, but changed his tone when he saw her holding her belly. "The baby?" he breathed, coming to kneel next to her.

"My water broke!" Jackie's voice was strained, as she tried to speak between contractions. "I've made a mess!"

"Don't worry about the mess!"

"Ohhh God! It hurts!"

"You're not due for another week!

"TELL HIM THAT!"

Michael ran into the bathroom and grabbed several towels.

"Wait, wait," she breathed, as the contraction ended. "Okay, okay."

He helped her dry off and change her nightgown. "Come on. Can you get up?"

Jackie nodded and Michael helped her to her feet.

"Oh no! Ohhh!"

Yet another contraction, and Jackie was forced to sit down again.

"Maybe I should call an ambulance," Michael suggested.

"No!" she yelled.

"Well how the hell am I going to get you downstairs?" he

yelled back.

Michael stayed with her until the contraction subsided and then suddenly coherent, he ran out the door. He returned only seconds later with a wheel-bottomed office chair.

Michael helped her with her robe and sat her on the chair. He wheeled her to the elevator, which he'd forgotten existed at the far end of the hallway, knocking on his father's door as he passed.

Walter appeared at the door, confused from sleep. "What's the matter?"

"She's in labour; I'll call you from the hospital."

"Oh my! What do you want me to do? Shall I call anyone – your mother?"

"No! I'll tell her myself!" Jackie snapped.

"All right, all right. Go on, go on!" Walter seemed in a daze as he followed them to the elevator and down to the car.

"Call Dr. Francis, Dad. The number's in the study," Michael instructed as he helped his wife into the passenger seat of her BMW.

Jackie had three more contractions on the way to the hospital. Between two of those, Michael looked her way.

"Don't you want to call your boyfriend?" he asked accusingly.

"I hate you," she breathed.

"Thank you," he replied, the lump in his throat threatening to choke him.

At the hospital, Jackie was quickly whisked away to the labour room while Michael was asked to fill out the necessary forms.

"Quickly, quickly!" An elderly nurse came running towards him.

"What's wrong?" Michael was frightened.

"Your wife's fully dilated. You better get in there if you want to see your baby being born!"

The nurse helped him with the green hospital gown and tied a mask around the back of his head. She took his hand and led him to Jackie's side.

"Michael!" Jackie cried. "Ohhh! God!"

"Can't you give her something?" he asked anxiously.

"No, it's too late," one of the nurses told him.

Michael looked down at his wife. "What do you mean it's too late?"

"No, no," the nurse reassured him. "I meant, there's no time for anything to take effect now. Besides, your wife didn't want an epidural."

Jackie had another contraction. Again she screamed for him to help her.

Dr. Francis arrived, looking particularly funny with his hair standing on end. "Well, Jackie, I hope you're happy!" The doctor kidded. "I was having an absolutely wonderful dream when I was paged!"

Jackie didn't hear him – she barely saw him!

The elderly nurse at her side spoke gently to her, telling her to try and breathe steadily.

"I have to push!" Jackie cried.

"No, no. Not yet," Dr. Francis told her.

"Just breathe. Breathe," the nurse instructed. Then she turned to Michael, who stood there motionless, staring in astonishment. "Do something, deary; hold her hand! You're not one of those men that bow out when the tough part comes, are you?

And don't you dare faint on me; you'll just have to lay there if you do!"

Michael sat on the stool next to her. He took hold of her hand and looked down at her.

Jackie rolled her head from side to side. "I can't, I can't. Michael please… take me home, I want to go home…"

"Now, now. You're doing fine, honey," the elderly nurse said to her softly.

Barely two hours had passed, but to Jackie it seemed an eternity.

"Okay, Jackie," Dr. Francis looked up from the foot of the bed where her feet pushed against the stirrups. "Next contraction, I want you to push!"

Here it was.

"Push! Push, Jackie!"

"I can't!" she screamed.

Michael's hold tightened, as did Jackie's. In fact, she squeezed his hand so tightly against the steel bars of the bed that his wedding band actually cut into his finger.

Michael wiped her brow with a damp towel.

Was that concern she saw in his eyes?

Yet another contraction, and again she pushed. She pushed and pushed until she thought she would burst! And finally…

"It's a girl!"

Jackie let out an enormous sigh of relief. She was so tiny, so beautiful… so perfect!

In contrast, Michael's breathing seemed erratic suddenly.

The doctor placed the baby on Jackie's belly, and handed Michael a pair of surgical scissors.

"You may do the honours, sir!"

Michael cut the umbilical cord and soon after, the nurse took the baby away to clean her.

Jackie's body shuddered uncontrollably. She was so cold, so very cold.

"Why is she doing that?" Michael asked anxiously, his voice strained.

"Don't worry, it's just the shock to her body; she'll be fine." The nurse covered her with what seemed to be a thermal blanket, and not long afterwards the shuddering subsided.

"You can remove your mask now, honey; give your wife a kiss!" she instructed. "She did a good job!" She smiled and went to help the other nurse with the baby, while the doctor tended to Jackie.

Michael pulled off the mask and looked down at his wife.

Jackie was exhausted. She watched him as he obviously contemplated doing what the nurse had suggested. But it was too late for that. It was no use acting anymore. It was over.

Returning to them, the elderly nurse handed Michael a little pink bundle, and Jackie was amazed. There were tears in his eyes!

He sensed her eyes upon him, and looked over to her, but Jackie couldn't bear to hold his gaze; she turned her head away and cried. When she turned back towards him moments later, he was gone, gone without a word.

Several anxious hours passed before Michael returned to the hospital. Both Walter and Joan had already been to see Jackie earlier – thankfully not together.

Michael stopped at the nurses' desk.

"I'm sorry, Mr. Madison, but Dr. Francis is in surgery

this morning."

"He told me he'd have results ready… from some tests."

"Just a moment, sir," the nurse said politely.

Michael tapped his fingers impatiently on the counter while the nurse flipped through the pages of her chart.

"Mr. Madison, there are results here, but unfortunately, I am unable to discuss them with you."

"All right. When will the doctor be available?"

The nurse smiled patiently. "I don't know, sir. It was emergency surgery, but he was with your wife when he was called. Perhaps he has already discussed the results with her."

"I see. Thank you." Michael turned and headed towards Jackie's room.

His heart was in his throat by the time he reached her door. What were the results, he wondered? Who was the father of that beautiful little baby? Was it he, or John? And what about John? Where had he been during all this? And Jackie… Jackie never once called for John during labour. Why?

The important questions were answered, however, the moment he opened the door. There, on the edge of Jackie's bed, sat his friend John. He held the baby in his arms. Joan looked on like the proud grandmother.

Michael's breath caught in his throat, threatening to stifle the very life out of him. He had to leave before they saw him, but in his haste the door made a sudden noise and they all looked up.

John called out to him, but Michael didn't stick around; he kept on walking.

"Michael! Michael, wait!" John called after him, hurrying down the corridor.

Michael stopped in front of the elevators. He pushed the button and turned to look at him. His face was black with anger, his eyes murderous.

"I guess congratulations are in order," John started, as he slowly extended his hand.

Michael also extended his hand, albeit in a different way.

Before John knew what was happening, he was flying across the corridor, landing quite heavily on his behind.

Michael didn't think he needed to explain his actions, although the nurses that scurried around to help John demanded to know what was going on.

He didn't oblige. When the elevator doors opened, he disappeared behind them, and was quickly out of the hospital.

Within minutes he stormed into the house.

"Michael?" Walter called, stepping out of the study. One look at his son's face told him something was not right.

"Michael, has something happened?"

"I'd say!"

"Not the baby?" Walter asked, worriedly. He had been to the hospital earlier and both mother and child looked fine.

"Only that she's not mine!"

"What!"

Walter remained silent while Michael explained the wretched details of his so-called marriage, omitting only the part about Sam's business. His father was so silent that Michael thought that he had been struck down by a sudden stroke.

"Dad?"

This could not be happening. Walter thought his troubles had climaxed months ago, with a disturbing telephone call that had threatened to destroy everything. He'd been wrong. "You know…" he started, seemingly dazed. "I was bluffing. I never imagined that you would go to such lengths…"

"Don't you dare turn this around!" Michael lashed out. "I know what I did and I'm paying for it! Disown me; sell everything, give it away, do what you want! I just don't care anymore!"

"But how could you do this?"

"Drop it, Dad! I know you'll be sorry if this conversation continues!" Michael threatened. "I hold you directly responsible for everything! You remember that!"

"Me? *You* are the one who thought that arranging for a surrogate mother would solve your problems! How is this my fault?"

"You started it!" he spat, knowing full well that the answer did not satisfy his father. But Michael refused to disclose anything further. He stormed out of the house as forcefully as he had stormed in.

CHAPTER THIRTY-SIX

*T*he cold wind nipped at Michael's ears as he stopped in the entryway, his hand on the doorknob.

Walter and Elmer were on their knees trying to assemble a bassinet, and Michael, having been 'missing' for the last three days, was somewhat perturbed.

"What the hell are you doing?"

"Oh, you've decided to come home!"

"I asked you what you're doing!"

Elmer Delaney suddenly looked uncomfortable and rose to his feet. "I'm going to find a screwdriver," he announced unnecessarily.

Michael slammed the door shut. "Dad!"

"You wouldn't be asking if you hadn't taken off – or at least kept your phone on."

Michael stared at him. He seemed to be afraid to pose the next question. "What's going on?" His voice was suddenly quiet.

"What's happened?"

Walter slowly rose to his feet and took a seat on the stairs. "Dr. Francis called just after you left."

"Dr. Francis? And?"

"Yes. Apparently, you ran off in somewhat of a huff and didn't wait to speak to him."

Michael shook his head. "What was the point?"

"The point, my dear, impatient son, is that the child is yours."

"Mine?"

"Yes, yours."

"But I thought…"

"You thought wrong."

Michael suddenly needed to sit down as well. He walked over to the stairs and sat down next to his father. He held his head in his hands.

"Where is she?"

"The baby? With Jackie obviously."

"I meant Jackie."

"Oh." Walter paused. "I don't know where Jackie is now."

Well, it wasn't too difficult to conclude. "She must be with *him*."

"I don't know," Walter repeated.

"Have you seen her?"

"Seen who – Jackie?"

Michael bowed his head and sighed heavily. "The baby!"

"Ah! Yes, I've seen her. She's beautiful. I've seen Jackie as well," Walter added. Michael turned to look at him now. "She told me that she'd be in touch when she is ready to discuss the baby. That's good." He pointed to the bassinet. "I'm hoping she'll come visit soon."

His father was delusional. Shaking his head, Michael sprang to his feet.

"Where are you going now?" Walter wanted to know.

"I'm going to find her."

"The baby?"

"Jackie!" he growled, as he slammed the door behind him once again.

"I'm sorry, Mr. Madison. Dr. Bellows is busy," John's secretary was saying. "He's on the telephone."

Michael wasn't listening. He walked right by her and barged into John's office.

"Sir! Sir, you can't—" But Michael closed the door between them.

"Just a moment," John said into the receiver, and pressed the hold button. "Do you mind?"

"Yes, I do. Where is she?"

"Oh, I'm fine; besides a fat lip!"

"Where's my wife?" Michael repeated.

"Your wife? If you mean Jackie, I don't know where she is, and if I did, I'd be the last person to tell you!"

"Don't push me, John," he threatened, leaning across his friend's desk. "You might be on a liquid diet for the next couple of months!"

"Don't threaten *me*, Michael," John said calmly. "I don't scare that easily. Your best bet is to stick to poor defenseless young women. Leave her alone, Michael. She'll let you know when she's ready to talk."

Michael straightened to his full height, towering over him,

but John didn't buckle a bit under his menacing stare. Michael turned and left the office.

He paused in the corridor and leaned against the wall, his eyes raised heavenward, as if waiting for guidance. Perhaps John was right. Perhaps it would be right to give her some space. He should at least allow her that much after all that had been done to her.

A week had been long enough, however. He had to see his daughter; he had to see Jackie. The holidays had been horrible, miserable, lonely… The new year had not presented itself to be any better. It was up to him to try and change that.

Michael stopped his car next to the white BMW parked in the Ellis' driveway. He sat there for several moments before mustering the courage to go to the door.

Standing in the subzero temperature, his breath fogging around him, he knocked. He knocked again.

Finally the door opened and Michael's heart sank. The woman who answered the door was not Jackie, but her mother. Joan Ellis was not someone he was ready to face just yet.

Joan, however, had been prepared. At Jackie's request, she had remained quiet. But the moment she set eyes on the man who had taken advantage of her daughter, she flung out her hand and slapped him hard across the face.

Michael knew he'd deserved it, although that knowledge didn't make it any easier to accept. Raising a hand to his cheek, he looked past her to his wife, who had just come down the stairs with the baby.

"I had it all planned," Joan's unsteady voice brought his eyes back to her. "I rehearsed in my mind, over and over again, what I was going to say to you. But now that you're standing here, I've decided that there are no words to describe what I think of you. You're not worth wasting my breath over!"

"I never wanted to hurt you," Michael began.

"No, just my daughter!"

Michael looked at Jackie again, but Jackie didn't say a word.

"That wasn't my intent either."

"Oh good! I would hate to have seen what you would have done if it had been intentional!"

Michael was silent.

"I know full well why my daughter agreed to this ludicrous plan of yours! Because in spite of it all, she—"

"—Mother!" Jackie exclaimed, stopping her mother from revealing more than she wanted.

"What do you want now?" Joan asked instead. "Haven't you done enough?"

"I've come to see my daughter... and yours," he told her quietly, again looking towards Jackie.

Joan turned towards Jackie, silently questioning her.

"It's all right, Mummy," she confirmed.

"Maybe for you. I can't stand to be under the same roof with him! I'll be next door if you need me!"

Grabbing her coat, Joan pushed past him and hurried over the snow-covered lawn to the Lankowsky home.

Michael stepped inside and closed the door behind him. He stood there, not yet attempting to come forward.

"Did you tell her everything?"

"One shock at a time, dear," Jackie replied sweetly.

"How are you?" Michael's voice was quiet.

Jackie had been watching him. He looked tried, strained. He seemed to have lost the arrogance, the confidence in his stance. His beard had grown again, but that only enhanced his looks – and *that* was not what she wanted to think about.

"What are you doing here?" she demanded to know, ignoring his question. "I left word that I would call when I was ready."

"I know. My father just told me. He told me about the baby, too. I was away; I didn't know..." Michael slowly took the few steps towards her. "She's mine." He stated the fact.

And Jackie confirmed, "Yes."

Michael slowly raised his hand and gently touched a finger to the baby's soft pink cheek. His chest felt suddenly constricted by an enormous vise.

Jackie watched as his expression became softer, his eyes became misty and a trembling smile played on his lips.

"Do you want to hold her?" she asked, her tone cold.

Michael looked at her sharply, retrieving his hand.

"No, I... she's too little..."

"Well, you'd better get used to her, if you're going to be taking care of her at all," Jackie said logically.

"What does that mean?" Michael's tone was tentative.

"It wouldn't be fair to her to have to grow up not knowing her father, regardless of what I think of you." She didn't elaborate further as she placed his daughter in his arms.

Michael looked as though he had just been handed a delicate piece of crystal, liable to break at any moment. The baby seemed even tinier in his arms.

"Is she all right?" he asked.

"Yes. She's perfect."

"Are you – all right, I mean?"

"Yes."

He gazed lovingly at his little daughter, taking in her perfection, the miracle of life... the fact that she was his... "Why are you not with John?" he asked suddenly, looking up at her. "Is he upset about the baby not... being his?"

Jackie paused for a moment, making certain she knew what she wanted to say.

"No, he's not upset. I needed some time to myself, to get used to her. Besides, I couldn't burden John with a newborn, someone else's at that."

A muscle started to twitch at his jaw. That really didn't answer the questions that flooded his brain. That response didn't tell him what he wanted to hear.

The baby started to squirm and he nervously handed her back to Jackie. She placed her in the bassinet, delicately adorned with white satin and lace, a large pink bow on either side.

"I... about what you said..." Michael started.

"What about it? You were contacted by my lawyer; you must know I'm not making idle threats."

"Yes. I know that. Frank is taking care of everything. Letters regarding your father have been drafted and in some instances issued. The companies affected will be contacted soon, if they haven't been already. I've done what you asked." Michael paused as he searched her blank expression. "I meant... what you said before... about her growing up knowing her father... does this mean you're thinking of granting me some sort of custody?"

"I don't know. Possibly in the future. But she needs to be

with me now."

"I realize that, but I don't want to miss this time in her life. It passes too quickly." Jackie only shrugged and Michael tried to muster the courage to continue. "Actually, I was thinking that… well, are you willing to settle with only partial custody?"

"What are you getting at?" Jackie asked suspiciously. She sat down, unable to stay on her feet any longer, and Michael did the same. "Don't push me. I said not now, but maybe not ever. By the time she's old enough… I might get used to the idea." Jackie's words sounded synthetic, even to her.

"Do you honestly believe that?"

Jackie rose to her feet again and walked away from his questioning stare. She shrugged again. "That I'll get used to letting her go? I don't know."

"Why don't you just come back?" he blurted.

Jackie swung around. "Pardon me?"

Michael too got up and walked towards her, making certain to keep his distance. "I want you to come home."

"I beg your pardon?" she rephrased her question.

"I want you to come home."

Jackie couldn't believe her ears. "What? No! I can't."

"Is it because of John?" Michael asked tentatively, afraid to hear the truth.

"John?"

"You can't marry him. You're still my wife," he said softly.

Jackie's eyes rounded in surprise. "No, I signed the divorce papers."

"*You* did. I didn't."

"Why not?" Jackie was incredulous.

Michael closed his eyes and sighed. "So much was going on…" he began, and Jackie raised an eyebrow in suspicion, forcing him to continue; forcing him to tell the truth. "I didn't want to."

"Really? And since you're so used to getting what you want—"

"—No. Not necessarily," he told her, stopping her from continuing.

Michael paused, taking in the wide, wondering eyes that looked so tired, the soft cheeks that seemed to have lost all colour, and the full, parted lips that he so longed to kiss.

"If you come home," he continued, forcing his mind to stop wandering, "we can raise her together. Neither of us will have to miss any precious time."

Jackie was speechless. Her mouth opened, but no words were able to escape.

"All your requests concerning your father have been met. I told you I have most of the legal documentation ready. If there is anything further, I promise to listen, and hopefully, to take care of it to your satisfaction. I think you have to choose now between John and your daughter."

"Leave it to you to manipulate the situation, once again!"

"I'm not trying to manipulate anything. It's fact. If you decide not to come back, if you marry John, you'll have partial custody. And—"

"I'll have partial custody – if I see fit to grant it to you. I don't have to give you anything!"

"Yes… I realize that, but you just said you think it best that our daughter know her father," he repeated, and Jackie rolled her eyes.

"She can *know you* from across town!"

Michael sighed. "I understand if you want to be with John, and that the baby needs you right now. I know I don't matter at all to her, at least, I won't for a while, but… if and when you do decide to grant me either custody or even visitation… you'll eventually be as I, a part-time parent. If you come home, you'll be with her all the time."

"I'll also be with *you*, all the time!"

"Do you hate me so much that you wouldn't even consider my suggestion?"

"Yes! Has it finally seeped into that thick skull of yours?" Jackie shook her head. "Do you think this child would not be affected? And what life would I be living? I told you, I'm through pretending."

"I'm not asking you to. I told my father about us. The only thing I do ask, is that you don't tell him about the rest."

A cynical smile turned the corners of her mouth. "You're still afraid he'll disown you, aren't you?"

"No," he told her, exhaling a breath. "None of that matters to me – not anymore. It's just that his doctor told me that he's developed high blood pressure; he shouldn't have any more revelations dropped on him. He's been acting strange these last few months and his appearances at the office have progressively decreased. He's not well."

Jackie pondered that information. "Why?" she asked.

"Why?" Michael was unsure of her question.

"Yes, why? Why would you ask me to come back?"

" … I was hoping that my daughter wouldn't have to be raised in a broken home as I was."

"And you think that raising my child in an *unhappy* home is better? John would be a wonderful father—"

"—Well, she's not John's. She's *our* child, and no I don't, but," he continued, knowing she expected more, "I know that I've put you through hell…"

"Do you?" Jackie was sarcastic. "So, what is it, you haven't finished yet?"

"No – I mean, yes! I want to make it up to you." Michael raised a hand and rubbed his temple. "Look… I admit that I was the one who suggested to Frank that he approach you from the start."

Jackie listened; her arms folded across her chest.

"I knew that you would be perfect for the plan—" he confessed.

"—Lucky you," she interrupted.

"But that wasn't the only reason. In fact, I asked Frank to offer you the job in the first place, not my father." And Jackie digested that piece of information. "Remember when you told me that our paths had crossed a long time ago? I never forgot seeing you that day… You and your father had come to the office… I'd asked my father about you, but he was adamant – you were much too young and absolutely off limits. You made an impression on me back then. There was something about you… When we met again… I wanted you—"

"—*And*, as I said before, you're used to getting what you want."

"No," he stopped her, pausing for a moment. "You were different than the women I'd known; a challenge. That's what I told myself, that I wanted you because of that. I just didn't want to admit… I was afraid to admit…"

"Admit what?" Jackie looked at him through narrowed eyes. Her head tilted to one side, waiting for him to admit to yet one more wrongdoing!

"Our meeting – even the situation that presented itself, was like a sign to me. I wanted you, but I didn't know how to go about winning you. I felt… I wasn't sure *what* I was feeling! I was afraid to admit that you got under my skin right from the start – that I fell in love with you when you poured that pitcher of water on me!"

Jackie blinked, and blinked once more. That night, long ago… she had thought she had only imagined Michael uttering those words…

Jackie bounced back quickly. "Was that between your visits with Brenda?"

"Brenda?" Michael's eyes narrowed and he shook his head in disbelief. "I was with Brenda once since we were married. I know it was once too many, but that's what it was – once."

"No, you think I *caught* you only once!" Jackie laughed bitterly.

"Because it *happened* once. That's the truth. I haven't seen her since I let her go, I swear. And by the way, I didn't know that Nyland was her brother. They used different names," he shrugged. "I suppose that's why they 'worked' so well together."

Jim Nyland had more or less proven that Michael had been with Brenda while they were married. Nyland had given her proof of Michael's other wrongdoings, why should she believe Michael now?

"So I'm to believe you weren't with her in Chicago?"

"Chicago? If I remember correctly, that was during the time of your Oscar winning performance," he said, his tone bitter. "That's when I thought you loved me, why would I have been with her?"

"He dialed your hotel number; she answered your phone. That's cut and dried in my book."

"What? When? When did he call?"

Jackie threw her hands up in frustration. "I don't know! What difference does it make?"

"A great deal if I can prove my innocence!"

"All right. It must have been... the day after you left home. There," she huffed, waiting for his response.

"Jackie... I was with Gene Feldberg all day *that* day. I had a late dinner with *him* and I was with him again the next day. I never saw Brenda, but judging by what you've told me about Nyland, it wouldn't surprise me that his *sister* is just as devious. Do you honestly think that she wouldn't be able talk a bellboy into letting her into someone's room – my room? God! Why would I want to be with *her*?"

Could he be telling the truth? He must know that she could very well investigate – in fact shatter – his alibi... Her ever-ready pride kicked in. She wasn't going to buckle now. "How the hell should I know? Maybe you like variety. In any case," she shrugged, "if you weren't with her... that's too bad. Maybe you're not so fortunate, after all."

Michael bowed his head for a moment, as if trying to find the strength to go on. "It obviously doesn't matter to you, but I wasn't. Even that one time, she came on to me. I didn't want *her*, I wanted *you*, but you were so hell-bent on hating me..."

Jackie raised an eyebrow. "You blaming me again?"

"No. I'm to blame." He looked up at her now. "I'm saying that I was wrong. I accepted her advances because I couldn't have you. That was stupid, and I'm sorry." Jackie's expression remained the same, and he continued. "I know how you feel about me – and yes I know you've had just cause – our wedding night, Brenda, the miscarriage… everything! Your feelings have never been a secret; I was an idiot to think otherwise. The thought that it had all been an act to cover your affair with John never entered my mind."

Jackie shrugged indifferently. "I was only following orders. I was acting as though I liked being your wife. Wasn't that the plan?"

"Yes," he said, admitting defeat. "That was the plan."

"I'm fresh out of acting skills."

"I know. I told you, no more pretending. Couldn't we at least give it a try?"

Jackie took a few steps away. Was she actually considering yet another proposition? She turned to look at him. "How can I live with you, when I detest you?"

"I'll keep my distance, I swear. I'll do whatever you want."

Jackie slowly shook her head from side to side.

"Jackie… I love you, but I am blatantly aware of your hatred towards me and I doubt that'll ever change. I'm hoping to do this for the baby more than for myself. I'm hoping we could learn to live with each other, that you could… at least tolerate me… Wouldn't it be best for her?" he begged.

"It would most likely be worse, not better." Jackie was tempted to ask how he could still love her when he thought she'd been with John, and intended to be with John still, when he was so certain of her feelings, but she didn't bother… she knew first-hand how fickle that emotion could be…

"Will you at least think about it?"

She watched him; her head hurting from all the conflicting

thoughts that dodged around in her brain. This would be madness. This was something she could not do.

With desperation in his voice, in his eyes, Michael repeated his plea. "Please, think about it?"

CHAPTER THIRTY-SEVEN

*T*hink about it? That's all she *could* think about during the next few weeks. Could she go back to him, for her daughter's sake? Could she tolerate being called Mrs. Madison, after what she'd learned? She and the baby would probably be better off remaining with her mother. Joan would love nothing more than to help raise her granddaughter. On the other hand, could she walk away, never to see him again? Jackie shook her head vigorously. Where did that thought come from? It was the baby, the baby... Even if not now, but later, could she bear being away from her daughter for more than mere moments? No, she could not. She didn't need him or John for that matter to provide a loving environment for her daughter, but did this innocent child deserve to be raised in a broken home when she had the power to prevent it? No, she concluded, she did not...

With the baby and car seat in one hand and the diaper bag in the other, she slammed the car door shut using her booted foot.

Awkwardly, she made her way up the steps to the Madison home, her home – *their* home.

The door opened suddenly, revealing a startled Michael standing in the foyer.

Quickly, he regained his composure and reached for the precious cargo, setting her just inside. He turned to Jackie, a strained smile curving his lips.

"I promise you won't be sorry," he said quietly.

"We'll see," Jackie replied, and watched him as he knelt down and reached for his daughter lying under the protective blanket. "I don't know if I can handle this. I'm… just willing to give it a try. Don't see this as permanent."

"All right. I understand."

Jackie followed him into the living room and draped her coat onto a nearby chair. "Where's your father?"

"He's out. Why?"

"You'll do the explaining. I'd rather not be grilled."

He agreed willingly. Just to have her here, he thought, he'd agree to just about anything. "Yes, don't worry, I'll take care of my father. In fact… my father has suggested he move out. He's looking for a place…"

That was strange news. This was Walter's home, the home he had built for his family years ago, why would he offer to leave now? Had he learned about what Michael had done? Was he trying to make amends for his son's indiscretions?

"Why?" she asked simply.

Michael shrugged. "I offered to move out instead, but he insists. It might work out best for now," he shrugged, looking up at her.

"And why is that?" Jackie couldn't douse her suspicions.

"I just think we have a lot to deal with. It'll be difficult enough for you to be here, without having an in-law in the way."

Jackie digested this information and his explanation. He was probably right, but she didn't need to tell him that. "I don't care either way," she said instead.

Michael sat down on the big chair and held the little bundle in his arms.

"God, I missed you…" he whispered, and only he knew that he had meant he'd missed both mother and child. "She's beautiful."

Yes, she was, but Jackie wasn't going to engage in any more conversation. She was not going to fall for that!

Michael watched her as Jackie dropped the diaper bag on the floor next to the entrance of the room. "I received the forms from the government regarding her birth certificate. I suppose they assumed that you were still living here. It's been a month since she was born; you haven't named her?"

Jackie placed a pacifier on the coffee table next to him. "No." Choosing a name for their child was something she'd hoped they would do together, so she kept putting it off, hoping for some miracle…

"No?"

"That's what I said," she said extra sweetly.

"I was thinking… what about 'Samantha'?"

Jackie was surprised at his suggestion, and naturally suspicious. "Samantha?"

"After your father," he elaborated.

"If you're trying to win points, it won't happen," she said with a cynical laugh, and Michael became serious, a frown creasing his brow.

"I'm not trying to do anything – least of all win points. I've lost the game. I'm fully aware of that," he assured her. "If you don't like the name, choose another; it doesn't matter. I just think we ought to name her."

Jackie bit the inside of her lip. It had been a nice gesture; why not simply accept it as such? "Samantha's fine." Actually it was perfect, but she'd keep that opinion to herself.

"Fine."

"Fine."

Didn't they do this before, she thought to herself?

Jackie was deluding herself.

No matter how much she denied it, she knew full well that Michael still affected her senses. When he'd come near her to kiss Samantha or take her from her arms, Jackie would force herself to look away. If she didn't, she would notice that once again the coldness had gone from his eyes. The sardonic laughter, the harshness of his manner, it was all gone. A gentleness had replaced all that, as it had before she learned about the sabotage.

The sabotage… Yes, she should just dwell on that. That would keep her focussed! That would keep her from falling for him again! Unfortunately, something didn't sit right. She couldn't comprehend why he had not even tried to deny the crime, or why he had agreed to her demands so quickly, without question…

John had found nothing strange about Michael's willingness to adhere to her demands. "Jackie, he screwed up – badly – but he loves you. He'll do whatever it takes to make it up to you. Of that much I'm certain. Your willingness to return…"

"You think I'm crazy don't you?"

"Yes, I do. You're crazy about *him* – and please, please don't deny it. After everything you've learned, after your determination to lead him to believe we'd been together… you went back to him."

"I wanted to cause him distress and I succeeded. I'm going back for Samantha, not for me," Jackie had been adamant, but John would not be fooled.

As for Michael – he was just happy to have her back, to have his daughter with him. He told himself the reasons for her return didn't matter. However, his wife's cold, forceful words tore at his heart. The phone calls that he assumed to be to John's were destroying him. Jackie had obviously given up John to live with Michael, but he couldn't believe that whatever she and John had shared was actually over. That was a subject Michael was reluctant to discuss with her. He was afraid of the answer. He refused to think that Jackie would eventually leave.

Michael had added another door between the nursery and the master bedroom before she'd returned, in the event that Jackie would grant him time with his daughter. Now that Jackie was back he offered his room, their former bedroom, to her, but she declined. Instead, she opted for the guestroom, which also had a connecting door to the nursery.

She had to admit he had done a wonderful job of decorating Samantha's room. Walter had told her that Michael had insisted on doing everything himself, even the painting. And she was impressed.

The walls were of a pale shade of pink, with white satin moons and stars scattered about. Her furniture and crib were white. A soft tulle canopy draped from the ceiling, cascaded around the headboard of the crib and down to the floor. The bedding was made of white silk, with little pink hearts and bows embroidered throughout. It all came together with the plush carpet, perfectly matching the pink of the wall.

Jackie looked around the room as she sat in the rocking chair, nursing Samantha. She could not have asked for a more delicately and beautifully decorated nursery for her baby. She appreciated that, since the nursery was where she spent most of her time – she tried to avoid Michael as much as possible.

Walter had been very apologetic over this entire ordeal. He told her that he regretted being the cause of his son's manipulation of her. Jackie accepted his apology. After all, there was so much more for which his son was responsible!

"I suppose Michael told you I was looking for a place of my own."

"Yes he did. Look… this is your home… I agreed to come back for the baby's sake, but perhaps we should look for a new home, not you."

"Nonsense. What would I do with this place? I'd go stir crazy. No… actually my offer has been accepted. I purchased a condo down by the lake. My friend Marty lives in the same building, so I'll have company. It won't be ready for another couple of weeks or so, but… what do you think?"

Jackie shrugged. "Sounds nice. If that's what you want…"

Perhaps it wasn't want he wanted, but it was for the best. Walter knew that.

"Miss Jackie," Elmer Delaney approached her one morning after breakfast. Elmer was a quiet man, friendly, yet quiet. He

rarely started conversations with Jackie. "I just wanted to say...
that we, Alice and I... are very happy to have you back."

Jackie's emotions had apparently not yet returned to normal,
for suddenly a lump formed in her throat and Elmer's face
became blurry through her tears. She wondered what they must
think of her.

"Thank you." Jackie wasn't quite certain what to say. She
and Michael were certainly not a typical married couple. "I
know things have seemed extremely strange... I—"

"You don't have to explain, Miss. Michael filled us in. I hope
that's okay!" he added as an afterthought, and when Jackie nodded,
he continued. "I have to tell you, it didn't sound like something
Michael would normally have done... All I know is that he is
very much in love with you. He's been miserable without you.
I know that things are not normal between you, but he is willing
do anything to win you back. He may have faltered, but he really
is a good person. Give him the opportunity, will you?"

"Although I did come back, I don't know if things will ever
be right," Jackie extended her hand to Elmer. "I mean our entire
relationship was based on lies, how does one overcome that?"

"I understand. But you would not have returned if you didn't
feel something for him. You would not have returned simply for
the sake of your child," he said knowingly, patting her hand, and
Jackie found it necessary to avert her eyes.

She shrugged, wanting to end the conversation. "I don't
know. I can't make any promises."

Michael walked into the nursery one evening while she fed
Samantha. During the past few weeks he had made a point of

disappearing when she nursed. He knew that he would not be welcome to share that experience. This night was no different.

"Oh, I'm sorry," he said, lowering his eyes. "I just wanted to say good night to Samantha."

Jackie covered herself. "You should knock."

"Sorry, I'll come back later."

"No. She's had enough. You can burp her." Jackie rose from her chair and Michael accepted the invitation to enter. She kissed the baby and handed her to him as she stifled a yawn.

"Make sure she burps and put her down on her side," she instructed, and then stopped at the door. "Tomorrow we should discuss Samantha's baptism. I don't want to wait any longer."

"Okay... Do you want to talk—"

"Tomorrow. I'm tired, I have to get some sleep."

Michael stood in silence, watching as she retreated into her own room.

It wasn't much later when Jackie heard a faint cry. Jackie moaned and whimpered. She couldn't get up; she couldn't...

Suddenly, she jolted out of bed. The baby!

She rushed into the nursery, but Samantha was not there!

"Oh God!" Jackie cried. "My baby!"

Forgetting about the connecting door, she ran blindly into the corridor and over to Michael's door. She didn't knock; she burst right in.

"Where's Samantha?! She's not in her crib!"

Michael turned to look at her curiously. He held his daughter against his bare chest as he gently patted her back. "It's okay. I have her."

"What are you doing?" Jackie accused, her heart starting to

settle once she saw her daughter.

Michael spoke softly and calmly, trying to reassure her. "She was crying, but she's fine."

Finally, Jackie took a few calming breaths. "I didn't hear her..."

"I know. She had a bit of gas, but she's almost asleep; I'll put her down in a minute. Go back to bed."

Jackie shook her head, watching Samantha intently.

The baby stirred again, and Jackie reached for her.

"I have her; go to bed," Michael repeated.

Again Jackie shook her head. She was so tired, but she didn't want to leave until she knew Samantha was asleep. She sank down onto the edge of Michael's bed, her eyelids weighing heavily over her eyes.

Sleep was not something that had been coming easily these last few months, but her lack of sleep was not solely due to a newborn. She'd lie awake night after night pondering her decision to return, replaying in her mind all that she'd learned, all that Michael had said. Her head ached from all the mixed emotions that threatened to send her over the edge. She was exhausted. No wonder she hadn't heard the baby's cries. No wonder she leaned over, resting her head on the pillow...

For two short hours, Jackie lay in a deep sleep. Again Samantha awakened and needed to be fed. Again Jackie didn't hear her.

Obviously unable to feed the baby himself, Michael reached over his daughter and gently shook Jackie's arm, but Jackie didn't budge. Moving the baby over to his side of the bed and blocking the edge with his pillow, he went around to Jackie's side and sat down beside her.

She must be exhausted, Michael thought to himself. All that had happened had to have been difficult to deal with. Adding childbirth and the little sleep that comes afterwards could only have intensified her weak state.

Michael couldn't resist. He extended his hand to her cheek, caressing it gently, calling her name...

But Jackie's head rolled from side to side. She was being held down against her will. Michael was telling her that he would force her to into submission, no matter what it took. Brenda was there too, and she was rocking Samantha in her arms, laughing while Michael kept her from her daughter.

Suddenly her eyes fluttered open. "No!" she yelled out. "No!" Jackie seemed dazed, but her face contorted to a strange expression of confusion and panic.

Michael quickly rose from the bed as Jackie swung her fists towards him, crying hysterically.

"You can't do this to me! You can't do this!" she cried, stumbling to her feet.

Michael watched her in astonishment as she continued to hyperventilate.

"Jackie..."

Michael attempted to take a few steps towards her, but Jackie backed away, as if afraid of him.

"What are you doing here? You can't do this! Where's my baby? Where did she take her?"

"Where did who take her? Jackie... Samantha's here. You're in my room," Michael explained calmly.

Jackie's breathing came in spurts. In a daze, she looked around, realizing where she was. Spotting her infant daughter in the bed, she started to reach for her.

Michael again put a hand on her arm and again she lashed out irrationally.

"Don't touch me! I have to feed my baby!"

"Calm down first. Your milk must be curdled by now!" he exaggerated.

"I said don't touch me! Stay away from me!"

"Jackie, calm down. I'm not trying to do anything. I had Samantha, remember? She had gas. You fell asleep and I didn't want to wake you, that's all. I wasn't trying to do anything!" Michael pleaded.

Jackie watched him through teary eyes, her breathing still erratic, and she realized she was finally starting to awaken from whatever nightmare she'd been having. It had been a dream, a horrible dream. Her daughter was safe... she was safe...

Samantha began to cry again, wanting to be fed.

"I have to feed her," she said again in a strained voice as she gathered her child into her arms.

"Jackie, you shouldn't nurse her while you're like this."

Jackie ignored him and walked out of the room, leaving Michael to stare after her.

He sank down on the bed, himself in a daze. What had happened?

What was all that about? He didn't know. Michael was certain of one thing, however. He could no longer live like this. He had been selfish and it wasn't right.

It was barely five in the morning. He got up, showered and dressed. It was early, but there was much to do that day.

CHAPTER THIRTY-EIGHT

Michael came home very late that evening and was gone early the next morning. This was repeated for the next two days.

Jackie hadn't seen him since that night, a night that remained quite fuzzy in her head. She remembered that she'd been somewhat hysterical, but nothing more. And she decided that she didn't want to remember the details anyway.

After breakfast she gathered the diaper bag, secured Samantha into her car, all warm under a protective blanket, and ventured out to visit her mother.

They had just finished lunch when there was a knock at the door.

Jackie, her nerves still a little raw, jumped at the sound.

"Jackie, it's the door! Calm down!" her mother laughed. Joan patted her daughter's hand and Jackie, in turn, gifted her with her smile.

When Joan returned to the kitchen, however, she was less jubilant, and again Jackie panicked.

"What?"

"I don't know. That was a messenger from your lawyer's office."

"My lawyer? How did he know I was here?"

Joan handed her the envelope.

Jackie had already painfully recounted to her mother the manipulations of her beloved husband, and the reason she was now a grandmother, but she had not yet disclosed to her what Jim Nyland had told her. She didn't have the heart.

These could be the papers concerning the transfer of funds to her mother's name. It was time now, Jackie realized, to tell her everything.

Joan pointed to the large envelope. "Aren't you going to open it?"

With trembling hands, Jackie did as her mother suggested.

It was a letter. Handwritten from Michael, along with affidavits and other documents.

"What is this?" Jackie was annoyed.

"Sweetheart, just read it."

She did. The letter read:

Jackie:

Two years ago today I came to your home. This visit started a chain of events that, however painful, I would not change for the world.

Enclosed you will find three documents. The first is documentation of an account that has been opened in your mother's name. Amounts are specified on the statement.

All companies that suffered as a result of the virus have been informed that the chip purchased from Ellis Electronics was dysfunctional only due to sabotage. If any further compensation is necessary, it will be done so in your father's name by Madison Electronics.

Tears started to flood her eyes.

"Jackie? What it is?"

But Jackie just shook her head and continued to read.

Everyone in the business knows that the microchip we have used as our own was indeed created by Sam Ellis.

I regret the events that caused such destruction to your family. Although I cannot change everything, I hope to at least give you satisfaction, as well as compensation.

The second document is your copy of our divorce papers.

Jackie's heart pounded painfully in her chest.

You will see my signature in the appropriate areas.

You are now free.

The third is an affidavit, which states that I grant you sole custody of Samantha.

"What!" she breathed, as she quickly searched for the document. It was true!

I have opened another account in your name, leaving you sufficient funds for both of you to live an extremely comfortable life. A trust fund for Samantha has been set up. It will be in trust to you until her 21st birthday.

I thought that the fact that you were not with John, and were instead living with me, would be sufficient. I was wrong. You, once again, were right. This is no life. To have you so close and yet to have to force myself to keep a distance is unbearable. The realization that your hatred for me will never diminish is killing me.

I choose to leave.

Joan watched her daughter's face become more and more pale.

I'm not yet certain where I'm going. I'll let Frank know as soon as I'm settled. If you need more funds, or have any further requests, Frank will make the necessary changes or adjustments.

If one day you decide that you want Samantha to meet her father, Frank will know how to reach me. I've been selfish and I have nothing to show for it. I love you, and the only way to show you is to let you go.

Michael

Jackie put the letter down, tears streaming down her cheeks.

"Jackie? Will you tell me now?" Joan asked slowly.

"It's for the best," she said into her tissue.

Joan was afraid for her daughter. What else could go wrong? "What is? What's for the best?"

"There's something else that you should know, Mummy," Jackie started. "But maybe you should just read this."

Jackie handed her the letter and watched her mother's face as it too became pale.

"Oh my God," she said quietly. "What does this mean?"

"Mummy, it means that he was behind all that happened with Daddy. They sabotaged Daddy's chip. That's why he lost everything! And he was there to pick up the pieces – I was one of them, actually," Jackie said through her tears, as if only just realizing the connection.

"Good heavens!" Joan put her hands to her face. But suddenly, her mother looked up. She wiped her tears. "Jackie… maybe I'm all mixed up," she said holding her head. "But when did this take place?"

"What do you mean? Daddy put the chip into production just before I went back to school," Jackie explained.

"And things went wrong soon afterwards," Joan said slowly.

"Yes, like I said—"

"—But, Jackie, that was three years ago, almost four!"

"Yes, so?"

"Honey, Michael wasn't in Toronto then. He was setting up their plant in Montreal."

Jackie looked up at her mother.

"Michael took over the year that Daddy died. Remember, when he first came here? He told you that his father had just turned the company over to him?"

Jackie's mouth opened, but no sound came out. There was a tremendous blockage in her throat. "Mummy? What are you saying?" she whispered finally.

"It wasn't Michael, Jackie. He was not behind this. He's taking the blame... for his father!"

"No! Why? Why would Walter...?"

"Get the baby!" Joan instructed as she quickly gathered the papers and shoved them back into the envelope.

Jackie was all thumbs as she tried to literally stuff Samantha into the pink snowsuit. "Mummy... he might not have been in charge then, he might not have initiated it, but he must have known!" Jackie couldn't bring herself to believe otherwise.

"There's only one way to find out!"

During the ride home, Jackie tried to understand what was happening. Could it be true? Could Michael be taking the blame to save his father from a fate not so unlike *her* father's?

Even with the current turn of events, however, Jackie felt compelled to confide to her mother the state of Walter's health before confronting him.

"Ask me if I give a damn! Did he stop to think what he was doing to your father?"

Joan brushed past her daughter and entered the Madison home unannounced.

Mrs. Delaney was hurrying towards them. "Hello! I thought I heard voices."

"Hello, Mrs. Delaney. Is Walter in?" Joan asked, her tone crisp.

"Yes, he's...."

Just then, Walter appeared from the study.

"Joanie!" he smiled, extending his hand.

"We have some things to discuss, Walter." Joan's face did not invite a handshake.

Obviously sensing impending disaster, Mrs. Delaney retreated into the kitchen.

"How could you, Walter?"

"What is it? What's happened?" he asked, obviously alarmed.

"How could you look my daughter in the face every day, knowing full well that you are the one that caused her father's destruction − her father's death!"

Walter's face suddenly became a traffic light on the blink. It turned red, then yellow, then green, and finally it lost colour altogether!

"Joanie..."

"And don't call me Joanie!" she hollered, her body trembling with anger.

Jackie took the baby to the kitchen. Mrs. Delaney looked anxious. "Is everything all right, Miss Jackie?"

"I don't know, Mrs. Delaney. Could you watch Samantha for a little while?"

"Yes, yes, of course. I'd be happy to!"

Jackie left a joyous Mrs. Delaney with Samantha and returned to the yelling, which had now moved to the living room.

"How could you? How could you?" Joan demanded.

Walter bowed his head, knowing that he'd finally been caught. "My God, Michael..." He wiped his brow with a large white handkerchief and faced Joan. "Joanie – *Joan*... it started out as a simple business transaction. It got a little out of hand. When I realized that, I tried to fix it; I tried to help, but Sam... he was too damn proud!"

"Yes, Sam *was* proud! And he was honest! Unlike you!"

Walter sank down onto a chair.

An incredulous Jackie stood at the doorway. "Then it's true? Oh good heavens! How did you do it?" she demanded. "How did you get your hands on that chip?"

"I... had an engineer working at Sam's plant. I instructed him to install a virus," Walter confessed, and Jackie felt something jab her heart.

"Why? Why would you do this to him?" Jackie couldn't understand his motives.

"Like I said... it started out as simple rivalry. He had created something that would make millions. Relieving him of that chip... gave me the opportunity to get back at him, and I took it!"

Walter's voice had taken an angry tone and Joan looked as though she wanted to lash out at him, to grab him by the throat. "Get back at him? Get back at him for what? What did he ever do to you?"

"He took you away from me!" he blurted, his voice rising.

Jackie was flabbergasted! "What?" she yelled, but neither

heard her. She looked from one to the other, in utter shock. She couldn't believe what she was hearing!

"He didn't take me away from you, Walter!" Joan said forcefully. "You just couldn't handle the fact that I fell in love with Sam! I chose him over you and for that you had to destroy him!"

"Joan, he destroyed *me*! I married the first woman that would have me, and you know how disastrous that was!"

"That was your choice! It was your sulking that made you jump into marriage without a second thought! None of it was Sam's fault! I loathe you, Walter Madison! I loathe you for what you did. You've not only destroyed my husband, but now my daughter's life. Although, I'm sure you feel some sort of poetic justice now that my daughter married your son and gave you a grandchild – my husband's grandchild!"

Jackie intervened, her voice trembling. "I have to know... was Michael part of this? Did he know?"

"No! No! He knew nothing of this! I swear it!" Walter was adamant. "I had no idea Nyland was blackmailing both of us – the bastard!"

Jackie's breath caught in her throat. This was far too much for her to handle. She sank down in a chair.

"Jackie, dear..." Her mother came to her, placing her hand on her daughter's forehead.

"Nyland was blackmailing you?" Jackie asked, her voice strained.

"Yes. Yes, for tens of thousands, hundreds of thousands. I've... paid him to keep the truth hidden. He threatened to call the authorities, but what was worse... I knew my son would hate for me for what I'd done to his wife's family, but that bastard told him anyway."

Jackie leaned forward in her chair. "Nyland wasn't blackmailing Michael. Nyland supplied the information to me free of charge knowing full well that it would lead me to believe my husband was involved, that it would destroy us. *I* am the one that confronted your son; *I* am the one who made demands of him. Your son, knowing of your ill-health, took the blame for you!" Jim Nyland, Jackie realized now, had also lied about Michael's infidelities. Michael had been faithful. She was positive of that now.

Walter held his head in his hands. "I'm sorry, I'm sorry."

Suddenly she jumped out of the chair. "Where is he?"

"Jackie, I'm sorry. I never meant—"

"—You never meant for anyone to find out! But *I* did, you see, and just as Nyland had hoped, I jumped to conclusions, assuming that Michael was behind it all. I would never have believed that it had been you all along. Your son's coercing me into marrying him was wrong, but that plan was initiated because of your ultimatums, your selfish need to control his life. Fortunately, something happened that neither of us would have imagined! Our union, however unorthodox, intensified the feelings we already had for each other. We actually fell in love!" she said, her voice breaking with emotion. "I asked you where he is!"

"I… he was at the office a short while ago. I spoke to him."

Jackie was about to turn towards the door, but she had something more to say.

"I have a news flash for you, *Dad*," she told him, a smug look on her face. "Your son is leaving! Did you know that? He's leaving his daughter, just to keep the truth about his father hidden! He's leaving *me*, because I made him believe that I didn't care about him, that I was involved with another man! Is this what you wanted? Is this what you've waited for – for the last forty years? Was revenge so sweet after all?" she nearly screamed. "I know now," Jackie continued in a quieter tone, "that everything he's done, you've pushed him to do. *You* are the manipulator, not him!" Jackie turned sharply, as if no longer able to look at him.

Jackie rushed to the door. "Mummy, Samantha's with Mrs. Delaney."

"Jackie, where are you going?" Joan called after her.

"I have to find him; I have to stop him."

Slamming the door behind her, Jackie ran to her car and sped along the long driveway and over to the Madison plant.

She stormed into Frank's office, the two men sitting across from him turning to look at her.

"Jackie... I'm in a meeting." Frank rose from his chair.

"Where is he?" Jackie demanded to know.

Frank excused himself and came around his desk. He placed a hand on her arm, and she allowed him to lead her out of the office.

"Frank, where is he?"

"Jackie..."

"I know, Frank. I know the whole ugly truth!" she cried. "But right now, I think it's the most wonderful news I've heard in a long time!"

Frank watched her, realizing what she meant.

"Where is he, Frank?" she begged.

"He... he's at the airport!" Frank looked at his watch. "He's leaving for France... Paris," he elaborated, as Jackie started backing away. "I don't know if you'll make it!"

"I have to!" she called out as she ran from the building.

Jackie ran every stop sign and every red light until she reached the highway. Then she drove at dangerous speeds through the snowy slush until she finally stopped in front of the terminal.

"Lady!" An officer of the Royal Canadian Mounted Police, the federally licensed police force that patrolled the international airport, called out to her, waving his arms. "You can't stop here; you'll be towed!"

Jackie couldn't care less! Jackie didn't even care if he arrested her, but only after she found her husband. She ran inside, knocking over luggage and dislodging purses on the way.

She reached the departure counter, but there was no sign of Michael.

"The flight to Paris," Jackie yelled at the attendant, breathless from running. "Has it left?"

The people in line were annoyed at her interruption.

The woman behind the ticket counter looked at her strangely, but answered politely. "No ma'am. It will be boarding at gate nineteen in just—"

"—I have to get there!"

"Ma'am!" The woman stopped Jackie from stepping by the counter. "You can't go through, ma'am!"

"Fine!" Jackie fumbled in her purse for a wallet. "I'll buy a ticket!"

"Excuse *me*, lady, but am I invisible?" The man at the front of the line spoke up. He was being served when Jackie had stormed through.

"I'm sorry, but I have to stop my husband!"

The man watched her anxious face, the trembling hands that fumbled for a credit card.

"All right, go ahead," he told her, stepping back.

"Thank you, thank you," Jackie told him and turned to the attendant. "Here," she said, handing her the card.

"But ma'am, the flight is sold out."

"Sold out?" Jackie panicked and unwittingly raised her voice. "I don't care! I'm not flying, I just want to stop my husband!"

"Can't you make an exception?" The man at the counter came to her rescue.

"No, I'm sorry. But… but I'll sell you a ticket to Lisbon. It's boarding at gate seventeen."

"Fine! Fine! That's good!" Jackie took the ticket from the attendant. "Thank you. Thank you!" she called back to the man at the counter as she ran down the corridor towards the gates.

The keys that she'd shoved into the pocket of her long camel coloured coat buzzed noisily when she passed through the security check.

Security guards came forward, asking her to empty her pockets and stand still while they passed a wand over her body. The safety of passengers secured, they allowed her to continue.

Gates ten through twelve, thirteen and fourteen, she shed her coat and dropped it somewhere near a chair. Gate fifteen and sixteen… Jackie was ready to drop!

Finally, she spotted him. "Michael! Michael!" she called.

At least five men named Michael turned to look at the crazed woman jogging alongside the mobile sidewalk, trying to keep up.

Finally, *her* Michael, recognizing her voice, turned as well.

"Michael, wait! Don't go!"

Michael watched her, he listened, but he continued to walk, making no move to step off.

"I know the truth. My mother confronted your father. He admitted everything! Why didn't you tell me?"

"What difference would it have made?" he asked her, finally speaking. "Go home, Jackie. Go call John."

"Michael!" she called again, starting to feel faint from exhaustion. "There was never anyone else! John just played along. I was so upset about my father and... and Brenda..."

"Brenda? I told you!"

"I know. I didn't believe you! I was afraid to. I just couldn't, but I was wrong. I know now it's not true... Michael, please," she begged. She slowed her pace, unable to go on. "Don't go. I love you... Ouw!"

Jackie stopped; a throbbing pain in the ankle she'd just twisted halted any further attempt to follow him. She held a hand on her chest, hoping that her heart would stop pounding, hoping that her breathing would return to normal before she fainted. She watched him slowly move farther and farther away from her.

She had been too late. Admitting defeat, Jackie limped to a nearby chair and sank down into it. She was physically and emotionally exhausted. Her elbows resting on her knees, she placed her head in her hands and cried. If only she hadn't been so quick to believe the worst... if only she hadn't let her pride rule her life...

Suddenly, a black leather bag was dropped by her feet. Round-eyed and teary-faced, she looked up.

Michael was standing in front of her. He said nothing.

Without a word, he reached down. His hands gripped her shoulders and lifted her to her feet. He searched her startled face for a second longer before finally closing the gap, pressing his lips to hers in a kiss that had been forbidden for far too long.

"Ouw!" she cried out against his mouth when she accidentally put weight on her sprained ankle. "See what you did!"

"What?" he exclaimed worriedly.

Jackie pushed at his chest. "You made me twist my ankle!" she accused.

"I'm sorry…" Michael chuckled, and kissed her again. "You love me," he whispered. After all that had passed, this revelation was almost too wonderful to be true.

Jackie was silent as tears welled up in her eyes again. "I shouldn't…" she managed in a tight voice.

Michael smiled. "I know," he admitted, gazing lovingly into her eyes.

"Why? Why didn't you tell me the truth? I know you wanted to protect your father, but you were going to leave us…"

"I was going to leave because I thought you hated me, that you wanted John."

Jackie shook her head. "I made you think that because I thought you—"

"—You're the only one I ever wanted, the only one I've ever loved."

"I love you, Michael," she whispered, caressing his cheek.

"No more assumptions, okay?" he begged.

Again she shook her head, "Never, I promise," she smiled. "Let's go home… our little girl is waiting…"

Michael swung her up into his arms and happily obliged.

THE END

Don't miss

Someday My Prince

and

Second Chance

TWO NEW SCINTILLATING ROMANCE NOVELS

by

J.E. D'Angelo

J.E. D'Angelo

J.E. D'Angelo's active imagination was fostered through childhood years spent watching and discussing thousands of movies and dozens of operas with a creative father who inspired her passion for storytelling. It wasn't long before she began to re-imagine personal versions of these stories, which finally led to creating her own. Ms. D'Angelo is a member of the Canadian Authors' Association, Toronto Romance Writers, and Romance Writers of America. Visit her on the web at:

www.jedangelo.com